PRAISE FOR MICHELLE MARCOS

"Michelle Marcos has a fresh and lively style, and a natural feel for romance...When I want a great historical romance, I'll reach for anything by Michelle Marcos!"
—Lisa Kleypas, bestselling author of
Love in the Afternoon

"A talented storyteller, Marcos gives a very human face to all her characters." —*Fresh Fiction*

"A bold and creative new voice in the romance world... Marcos is an author to take note of."
—*Romance Reviews Today*

Praise for WICKEDLY EVER AFTER

"A scrumptiously sensual and delightfully witty historical romance...I absolutely loved this story. Brimming with mystery, humor, witty repartee, an interesting plot, charismatic characters, and intrigue, this book is a winner! I look forward to reading Ms. Marcos's future works as well as those she already has out. I highly recommend *Wickedly Ever After* to anyone looking for a terrific read." —*Romance Junkies*

"4½ stars! For this installment of Marcos's Pleasure Emporium series, the once infamous brothel becomes a school where young ladies learn the art of seduction. Playing on several erotic romance themes and adding her own delicious brand of sensuality, Marcos delivers a fast-paced, sexy tale."
—*Romantic Times BookReviews*

Praise for WHEN A LADY MISBEHAVES

"Debut author Marcos delivers a refreshing, creative take on the typical Regency, carried by the spirited April and buoyed throughout by lively plot twists."

—*Publishers Weekly*

"Her heroine is a spunky delight, and her dark, hostile hero is an ideal foil...Marcos displays talents that are sure to grow with each new title."

—*Romantic Times BookReviews*

"*When a Lady Misbehaves* is the first in a bold and original new series by a bold and creative new voice in the romance world. Michelle Marcos is impressive in her debut. The characters in *When a Lady Misbehaves* are complex and immensely fascinating, the story is imaginative, and the plotting is excellent. Ms. Marcos makes some clever twists on the traditional romance. I highly recommend *When a Lady Misbehaves*...new-comer Michelle Marcos is an author to take note of."

—*Romance Reviews Today*

"This rags-to-riches story by debut author [Marcos] absolutely sizzles. *When a Lady Misbehaves* is beautifully done and I highly recommend it." —*Fresh Fiction*

"*When a Lady Misbehaves* is loaded with smolder and charm...It was a joy to read this inventive, sexy, and ultimately moving story."

—Lisa Kleypas, bestselling author of *Mine Till Midnight*

St. Martin's Paperbacks Titles by
MICHELLE MARCOS

Wickedly Ever After

Gentlemen Behaving Badly

When a Lady Misbehaves

Secrets
to Seducing a Scot

Michelle Marcos

St. Martin's Paperbacks

For God

This is a work of fiction. All of the characters, organizations, and events portrayed in this novel are either products of the author's imagination or are used fictitiously.

SECRETS TO SEDUCING A SCOT

Copyright © 2011 by Michelle Marcos.
Excerpt from *Lessons in Loving a Laird* copyright © 2011 by Michelle Marcos.

For information address St. Martin's Press, 175 Fifth Avenue, New York, NY 10010.

ISBN: 978-0-312-38178-3

Printed in the United States of America

St. Martin's Paperbacks edition / August 2011

St. Martin's Paperbacks are published by St. Martin's Press, 175 Fifth Avenue, New York, NY 10010.

10 9 8 7 6 5 4 3 2 1

ACKNOWLEDGMENTS

The cover of this book may have my name on it, but that's only because there isn't space to credit all the people who helped in its creation.

I'd like to thank my editor, Rose Hilliard. It was her suggestion that I consider writing a Scottish historical, and that idea opened up a whole new genre (and a new set of heroes) to my imagination. Her insight, guidance, and creativity have helped make this book so special. Rose, you are a treasure!

I'd also like to thank the team at St. Martin's Press for their collaboration in putting this book together. You are amazing.

I have to thank my parents, Lino and Juana Marcos, for their example of love. Fifty-eight years of marriage and they're still together.

Finally, thanks to Jesus Christ, for loving me.

GOD, GIVE US MEN!

God, give us men! A time like this demands
Strong minds, great hearts, true faith and ready hands;

Men whom the lust of office does not kill;
Men whom the spoils of office can not buy;
Men who possess opinions and a will;
Men who have honor; men who will not lie;

Men who can stand before a demagogue
And damn his treacherous flatteries without winking!
Tall men, sun-crowned, who live above the fog
In public duty, and in private thinking;

For while the rabble, with their thumb-worn creeds,
Their large professions and their little deeds,
Mingle in selfish strife, lo! Freedom weeps,
Wrong rules the land and waiting Justice sleeps.

—Josiah Gilbert Holland (1819–1881)

Secrets
to Seducing a Scot

PROLOGUE

RAVENS CRAIG HOUSE, SCOTLAND
TWENTY YEARS BEFORE

It was a beautiful knife. Blade sharp enough to cut metal. Handle hewn from the stag his brother had hunted. Sheath made from thick bull hide.

Malcolm held it up to the light. Sunshine from the window slid down the edge of its eight-inch blade, as if the knife could slice the very light.

And in just a few moments, his father was going to die by the weapon.

But Malcolm was unaware that such bad things could happen. He was angry that his father had taken his two older brothers hunting and not him. He was upset that he was left to mind the home as "man of the house" while they were out doing the really manly things. Malcolm had insisted that he wasn't too young for boar hunting—he was past thirteen and covered in hair where it counted—but his father hadn't permitted it.

The front door slammed, heralding his father's arrival. Malcolm peered over the wooden balustrade, the sheathed knife still clutched in his hand. Below stairs, his mother wiped her hands on her apron as she stepped into the hall. A relieved smile warmed her face as she greeted the hunting party. His father gave her a hummed kiss and a lingering hug, while his older brothers staggered under the weight of the pole between their right shoulders from which hung the slaughtered pig.

"'Tis a fine big one, John," said his mother. "We'll be feasting all winter on that one."

"Aye," his father replied, when his sons were out of earshot. "And not the only big thing I've brought for ye."

"John!" she giggled as she slipped out of his grasp. "No' the now."

His little brother and twin sisters squealed in childish curiosity when they saw the fresh kill. Sullenly, Malcolm trudged down the stairs. It should have been him bringing the boar in on his shoulders. It should have been him winning the admiration of his brothers and sisters. But as his family circled the large animal on the table, he felt bereft of honor.

His father took a draft of ale from his tankard. "Malcolm! Come see what we've brought."

The large animal lay lifeless on the butchering table, its eyes half closed as if it were just falling asleep. It was massive, too, at least eleven stone. A masterful kill.

Malcolm nodded silently.

John set down the tankard and took Malcolm's face in his hands.

"I know ye wish it had been ye to bring in the hunt, son," he said with characteristic understanding. "But boar hunting is too dangerous for a man who's yet to grow."

"I'm big enough, Da," he retorted, a little more petulantly than he intended.

"Aye, ye are," John said, reaching across and tousling his son's black hair. "But tall is no' the same as grown. Have no fear . . . we'll get some weight on yer arms over the winter. Next season, I'll take ye with us. And *ye* can be the one to wrestle the boar to the ground."

Malcolm smiled at the thrilling prospect. "Promise?"

John smiled. "Aye. That I do."

The door exploded inward, shocking a startled scream from his mother and the little ones. A frigid draft filled the house as twenty armed men pounded into the hall.

John threw Malcolm behind him as his mother gathered the young ones around her. Malcolm looked at each of the intruders in turn. They reeked of blood and liquor, and they brandished their weapons at every single one of his family members, murder printed on their faces.

"Who the devil are ye?" demanded his father.

A tall man with a ginger beard spoke. "Aye, the de'il indeed. Did you no' expect a visit from yer own clan? Or did ye think yer cowardice would go unnoticed?"

John picked up his hunting dagger from the table. "Get out!"

The bearded man laughed hollowly. "Ye see that, lads? Now he's found his balls!" He turned back to Malcolm's father. "Where were they when the clan was musterin' for battle yesterday, eh? Where were *ye*?" The tip of the man's sword pushed against John's chest.

His father never backed down. "I'll no' say again. All of ye, get out of my house! If ye've a quarrel with me, we'll discuss it outside."

The bearded man's sword swung over to the dead animal. "Ye'll fight a boar but ye'll no' fight a man. Ye're nothing but a cringing coward."

The word made young Malcolm's blood boil. "My father is no' a coward!"

"Keep quiet!" shouted his own father back to him.

"Tell me, boy, what would ye call a man who does not show his face to a battle alongside his own clansmen? A battle in which he is not only duty-bound to present himself, but honor-bound by the loyalty he's sworn to the chief?"

Malcolm didn't recognize any of these men, but they were unified by the tartan that made up their kilts. The same tartan that Malcolm wore.

"I made my case before the chief personally. I have no quarrel with the McBrays—my son Hamish is to be married to a McBray lass. I could no' fight them."

"Ye mean ye *would* not fight them. Ye and yer tenants would have increased our showing on the battlefield. It may not have come to a head if they had seen us strong in number. But without ye we were outnumbered, and the McBrays saw it. They tore us to strips. The battle was lost in only two hours."

A sheen of perspiration broke out on his father's lined forehead. "I'm sorry."

"Sorry?" A man stepped out from the pack. He was unwashed, his thinning hair matted to his head, and he had deep, dark circles under his eyes. "I saw both my sons slain on that battlefield. I found my William with a claymore in his chest. My boy Robert had his neck broken. It took an hour for him to die." Despair gnarled the man's face. "Ye don't know the depths of sorry yet!"

John swallowed hard. "I know ye're grieving. But the blame for yer boys does not rest on me."

"Aye, it does," said the bearded man. "His sons' death, as well as every man out there who lost life or limb, is on *yer* head. Ye and every man jack of yers who hid with yer womenfolk inside the safety of yer homes. Lads, let it no' be said that there is no justice among our clan. An eye for an eye. If Angus here lost two sons, then John must not be allowed to keep his!"

"No!" his mother screamed as she dove in front of her older sons.

A heavyset man punched her in the face, and she crashed to the floor. Malcolm's brother Thomas barreled into the man, but he was overtaken by two more. John flew to his rescue, his dagger raised in the air.

War had broken out in Malcolm's home.

Malcolm's heart pounded in his ears. His breathing raced inside his hairless chest as he helplessly looked on at the melee.

And suddenly he remembered . . . he was not helpless. In his sweaty palm was the sheathed dagger he had taken from Thomas's room.

Could he do this? Could he use this knife to kill a man?

He heard his father scream in pain, and a geyser of righteous anger spewed from inside Malcolm's belly. He unsheathed the weapon and flew into the tangle of men, a war cry tearing from his adolescent throat.

But before he could plunge it into a man's back, someone grabbed him from behind and threw him to the wooden floor. The man with the ginger beard fell on top of him, driving the air from his lungs. Malcolm tried to wriggle out from underneath him, but the man didn't let him go until he had wrenched the weapon from Malcolm's weakened hand.

Malcolm came to his feet, snarling. Hatred welled up inside him as he stared at the bearded man. Fear dissolved into bloodlust, and Malcolm now knew that he needed no weapon to kill his opponent. His fingers curled like claws.

The man didn't show the slightest fear of Malcolm, but Malcolm was about to make him regret that. A wildness came over him, like the fight of a cornered animal. Though he was unarmed, Malcolm lunged at the bearded man. He used his fists, his feet, his teeth . . . anything to defeat the man who had brought the attack against his family. In the back of his mind, Malcolm knew that the man held not only a claymore, but also Thomas's dagger. Any minute now the bearded man would plunge the dagger into Malcolm's body. But he didn't care. Malcolm had lost all fear of death.

What he lacked in strength he made up for in speed. Again and again, Malcolm pummeled the man in the face and body. Finally, the man dropped the dagger on the floor, and Malcolm dove for it. He seized the dagger from the floor. But just as he straightened up again, he realized he had walked into a trap.

The bearded man swung his meaty fist into Malcolm's face. It hit him squarely on the cheek, and the force of it spun his head. The intense pain disoriented him long enough for the bearded man to swing his other fist into the side of Malcolm's head. A burst of pain filled his head, and Malcolm felt his world sputter like a dying candle.

Finally, the fist came flying at his chin.

And all went dark.

A sound was breaking through the quiet darkness. It punctured a hole through his syrupy sleep, and though he didn't know what it was, it demanded that he wake up.

Malcolm's eyes fluttered open, and the pain in his head came flooding back. He didn't know how long he had been out, but he no longer heard the brawl.

There it was again . . . a high-pitched scream. A child's voice.

He tried to make his eyes focus. Through the haze of consciousness, he saw his little sister, Willow. She was being dragged to the kitchen fireplace.

The man with the ginger beard held her eight-year-old body against his chest, her feet scissoring helplessly in the air. In his other hand, clenched in his fist, he held out her wee hand.

A kilted man pulled an iron out from the fireplace, its tip glowing orange from the intense heat. She struggled against her captor, her pretty blond hair whipping around her, but her strength was no match for his. Shrilly she screamed as the hot end of the iron neared her hand.

Malcolm tried to come to her rescue, but his limbs were not responding to the cry of his mind. *Stop it,* he wanted to shout, but no sound could come out of his mouth.

Suddenly he felt himself being dragged across the floor. Though one of his eyes had swollen shut, the other one could see blurred images. They dragged him past the body of his mother, lying lifeless on the floor. Then past his brothers, Thomas and Hamish, who lay in a pool of their own blood. Finally, he saw John, his father, his eyes half closed in encroaching sleep. Just like the boar's had been.

The beautiful handle made from the stag's antler was protruding from his father's chest.

Malcolm closed his eyes to the horrifying vision. A scream, even if he could make it, would not erase the images from his mind. His twin sisters, Shona and Willow, and his little brother Camran cowered in a corner, tears drenching their faces as they clutched their burned hands.

"And this one?" said a voice far above his head.

"We'll brand him, too."

"Then put the iron back in the fire."

Seconds later a white-hot bolt of pain shot down his arm. He was helpless to prevent it, helpless to fight back, helpless even to cry out. But his unresponsive body could still sense every painful nuance of the searing on the back of his hand. Even the smell of his own charred flesh filled his nostrils with repugnance.

"We can't take this one."

"Why not?"

"He's bleeding out of his ear. The boy's as good as dead."

"He might recover."

"Think, man. The others can walk. But this one is unconscious. We don't have the horse to take him. Three *slaighteurs*. That's more than enough recompense."

All Malcolm's entrails seemed to scream from the pain on his hand, even more than from the terrible throbbing in his head and neck. But no pain was greater than the sight of his little brother and sisters being hauled away. Orphaned, mutilated, and terrified—and forced to go with their captors. And just before he drifted out of consciousness, only one thought filled his head.

Hunt them down.

ONE

A royal ball is very much like any other ball. One sees many of the same guests, eats many of the same dishes, and has many of the same conversations. But juggle enough balls, and one is bound to fall.

And so it happened to a certain gentleman and his lady who found themselves discreetly escorted from the Princess's birthday fête. Perhaps too much wine led to too much whine, but this unwise man balked about the selection of spirits at the Duke of Kent's table, and he decided to boast to the Prince Regent about his own collection of expensive liquors.

A word of advice to those who attend at court: Never complain about the champagne. It is one thing to be considered a connoisseur of the finer pleasures, but it is quite another to be demanding of them.

Unhappily, this particular man (and his particular tastes) will never be invited back. You may be called fussy, you may be called arrogant. But the one thing you don't want to be called is gone.

Serena Marsh tilted the champagne flute into her mouth.
The champagne wasn't as bad as all that. Come to think
of it, neither was her article. The polite yet forceful expulsion of Lord and Lady Lamoreaux tonight gave her
just the material she needed for this week's contribu-
tion to the "Rage Page." The column practically wrote
itself.

She gazed out over the stonework balustrade. Below,
people dressed in their royal finery swirled about the
sunken garden like fluttering confetti. Over by the rose-
bushes, Princess Augusta chatted amiably with a flock
of parliamentarians.

"Are you Serena Marsh?"

Serena turned around. Two ladies approached her,
and she could tell they were related. One was in her
early dotage, with a face like a gnarled tree trunk, and
the other looked to be her daughter.

"Yes, I am."

The wrinkles in the older lady's face deepened as
she beamed at Serena. "Oh, Miss Marsh, it's so good to
finally meet you. I simply adore your column! I read it
every Wednesday in the *Town Crier*."

"As do I," insisted the younger.

"You're too kind, Mrs.—"

"Lady Geraldine Hewitt. This is my daughter, the
Lady Marie Enstrom. My friends and I have such fun
with the clever things you say. Why, just yesterday we
were having tea with the Camberwells, and your column was the sole and exclusive topic of conversation
all afternoon. What was it you called that Dutch court-
ier, the one who loved to eat? Ah, yes, I remember . . .
'a man for all seasonings.' "

Lady Hewitt cackled, making Serena smile.

"I'd never laughed so hard in my life. Was he really
so *gauche*?"

Serena rolled her eyes prettily. "Unrepentantly so. Be glad you were not a witness to the awful wig he wore. I'm certain his hair wasn't that color even in his youth, which had to have been about three centuries ago. He can't possibly fool anybody. One's hair does not turn *black* with age."

The ladies laughed gaily.

"My favorite," remarked Lady Enstrom, "was that story you told of the French noblewoman who divorced her husband because of his profligate spending." Lady Enstrom turned to her mother. "She titled the article, 'Till Debt Us Do Part.'"

Their giggles could be heard well down into the garden, gladdening Serena's heart. If there was one thing she relished, it was having her words quoted back to her.

Lady Enstrom's eyes beamed at Serena. "I must remark, Mama, on the exquisite gown that Miss Marsh is wearing."

"Yes. Quite enchanting," confirmed Lady Hewitt.

The dress Serena had on was fashioned of blond silk embroidered with gold thread at the neckline, sleeves, and hem. A wave of starched lace fanned out behind her neck, and her golden hair was collected high upon her head. A string of pearls cascaded through the artfully placed curls.

"Thank you very much," she replied, a surprised blush rising to her cheeks. Modesty prohibited her from mentioning that she herself had designed it. "It was crafted by a very talented *couturier* from Orléans. The French seem to be better with a sewing needle than a bayonet."

Lady Hewitt smiled as she lay down her glass on the stone balustrade. "Tell me, who will you be writing about in your next column?"

Serena grinned. "My dear Lady Hewitt. You know I do not divulge any names in my column. And even if

I were to write about someone attending this ball, I
should not be so heartless as to break in upon his in-
cognito."

"His?" Lady Enstrom replied with a curious gleam
in her eye. "Oh, do tell us what you know."

Serena smiled benevolently. "I will only hint enough
to say that if I were you, Lady Hewitt, I would pick up
that drink again and make a great show of enjoying it."

The crinkles in Lady Enstrom's eyes deepened. "Oh,
I can't wait. Miss Marsh, you simply must come to a
party we're holding at the end of the month. I'm inviting masses of people. There will be lots for you to
write about."

"I'd be delighted."

"Where is your honored father? I shall invite him
personally."

Serena had lost track of Earlington Marsh when the
Prince Regent pulled her aside to have a good rail over
Lord Lamoreaux. She craned her neck over the garden
below. "I don't see him. But I shall look for him presently, and I'll be sure to convey your invitation."

"Good! I can't wait to tell everyone you'll be coming!"

Serena grinned as she walked away from the effusive women. Her social diary was full almost every
night for weeks. There was something to be said for
being the writer of a renowned Society column. Although she enjoyed a certain respectability from being
the daughter of an ambassador, the "Rage Page" had
put her name on everyone's lips. There wasn't a rout or
ball to which she was not invited, and her absence was
a shame upon the hostess. Her column had an enormous following, as everyone who read her column
wanted to be featured in it—even in a less-than-
flattering light. The editor of her paper once remarked

that Serena churned the cream of Society so much that one day she would end up with butter.

And her dance card was the envy of any duchess. The current of gentlemen that swirled around her always made her feel giddy with desirability. How she loved their attentions! She drank in their furtive looks, bathed in their endless flattery. She lost count of the number of marriage proposals she had received, knowing most of them to be born of unbridled lust to possess her. But she collected them anyway, like trophies that proved she mattered.

The exotic night-blooming jasmine offered up its heady scent as she strolled across the courtyard of Kensington Palace. Conversations drifted in and out of her hearing. Raised glasses shimmered in the glow of the full moon. The party was fizzing with festivity. This was London at its finest and grandest, and Serena hummed with pleasure.

A flash of red intruded upon her cheerful mood, and made her turn her attention toward the south garden. It was an army uniform.

Strange thing to see at a ball like this, a celebration of the birth of the infant Princess Victoria. Amid the cheerful pastel fabrics, a redcoat—especially that of a major general—brought an inexplicable sense of foreboding upon the jovial mood.

Her concerns were reinforced as the general walked up to her father and whispered something into his ear. A strange expression came over her father's face, and he followed the officer to a separate part of the garden.

Though he was only in his early fifties, Earlington Marsh looked a good deal older. His broad shoulders now drooped slightly, and his strong, intelligent eyes were weighted with experience and regrets. His sandy hair was salted with gray, which was echoed in the slight silver sheen just below the surface of his chin.

The two men disappeared through the ivy-covered archway, leaving Serena to stew in her curiosity. Anxious minutes passed as she debated the wisdom of intruding upon their meeting. But concern for her father drowned out the warning voice of propriety, and she took a step inside.

Her slippered feet made no sound on the soft earth. Instantly she spotted the red-coated general. He was locked in a whispered conversation with her father and a cluster of men. She strained to listen, and managed to catch just a few words. *Rebels. Uprising. Treason.*

One of the men caught sight of her and hushed the others. Suddenly every face turned to look at her, stopping her dead in her tracks.

"Serena?" said Earlington quietly. "What are you doing here?"

"Father. I-I was looking for you."

Earlington shouldered away from the somber-faced crowd. "These gentlemen and I were just having a word in private. You should return to the party. I'll be there in a few moments."

"Is anything wrong?"

"Nothing that should concern you, my dear," he said. "Let me escort you back to the gathering."

"Father," she began, a note of asperity in her voice. "I do hope you're not considering returning to work. You're not yet fully recovered!"

"Serena," he said. "You worry too much about me. It was only a mild seizure of the heart. I'm perfectly well now. Besides, we were just talking."

Serena shook her head, glancing at his dark green double-breasted tailcoat. He was wearing the same coat the night he collapsed at the Prime Minister's office. "It's too soon. I won't have it. If you won't have a care for your own health, then I will. I shall march right over there and tell them to leave you alone."

"Serena." There was that tone again, the one that she knew to be heavy with wisdom. "What have I told you about fear?"

She sighed. "There is a difference between fearing a real danger and fearing an imagined one."

"That's right. It is not meet that we should be afraid of what *may* happen. That would simply be an exercise in futility."

The general stepped forward. "Ambassador. The Privy Council is awaiting your answer, sir."

Serena looked up into her father's face. Though the circles under his eyes were darker and his skin had grown paler, the strength in his eyes had never diminished.

"Go back to the garden party. I'm certain there are some very handsome young men who are wondering where you've gotten to."

"If you send me back, I shall tell the Prince Regent on you," she threatened impotently.

His eyes smiled in return. "I'll rejoin you both presently."

Present. It was a word that grew more precious with each passing day. She wondered how much more of a present there would be with her father. Of one thing she was sure. It was a present she would not be able to keep.

TWO

He had him.

Silently, the hunter crept up on his unsuspecting prey. Malcolm squeezed the grip of his bow, all his senses leaping into heightened awareness. His heart hammered, his breathing quickened, his balls tightened. Though a chill night breeze wafted through the trees, he began to perspire. Time seemed to slow, an eternity fitting into a single heartbeat.

Sheltered within the womb of a small clearing, his prey was huddling over a meager fire. Malcolm watched as the man tossed a handful of twigs on the weak flames. The man shivered, tightening the McInnes plaid around his shoulders. Though darkness had finally fallen over the northern hills, Malcolm could see the pistol wedged into the waist of the man's kilt.

Slowly, he positioned the arrow across his bow. The distance was against him but the breeze now stilled. He shut one green eye, taking careful aim. This was the moment he had been working toward for nearly a fortnight, and the thrill of the capture began to flood his veins. He leaned forward, clearing the arrowhead out from behind a branch . . . when a twig snapped underfoot.

McInnes perked, gun brandished in Malcolm's direction. The man's vantage point rendered him practically

blind to where Malcolm was hiding. Even so, Malcolm
knew there was nothing more dangerous than a frightened man with a loaded gun.

"Who's there?" McInnes called out. Panic, mingled
with guilt, covered him like a sheen of sweat. "Show
yourself!"

In the dappled moonlight, Malcolm watched Mc-
Innes advance cautiously toward him. Perhaps his prey
was not so blind after all. Five courses of action with
varying degrees of danger streamed through Malcolm's
mind.

He untensed his bow, rendering himself defenseless.
Slowly, he picked up a rock from the ground. Cocking
back his arm, he threw it as hard as he could toward the
clearing.

The next moments happened in a blur. McInnes
spun around, a panicked response to the distracting
sound. Malcolm drew back the string on his bow and
let the arrow fly. McInnes fell to the ground, his scream
tearing through the forest.

Malcolm bolted from his hiding place, bounding effortlessly over a fallen birch. McInnes was writhing on
the ground, helplessly trying to pull the bloody arrow
from the back of his thigh.

McInnes rolled onto his side, his shaky hand aiming
the pistol at Malcolm. There was nowhere for Malcolm
to turn, nowhere to hide—the only thing that counted
was speed. He pounced full-body on the man in a desperate attempt to wrest the weapon from him.

Teeth bared, the men struggled with each other. Though
Malcolm towered over McInnes, McInnes was strong
and outweighed his hunter by a full two stone.

Risking his life, Malcolm released one hand from
McInnes's gun and pushed the arrow deeper into the
man's thigh. McInnes screamed, reaching for Malcolm's

arm. Then Malcolm swung a beefy fist into McInnes's abdomen. Incapacitated, McInnes released the weapon, and his opponent wrenched it from his fist.

Panting for breath, McInnes cursed. "Go on with ye, ye mangy cur. Shoot an unarmed man like the coward ye are."

Malcolm shoved the pistol into the waist of his black kilt. "Nothing would give me greater pleasure than to have at a thieving murderer. But luck is on yer side tonight, McInnes. The law demands her claim on ye first."

"Law? Ye're daft. 'Twas none but the English I killed . . . aye, them what was driving me off my own land."

"The Crown owns yer land now. Ye forfeited it when ye poisoned the stream that killed all of Lord Rutledge's cattle . . . and his infant son."

"What's this talk of the Crown?" he asked incredulously as Malcolm bound his wrists behind him. "Ye're a bloody Scotsman! Have ye no pride, man? Why do ye not support the rebellion?"

Malcolm was silent, making quick work of tying knots around the man's wrists.

"What clan are ye?"

Still Malcolm did not speak. It was a question he could not answer without a degree of shame.

Malcolm spun the man around and, holding him fast by his shirtfront, removed the *sgian dubh* from the man's hose.

McInnes glanced at Malcolm's hand. "I have ye now! Ye're a good-for-nothing *slaighteur*! Rejected by the clans. Ye're treacherous against yer own people!" McInnes spat at his feet.

Malcolm almost struck him for the insult. But McInnes was right. The scar on the back of his hand pronounced it. He was an orphan among Scots, living without the protection or the honor of belonging to a clan. It made him worse than nothing. But he would have it no other way.

Malcolm's emerald eyes bore into the man's face. "I owe m'loyalty to no clan. Scotland, England . . . it matters not who pays me to bring ye in. Personally, I'd do it just for the pleasure of seeing ye hanged."

"Slaighteur!" yelled McInnes as Malcolm jerked him forward by the arm. And though he was nearly bent over double as he dragged his wounded leg behind him, his voice carried above the treetops and reverberated in the forest. *"Slaighteur!"*

It was a name that Malcolm Slayter was forced to make his own.

THREE

"Scotland?" Serena repeated incredulously. "But there's nothing in Scotland except sheep and cows."

Earlington suppressed a chuckle as he poured the tea. "Serena . . . Scotland is an important part of Great Britain, and has very much to do with what makes Britain so great in the first place."

She screwed up her shoulders. "I still don't understand why you must be sent there."

Earlington spoke with the even tones and measured words that were his hallmark. "War with France has depleted Britain's treasury. In order to keep the country running, Parliament has had to impose yet another tax upon the people. But the Scots have complained, declaring that the additional tax is putting too great a strain on an already overburdened populace. Parliament heard their grievances, but has remained unmoved. Now there is widespread unrest in Scotland. The Prince Regent has asked me to relieve Anglo-Scottish tensions by keeping the rumblings from turning into outright rebellion."

"But why must *you* go?" she asked, taking the cup of honeyed China tea. "What about your health? You shouldn't even be traveling such a great distance, let alone embarking on such a delicate and worrisome assignment. Why can't they send someone else?"

"Serena, you know better than that. When your Prince asks you to go, you must obey. Quite frankly, I'm honored that he asked me. It shows that the Privy Council still has faith in my abilities."

Serena read the regret in his face. She reached out and covered his hand with her own.

"*I* have faith in you, Father. And if the sheep and cows are in revolt, I know that you will help them see reason."

Earlington chuckled as he brought the steaming cup to his lips. "My dear child, I do hope you'll behave yourself once you settle in."

Settle in. Serena set down her teacup, a worried look marring her forehead. "I've been wondering about that, Father. While you're busy talking sense to the Scots, what exactly will I be doing?"

He shrugged. "Whatever you please. Scotland is a beautiful country filled with many lovely landscapes."

"And after I've toured the surrounding countryside, what then?"

"How do you mean?"

"Well, here in London, I have my friends and my set. I shall miss them terribly."

"You are the most charming and delightful creature on God's good earth, with an innate flair for popularity. I'm certain that in no time you will make all new friends."

"Yes, but that will take some time. What shall I do in the interim?"

"You'll have your column to keep you occupied. You can still write it from up there."

She rose from the upholstered settee. "And write about whom? There is no Society in the Highlands, no social set as there is here in London. Who would want to read about Scotland? It's nothing in the middle of nowhere."

Earlington sighed. "The people are largely simple folk, it's true, but they have a wit and a warmth all their own. I'm certain you'll like them once you get to know them. And not all the people are farmers and herders. There are many families who are well off, who live in homes very much like ours. We will be meeting many of them as well."

Serena swung her gaze out of the window into the garden. The thought of trading the sparkle of London for the provincial Highlands depressed her. If she left London for any length of time, it might be the end of her column altogether. In no time, she could go from being among the "who's who" to being the object of "who's she?"

"I don't want to go, Father. But I don't want to stay here without you, either." She chuckled at herself. "I want it both ways, don't I?"

"Oh, poppet," he said, standing beside her. "I would love to give you what makes you happy. But I can't. Not this time." He put his hands on her shoulders. "This will be a dull diplomatic mission. You really needn't come. You can stay in London for the rest of the Season. I'll write to—"

The thought of him being so ill and so far away strengthened her resolve. "No, I won't hear of it. My place is with you. We go together."

Her father kissed her on the forehead. "It should only be for a fortnight. A month at the very most. We leave in the morning." Her father strode out of the morning room.

It wouldn't be so bad, she told herself. For four weeks, she could live without the balls and parties, and the accolades that came from writing a popular Society column. For a single month, she could do without the visits and surreptitious kisses from her gentlemen friends. It would be almost effortless to trade violins for bagpipes, and roses for thistles.

Wouldn't it?

FOUR

The Thorn & Thistle was bursting that evening. Each of the twelve or so tables in the pub was spilling over with men, and those for whom there was no seat packed themselves in front of the bar. The air was thick with the smells of roasting meat and unwashed bodies. Though the din of their combined voices was deafening, they were all speaking of the very same thing.

Malcolm Slayter had just left his capture at the Inverness courthouse and had collected his reward. He was bruised, exhausted, and thirsty, and he desperately wanted to wash McInnes's blood off his hands. A meal and a bed at the Thorn & Thistle would be just the thing to restore his depleted vigor. He tossed a coin to the stable lad with strict instructions to give his gray, Old Man, as much hay and oats as he could eat, and then opened the door to the pub.

There was hardly any room to walk around, dense as it was with men. Malcolm shouldered his way to the bar. At six and a half feet tall, no one impeded him. Still, the room got progressively quieter as he ordered a pint of ale and some stew and bread. By the time he made it to an empty bench in the back, the pub had silenced altogether.

A man wearing a Cameron tartan walked up to

Malcolm. "What're ye doing here? We'll have no *slaigh-teurs* here."

Malcolm hung his head, fighting to control his temper. He had forgotten to put on his gloves, which hid the scar that betrayed his dishonor. "I'm here for a meal and a bed, friend. I've no quarrel with ye."

"I'm not yer friend. And ye'll get no hospitality from any of us."

A Dundas man spoke next. "Leave him be, Charlie. The cause can use all the men it can get."

Charlie waved a hand at Malcolm. "Bah! Ye'll no' get help from the likes of him. He's a villainous *slaigh-teur.* Him and his kind are naught but rogues and knaves. They're traitorous all, to a man. Look at him! Why do ye think he wears a black kilt? 'Tis because he'll claim no clan . . . and no clan will claim him."

"Let the man speak his own mind." Dundas was a huge Clydesdale of a man, with shoulders heavy with muscle and a head of copper-tinged hair. "My name's Will. Ye've come opportunely. This here's a meeting to come to an accord about the tax. We're going to take a stand against the English. Are ye with us?"

Malcolm ran his right hand down his tired eyes. "I've come for a meal and a bed. If I can't get them here, I'll be back on my way."

"There. D'ye see?" exclaimed Charlie, loud enough for all to hear. "Weak as water! Go on with ye. Piss off."

Will looked Malcolm up and down, his intelligent eyes sizing him up. He pointed down at Malcolm's crimson-stained left hand.

"How bad are ye hurt?"

Malcolm looked down at the dried, rust-colored layer coating his fist. "It's no' my blood. It's someone else's."

A smile lifted the corners of Will's blue eyes. "Not

so weak as ye think, Charlie. At least we know who came out the winner in that fight."

A tide of laughter swept through the pub.

"Who lost his blood to ye?" asked Will.

Malcolm inhaled sharply. "Jock McInnes."

Will's auburn eyebrows flew up. Even Charlie's mouth fell open.

"Ye killed Jock McInnes?" asked Will.

"No. More's the pity," Malcolm answered. "But he'll be dead enough once he answers for his crimes."

A rotund man sitting at the bar slammed his schooner onto the table, the contents sloshing out onto the wooden surface. "Jock McInnes was a hero to the cause!"

A thundercloud darkened Malcolm's features. "Tell that to the mother of the bairn he killed."

The man's bushy beard bristled. "Freedom from the English carries a price."

"Oh? How many of yer own children are ye willing t'exchange for it?"

The man vacillated, his jaw tensed. "I wouldna turn over my own countrymen, that's for certain."

Malcolm's eyes stormed over. "Patriotism and justice are seldom compatible."

It was a sad truth that had changed the course of Malcolm's entire life. It was impossible for him to achieve one without forfeiting the other. Even now, at just past thirty-three years of age, he had probably amassed more enemies than most other men. He didn't have just the English to deal with—the Scottish, too, were against him. He belonged to an outcast kinship, a bastard clan with no lands, no heritage, no honor. All his life he had struggled to reclaim what was taken from him. And now he was being asked to help the very countrymen who denied him justice. Wearily, he lifted his satchel and stood.

"Carry on with yer meeting. I'll trouble ye no longer."

Will dropped a heavy hand on Malcolm's shoulder. Instinctively, Malcolm's hand flew to his concealed dagger.

"Friend," began Will astutely, "I'll wager ye've been ill treated by yer own kind. But ye'll get no bother from me. Let me buy ye a drop of whiskey. And if ye don't mind turning the blood on yer hands from that of the Scots to that of the English, ye may just find the justice ye are seeking for yerself."

FIVE

"Scotland? What the hell is there to do in Scotland?"

In the editor's office of the *Town Crier,* Archer Weston leaned against the four-foot stack of newspapers that formed his seat back. It was his trophy, that stack, and his goal was that when it got as tall as he was, he would start his own paper.

Serena chuckled at Archer's response, which echoed her own words to her father. "I told you I had unfortunate tidings."

Archer bolted out of his chair, his lean frame shaking loose his compact energy. "Unfortunate I expected. Not catastrophic."

She sighed. "Don't be so hysterical. Mine is just one column."

"Just one column?" Archer cocked his blond eyebrow. "Allow me to illustrate." He turned and pointed to a spot on his stack about a foot from the top. "This is where you started writing for this paper. And this," he said, about an inch from that point, "is where we finally started to turn a serious profit. Your column is the reason that women—and not just men—buy the paper. The 'Rage Page' has launched for us an entirely new readership— ladies of the upper classes. And more importantly, it's the reason a whole new segment of businesses have

started advertising in our paper. We are finally starting to emerge as a threat to the other major London
papers. Two months ago, the *Times* launched a column
similar to yours. But it had no cleverness, no sparkle,
and it was so disparaged by the readers that they dis-
continued it. The public loves your writing. You can't
stop now."

She was a kaleidoscope of emotions. From one moment to the next, she felt flattered, proud, needed, wanted,
and disloyal. It seemed as if she was abandoning not only
Archer but also the many readers who followed her work.
She looked into his pleading eyes.

"What can I do?"

Archer folded his arms in front of his chest. His
navy-colored tailcoat set off the windswept blond locks
that were just a shade darker than her own. "You must
stay in London! You can't make observations on what
happens in Society from the remote hinterland of Scotland."

Serena worried her lip. "Maybe Scotland's social set
is more interesting than London's. Maybe I can expose
a new set of stories to the readers."

Archer tossed his hands in the air. "London readers
don't want to hear about who is seen at the caber tossing. They don't know Lady MacWhatsit. And they
don't care what she's up to. They want to hear about
people they know, people they admire or admonish.
They enjoy guessing who you'll be talking about next.
You are their eyes and ears among Society's elite. If
you're gone for too long, you'll lose touch with all
those people. You can't leave London. You mustn't."

She covered her face with her gloved hands. "I can't
let my father go alone. He needs me, Archer. He's not
well, and I know he hides the truth from me. If he goes

to Scotland by himself and anything happens to him . . ." She dared not even finish the thought.

Archer went to her side and took her by the arms. "I'm sorry, Serena. Come here." He enfolded her in his arms. "I shouldn't make you feel accountable for our paper's profits. Of course you must go with your father. You'd only worry yourself sick if you let him go on his own. In fact, help him. The faster he brings order to that savage country, the sooner you'll come back, and the less the readers will miss you."

Serena gazed into Archer's caramel-colored eyes. Handsome and energetic, Archer was to Serena an exceptional man. At almost thirty, Archer was well aware of his power to change the world, one word at a time. His boldness and rapier-sharp intelligence excited her, and their conversations sometimes lasted hours. Of all the men she knew, only Archer made her toes curl. Maybe it was not her column or London that she'd miss the most. Maybe it was this embrace, and the gentle kiss he now placed upon her lips.

"Bugger the readers. *I'll* miss you."

She smiled into his cravat, her heart thrumming with excitement. "You've been absolutely horrid to me today. I won't miss you at all."

"Then I'll leave you with this to remember me by." He took her lips in a solid kiss that made her giddy with delight.

"If my father saw you kiss me like that, he'd have your head on a stack of your own newspapers."

"I'll cherish that thought," he said with a wink.

Serena contemplated that kiss as their town coach rumbled through the English countryside bound for an unfamiliar northern destination.

She looked across the seat at her father. He had been reading a sheaf of diplomatic papers until he quietly dozed off. He slept more and more, weak as he had become following his heart seizure, yet he was more determined to return to office. Nothing could keep her father from his duty to king and country.

Although her father was headed toward his destiny, she was moving away from hers. Not only was London her home, it was her delight, and each mile that she pulled away from it was a physical pain. It was as though an invisible thread tied her heart to that great and bustling city, and it grew tauter and tauter the farther away she drove. Until, she suspected, the cord would finally snap.

Now it became evident just how far she had traveled from the glittering London ambience. The landscape began to change as she traveled over the rugged terrain of Scotland. Gone were the vast manicured gardens and majestic mansions of England. Now she could only see the ruins of ancient castles and tiny crofts on the edges of farms. There were endless lonely miles between villages. Even the weather seemed to belong exclusively to this bleak country, as she left the summertime sunshine behind and entered a world grayed out by mist and rain.

And as they drove past a solitary croft enclosed on all four sides by a mossy stone dyke, only one thought filled her head.

How soon can I get back?

The woman leaned against the doorjamb of her two-room croft. Beyond the mossy stone dyke, a quarter mile from her farm, a beautiful black carriage rumbled down the lane.

There had been a time when she had thought she, too, might be riding a carriage like that one. But that was long before. Before she had married too young a man too old. Before the shine in her copper hair had tarnished to a dull bronze.

The good Lord had seen fit to deliver her of eight beautiful bairns, but now she wished she'd been barren. The crops hadn't come in yet, and there wasn't enough in the house to feed those who lived in it. The sheep had been sold off last year, and that money was long gone. And her a widow with no man in the house to look after them . . . It was a losing battle each day to keep body and soul together.

She lifted the lid on the cupboard she used as a larder. She counted its contents out into her apron. One leek, four potatoes, and maybe a pound of liver. She stared at the assortment in dismay. Nine people had to be fed on this.

Maybe if she had some oatmeal or flour, she could bulk up the meager offering, even make a crude haggis. But grain had become way too dear. The tax on it was beyond her ability to pay.

If only she had a bit more, her children might not cry in the night again. The old ones were used to the rumblings of their tummies, but the wee ones only knew to wail. To hear them cry was a physical pain for her, and her exhausted embraces were not enough to soothe their emptiness. She swept an alarmed glance down onto the ingredients for their supper, as if somehow wishing would make them multiply. But this was all there was. The liver, the five vegetables . . . and the apron.

An idea germinated in her desperate mind. She unfastened the apron from her waist. It might work. After all, the apron was made of soft cotton, loosely woven. If she tore it into strips, and ran it through the meat grinder together with the liver, it just might do. Minced together with the leeks and potatoes, and browned on the griddle over the fire, she might be able to turn a meal for four into a meal for nine.

At least she'd be able to fill the little ones enough for tonight.

But what would she do about tomorrow?

SIX

Though the long trip from London had been arduous, Serena and Earlington received a warm welcome when they arrived at Copperleaf Manor.

Their hosts, Lord and Lady Askey, were as pleasant and hospitable as Serena could expect. Though he was English by birth, Lord Askey's family had held lands in Scotland for generations, and he spent a great deal of his time there. He loved Scotland and its people, but he was a loyalist and he advocated a unified Britain. Politically, he was the perfect man to host Commissioner Marsh, being so well liked among the Scots. And personally, he and his wife made every effort to ensure that Serena and her father felt at home.

Josiah Askey was a man of fifty whose graying hair seemed to have melted from the top of his head to the sides of his face. He had a jolly air to him, and when he smiled his eyes became little blue crescents. Comfortable living had given him a paunch, but he was yet a man of unbounded energy.

His first wife had died of the fever, but she had given him two daughters: Lady Georgina, who had married the year before to a young man of means in Dumfries, and Lady Zoe, who was only fourteen. Although Serena was homesick for London, Zoe's youthful zest and irrepressible friendliness made the separation easier to bear.

Rachel Askey, his young wife, was only slightly older than Serena, but her May–December marriage seemed to have been made in heaven. Rachel Askey was a Scot from a noble family. She had a creamy complexion and strawberry freckles on her face that matched the rosy tones in her lovely hair. Recently delivered of an infant daughter, she was never seen without her nearby. She was bright in face and mind, and her kindness drew in the young Zoe, who embraced her as an older sister rather than as a stepmother. They were a warm family, and tried very hard to make Serena feel at home.

But home was back in London. Serena made every attempt to keep her chin up for the family's benefit, but she was secretly very unhappy. Being away from the City—at the very height of the Season—was a misery. At this very hour, she'd probably be climbing into a carriage, en route to a ball. She'd be wearing her new cornflower-blue confection with her pearl necklace and her white silk gloves, and her hair would be done up *à la cascade* with blue ribbons interwoven through the curls. It was a fashion she was looking forward to showing off. Her styles were always talked about and emulated.

She'd be drinking champagne and dining on lobster, Cornish hens, and vegetables in heavy French sauces. She'd be surrounded by peers, politicians, and playwrights—men of ideas and influence—and ladies who drove the culture of the day. She'd attend the theater, Almack's, museums. There'd be lawn tennis, picnics, card parties, and dancing. There'd be no end to her laughter and her discourse.

Until Scotland.

Zoe came in through the open drawing room door, munching on an apple. Her reddish brown hair streamed down her back. "The sun has come out. Would you like to go riding today?"

Writing was what Serena really hungered to do, and the activity she missed the most. But she didn't want to be a misery around the girl. "Certainly. Though I must warn you that I haven't had a chance to buy a riding habit this season, so please don't gasp in horror when you see me in last year's style."

Zoe rolled her pretty brown eyes. "Once we leave the stable, it wouldn't matter if you rode completely unclothed. There's no one to see you for miles."

Serena smiled, but there was no mirth behind it. She closed the book she was reading. "Zoe, I'm really grateful to your father and stepmother for sharing their home with us. And staying in Fort Augustus has been most restful. But sometimes I wonder if it doesn't get rather lonely here for you. Is there no set to which you belong, no place for you to enjoy the company of others your own age?"

Zoe sat next to Serena. "Of course! Sometimes I'll drive down to Dumfries and stay with my sister and her husband. Or we'll drive to Glasgow and stay with my cousins. They've just had their coming out."

Serena blinked, trying to phrase her question better. "What I mean is, is there anything for you to do that doesn't require two days' journey and several changes of horses? A party or ball to go to, at least once a week? Somewhere where there's food and entertainment, and lots and lots of people? Where you can see what ladies and gentlemen are wearing, and where you can show off your latest design, too? A place where people of all sorts get together, and they talk about things that matter . . . or things that matter just to them? Where people whisper their dastardly little secrets, and other people whisper them over to the next person? Fun places like that?"

"Well," Zoe began, "in the fall, when we return to

York, we reunite with our friends by organizing an autumn ball."

"In the fall," Serena repeated with an edge to her voice. "And meanwhile? What will you do here in Scotland during these interminable summer months?"

"Um . . . well, there will be the Saint Swithin's Day Festival in Invergarry next month. That's a great deal of fun, with lots of people. The Highland Games will be held then . . . apple juggling, caber tossing, and beer-cask rolling. And you can get all sorts of delicious sweets at the festival. That is, of course, provided there's no uprising to cancel it."

Next month? Serena smoothed out an invisible wrinkle in her new silk dress. There was no way she was going to endure another month without the distraction of a social gathering. It was bad enough that she was far removed from the thrilling bustle of London, but to have to wait another month for the relative excitement of apple throwing, caber eating, and beer bathing was just too much to endure. She had to do something about this.

She had to do something *now*.

SEVEN

" 'Tis an outrage!" Guinnein Kinross bolted out of his seat around the negotiating table, leaving the other three men feeling the weight of his displeasure.

Brandubh McCullough lowered his head pensively and took a deep breath. "It won't do to bring our feelings to the table, Kinross. Let the man speak."

Kinross grumbled, but he returned to the table. The upstairs room at the Inverness courthouse was as cold as a larder, but the tensions around the table seemed to have raised the temperature. He sat back down at the table, sending ripples through the untouched whiskey in all four glasses.

"Forgive us our outbursts, Commissioner," said Brandubh. "We Scots cannot stomach injustice."

Earlington Marsh regarded Brandubh McCullough thoughtfully. He was the youngest of the three emissaries who had come to the table, but unlike the others in the Council, he had a cool head and a face absent of expression. A handsome man, too, with a full head of dark brown hair and intelligent navy eyes that seemed wise beyond his years. Just the sort of man he would expect to find at a negotiating table in a seat of government anywhere in the world.

"There is nothing to forgive, gentlemen," Earlington said. "We are all here for the same reason—to find a

peaceful solution to the disharmony between our peoples.
I for one am willing to do whatever it takes to ensure
justice among all the king's subjects."

"Are ye now?" spat Kinross sarcastically, barely
looking at Earlington.

"It seems to me, Commissioner," began Hallyard
Skene, "that Scotland fared better when she wasn't
among the king's subjects." Like Earlington, Skene was
a man past fifty, but Skene seemed as if he had spent
every one of those years in battle. Scars glowed whitely
across his face, and he kept his arm tucked behind his
blue, red, and green fly plaid, concealing the spot below
his wrist where his hand was missing. "In the hundred
years since the Acts of Union, Scotland has never been
treated better than seventh-class citizens. We suffer like
any nation with a remote seat of government. Our liberties are taken away one by one."

"Aye," echoed Kinross, nodding his ginger head. "And
now more taxation, with no measure of relief or benefit? 'Tis an outrage."

Earlington was accustomed to dealing with politicians, men of words who utilized the subtle art of verbal manipulation. But these were not politicians. They
were plain-speaking people who voiced their true sen-
timents loudly. Nevertheless, the three Scotsmen were
powerful men with many holdings and much influence,
and if they called for an armed insurrection against
England, the people of Scotland would listen.

"Kinross, I can certainly understand your displeasure with the new taxes. Parliament wishes it were not
necessary to levy taxes on the people. But war with
Napoleon has nearly bankrupted the government. We
must rebuild, and to do so requires that we temporarily
assess a sixpence tax on grain and other foodstuffs."

"It's not just his displeasure you need to understand, Commissioner," said Skene. "People are starving because of the tax. It's gotten so that farmers can't afford to eat what they've harvested. If they don't meet the landlords' percentage for the tax, they'll be thrown off the land. Does Parliament mean to starve the Scots out of existence?"

"Not at all, Skene. This war has caused widespread suffering among all the king's subjects. The tax affects England as well as Scotland."

"But an Englishman earns more than a Scot," he countered quickly. "And he receives all the services the tax supplies. Good roads, more schools . . . better courts." He waved around at the room they were in, which was only slightly more dignified than a large barn.

"Aye," affirmed Kinross. "If there is to be a tax on the Scottish people, then the revenue should benefit the Scottish people."

"And don't forget, Commissioner," offered the young Brandubh, "an Englishman can sell his merchandise freely on the world market. A Scotsman is forbidden to trade directly, and so can't earn a profit. If I wanted to trade my cattle with Germany, I'd have to first sell it to England at the going rate. Is that fair?"

It wasn't, but Earlington couldn't say so. "These are all valid concerns, and you have my word that I shall bring these matters to the attention of Parliament."

"I'll tell ye what would bring the attention of Parliament. Refusal to pay the tax."

Earlington shook his head. "That is not a solution, Kinross. It would only embitter relations between our countries."

"No more bitter than the sight of a mother unable to feed her children," he retorted.

"No one wants that, Skene." As he spoke, Earlington detected a faint ache in his chest, and a thread of fear snaked through him. He waited for the crushing pain that had signaled his last heart seizure, but thankfully the ache went away. He took a sip of the whiskey to calm his nerves. "The king desires only peace, and to ease the suffering of the Scottish people. I am empowered to set a minimum fixed profit on livestock traded outside the country. You will henceforth receive a premium on every head of cattle you bring to London for overseas commerce."

"The tax, Commissioner," reminded Brandubh, pounding the table with a finger. "We are here about the tax."

Earlington nodded pensively. "The tax on the grain must stand."

Brandubh snorted. "Ye see, gentlemen? I told you as much. The art of government is to make two-thirds of a nation pay all it possibly can for the benefit of the other third."

Earlington lifted his head. "Those are the words of Voltaire, sir."

"Aye," replied the young man. "He was a great reformist."

"Reformist? Some would say a rebel."

"A rebel, aye. One on whose ideas stood the French Revolution. And the American. Perhaps the Scottish Revolution will be next."

"Forgive me, McCullough. But are you threatening civil war?"

"And what if he is?" chimed in Kinross. "It'd be no less than yer king deserves."

"And what do your people deserve?" asked Earlington. "The war with Napoleon has taken too many of your young fighting men already. Your remaining soldiers, for such I must call them, are either too young or too old for battle."

"No Scot exists who can't fight for his country."

"But will you deprive your women, who have already sacrificed their husbands and eldest sons to the war in France, of their fathers and youngest sons now? Be sensible, sir. Scotland has already lost too much."

"And now yer king threatens to take even the little that remains to us," said Brandubh. For the first time, Brandubh's face transformed into an expression. And it was not the one that Earlington wanted to see. "Ye speak the language of diplomacy well, Commissioner Marsh. But we will not be mollified any longer by soft words hiding whips and chains. There will be no tax. We'll not pay it."

"Think what you're saying, McCullough. You're talking about treason."

"Not treason, sir. Justice." Brandubh stood, and the other men did, too. "Take this message to yer king. Scotland rejects the British monarch as a tyrant. Our country's people will fight to the death to reclaim our honor and our rights."

"My lords," Earlington began in his most calming voice, "it is not in the best interest of your people to involve them in a revolution. They will be put down by dragoons. And there is too much misery already. Please sit down, and let us reason together."

"No more talk. The time has come for action."

Earlington stood and met his gaze squarely. "Then think on this as you are moved to action, McCullough. You—can't—win. You don't have the manpower, you don't have the money, and you don't have the weaponry."

Brandubh's face became one of resolute aggression.

"But one thing we do have, Commissioner—friends. France hates the English as much as we do. If they sided with the American colonials against ye, they'll side with us against ye, too. And with the Americans, the French, the Irish, and the Scots against ye, *ye're* the one, sir, who can't win."

Earlington sat down slowly, his knees weakening.

"And that is something, gentlemen," said Kinross, "that I'll drink to." He picked up the untouched whiskey and poured it down his throat. The other two Scotsmen did the same, and walked out.

Earlington sat at the table, the three glasses empty before him. He couldn't even contemplate what they had just threatened. Scotland, America, and France . . . all at once. These men weren't after justice. Or even a revolution.

What they wanted was world war.

EIGHT

In the study back at Copperleaf Manor, Lord Askey read the letter for the sixth time.

"This is horrifying." The crinkled joy at the corners of his eyes was replaced by an expression of dismay. "This is simply beyond any standards of honor and decency."

Earlington's face was only slightly more composed. He had spent the last twenty years learning and speaking the language of diplomacy, and it always meant hiding one's true feelings. But this was something he had never dealt with before. Concern marred his otherwise poised expression.

> *Sing a song of sixpence,*
> *Parliament to defy,*
> *Four and twenty Scots brigades,*
> *Baked in a pie.*
>
> *When the pie was opened,*
> *Their swords began to swing;*
> *Wasn't that a fitting dish,*
> *To set before the king?*
>
> *The commissioner in his countinghouse,*
> *Counting out his money;*

His daughter in the parlor,
Eating bread and honey.

And while in the garden,
Unmindful of her foes,
Came down a patriot Scot
And sliced off her nose.

A warning to you, Commissioner. England cuts off
her nose to spite her face. Have a care, or we shall
visit the same fate upon your daughter!

Earlington had read the threat dozens of times, but
each time he tried to analyze it his mind kept homing
in on the threatened peril rather than on any deduc-
tions about who had written it. "What do you make of
it, Askey?"

"I don't know what to say . . . I'm appalled. I didn't
think that tensions had come to such a head that men
would resort to this kind of tactic. I'm ashamed on behalf of all Scots. One thing is for certain: I'd like to
meet the evil, cowardly jackanapes who could con-
ceive of such an abominable thing."

Earlington lowered his head. The letter had achieved
its end: to elicit an emotional response. In both Askey
and himself. But he could not allow himself hysterics.
Calmly, he read the letter once more. Although it was
difficult, he could not take this personally. It was not
aimed at him, but his office. Whoever had been in his
place would have received the same or a similar letter.
Still, it was difficult not to take offense when the letter
threatened not him, but his beloved daughter.

Askey put his hand on Earlington's shoulder. "You
must know that no one will think any less of you if you

decide to return with Serena to England. They can send someone else, someone without so much to lose."

So much to lose. Yes, Serena was the whole world to him. She was the only family he had left. He could not risk her welfare. And yet . . .

He downed his glass of water with a shaky hand. "I cannot abandon my mission, Askey. The very fact that my family is being intimidated is emblematic of the need there is for continued talks. If an ambassador who brings peace can be menaced to so great a degree, what more will these people threaten to do—or do in fact— to an ordinary man and his family?" He sighed deeply. "It is . . . imperative . . . that I remain to discuss peace between our peoples. Freedom from strife is not meant only for one . . . it is meant for all."

Askey nodded, a proud smile on his face.

The ambassador folded the letter just as he had found it—speared to his carriage door with a black dagger. "Nevertheless, Askey, I refuse to put your family in danger along with mine. I will make inquiries right away, and Serena and I will move to a place of our own at first light, if that's agreeable to you."

Askey stiffened. "It most certainly is not. You will both stay here at Copperleaf. This is no fortress by any means, but there is still a measure of safety."

Earlington held up a hand. "No. I won't hear of it. We'll stay in Inverness. I'll petition His Majesty for a brace of English guards to protect Serena."

The crinkles returned to Lord Askey's eyes. "You can't surround the poor girl with uniformed guards, man. She's already champing at the bit to return home without you guarding her like a common criminal."

"I must shield Serena at all costs."

"Why don't you send her back to London where she'll be safe?"

The ambassador shook his head. "We've had this discussion a hundred times, she and I. She won't go, not without me. She desperately wants to return to England, but she adamantly refuses to go unless I go as well."

"What if you told her about the letter? Perhaps she'll go then."

The ambassador rolled his eyes. "Not likely. I know her too well. She'll only use it as an excuse to make me leave for London as well. Still, she must be told about the threat upon her person." He raked a hand through his graying hair. "Poor creature. She's miserable enough as it is without the added distress of this . . . menace. But there's nothing for it. I must ensure her safety at all costs. For her own protection, I shall just have to take her with me wherever I go. She'll be bored to tears, but she will just have to make do. At least until this whole problem is resolved." He waved the folded letter in the air. "Or this knave is caught."

"Knave," repeated Askey slowly, an idea taking shape in his mind. "Of course! I think I know who can help you."

"Who?"

The crinkles deepened at the corners of Askey's face. "Another knave."

Earlington's face was a mixture of hope and puzzlement. "Who do you mean?"

"His name is Malcolm Slayter. Well, Slayter is not his real name . . . that was sort of thrust upon him because . . ." Askey waved away the rest of the sentence. "Anyway, this man Slayter works for the British government. Mostly he's called on by the Crown to hunt down renegades and fugitives from justice. He's as cunning as a fox and strong as a lion, and he's never lost a man yet. He's an absolute master at predicting a criminal's movements, and no one can stop the devils better than he can."

"Do you think he'd be able to identify the man who wrote this letter?"

"If he doesn't know, he might be able to point us in the right direction. But of one thing I am certain. There would be none better to safeguard your daughter."

Earlington's bushy eyebrows drew together. "A protector, you mean?"

"Absolutely. He's as fearsome in appearance as he is in intelligence. No one will trifle with him. He knows more about the deceptions and violence of Scotsmen than any man still alive. His best skill is at preventing danger before there is even a need to counter it. He's the perfect man to secure the safety of your family."

"Is he a Scotsman?"

"He hails from the Highlands."

Earlington's eyes narrowed. "I don't think it would be a good idea to hire a Highlander, not with the current atmosphere of discontent among that population. It would be too easy for whoever sent this note to bribe or coerce him."

"Not Malcolm Slayter. For a start, Malcolm belongs to no clan. He has no loyalties to anyone. The Scots consider him too English, and the English consider him too Scottish. Why do you think that His Majesty's magistrates use him to apprehend Scottish renegades? He is faithful to his commission, and he feels no compunction about turning in another Scot."

"But is he friendly toward the English? I mean, where does he stand on the tax?"

"I don't know the man's politics, Marsh. As far as I know, he doesn't have any. This much I know: He won't be corrupted against us."

"How can you be sure?"

Askey shrugged. "Because the Slayters are an out-cast kinship. As far as clans go, they're the bastards. They don't belong to Scotland, and they don't belong to England. They're loyal only to themselves."

"Wouldn't it be better to send for an English man?"

"Hasn't the note implied that they want the English to leave? The last thing you want is another foreigner here. Malcolm knows the people, he knows the terrain, and he knows how to fight. He'll not disappoint you. I'll send for him. He can be here in the morning. All I ask is that you meet the man."

Earlington rubbed his forehead. "You're certain he can be trusted?"

Askey put a hand on Earlington's shoulder. "If it were my daughter needing protection, I'd use Malcolm. He's the best man for the job."

NINE

My dear Archer—

I am certain, with ever-growing conviction, that I'm about to go quite mad.

Scotland is a beautiful country, but I would enjoy it infinitely more gazing upon a framed canvas of it. It rains ten times a day here. Taking a walk through a Highland meadow should be an uplifting experience, until of course one stumbles upon the hidden danger of steaming cowpats. Then I'm afraid it quite ruins the mood.

The food is deplorable. The common people hold in high culinary esteem cuts of meat that are only suited for being applied to black eyes. Their traditional dish, called haggis, is a giant sausage into which they stuff all the parts of the sheep you and I would feed to our dogs. And I shan't disgust you by revealing the principal ingredient of something called "black pudding"—suffice to say that it is something only a leech could love.

How fortunate you are to be in London! How I miss the sounds of the market bells clanging, the clatter of carriage wheels on cobblestones centuries old, the noise of hundreds of thousands of people crowded inside a few square miles, and the infinite and varied entertainments. There are more diversions in London in a single week than there are in the whole of Scotland in a quarter of a year.

And what wouldn't I trade to be able to gaze upon the clothes of London once more? In Scotland, what is in vogue is actually quite vague. Fashions are at least ten years behind ... and only for those people who care enough to mind them. Most of the ladies I see wear clothing that seems more for comfort than for beauty, and the men wear things I've only seen in history books. I don't know whether to call it dress or dross.

I apologize once more for the circumstances that led to the temporary suspension of the "Rage Page." I am not unmindful of your predicament or your financial losses. I, too, yearn to return to the parties and social gatherings that were my bread and your butter. I hope to allay your concerns by informing you that a change is imminent. Something is about to happen that may return Father and me to London before expected. I shan't provide you with any details just now. But rest assured that circumstances may improve forthwith.

I look forward with great anticipation to sharing a dance with you before the Season is over.

Yours truly,
Serena

Serena signed her name with her characteristic flourish. It was so gratifying to have someone in whom to confide. She couldn't be so honest with Zoe or her parents, and her father was too immersed in the country's problems to be mindful of hers. At least Archer would be sympathetic.

As she folded the stiff lettersheet and addressed it, the maid came to her sitting room. Serena groaned. Although the girl was assigned to her as a lady's companion by Rachel Askey, the chambermaid was woefully inadequate for that station. There seemed to be no abundance of well-bred ladies in the Highlands of Scotland fit to serve this purpose, and even less concern among its people to observe the dictates of Polite Society in that regard.

To add to Serena's irritation, the girl's brogue was so thick that Serena could understand only every third word the mousy young thing said. And just calling her seemed an insurmountable task—her name, Caointiorn, was impossible for Serena to pronounce.

True to form, Caointiorn said something that sounded like words a drunkard would say. Backward.

"Pardon?" Serena said.

Caointiorn repeated herself, and this time, Serena could just make it out—her presence was requested downstairs, where the ambassador wanted a word.

"Thank you, Quint—Quinch—" Serena sighed. "Thank you, Quinny. Please tell him I'll be down directly. Oh, and Quinny . . . please ask the groomsman to saddle my horse. I feel like a brisk ride."

"Aye, miss," she said as she shut the door behind her.

Serena grinned as she sealed the lettersheet with a pool of red wax. She placed a hopeful kiss upon the letter before flouncing downstairs.

As she passed through the house, she silently wished good-bye to the smell of baking oatcakes wafting from the kitchen, the bleating of sheep whispering from outside the window, and the wretched quiet that pervaded the whole of her existence. She would never again take the intrusive smells, sounds, and sights of London for granted. The sooner she got to London, the better. Maybe her father was about to give her the news she'd been waiting for.

She smoothed out her lavender silk dress and breezed through the parlor door. "Good morning, Father."

"Good morning, Serena," her father responded.

He was wearing what she called his "official costume," a black coat and gold brocade vest that made him look distinctively statesmanlike. "I'm surprised to see you here today. I thought you were going fishing with Lord Askey on Loch Ness."

"I'm afraid there will be no such pleasures for the time being. Serena, there is someone I would like you to meet."

She saw no one else in the room. She looked at her father quizzically. "Who?"

"Me."

The deep voice came from behind her, startling her. She spun around to look at him, and her mouth fell open.

He was a man of unusual height, standing a full foot over her own five-and-a-half-foot frame. Like her father, he was dressed in a black coat and trousers, but the inferior cut and cloth of his coat gave him away immediately as a Scotsman. Coal-black hair undulated around his head, echoed in the wide eyebrows that feathered back toward his temples. A dark shadow spread across his chin and cheeks, bluing with the threat of tomorrow's beard. She craned her neck to look into his green eyes, which looked down upon her from underneath thick black lashes.

Her father came and stood between them. "Mr. Slayter, may I present my daughter, Serena Marsh. Serena, this is Malcolm Slayter. Your protector."

She halted in mid-curtsy, righting herself awkwardly. "My what?"

His forehead crinkled in bemusement as he straightened from his bow. "Mind ye don't fall over."

A crease formed between Serena's eyebrows as she eyed the man suspiciously. "Father?"

Earlington lowered his voice. "I've retained the services of Mr. Slayter to safeguard your well-being for the duration of our stay in Scotland, which will take longer than I had first supposed."

Serena began to reel from the words she heard. *Longer. Duration. Stay.* The permanence of it made her head spin.

"But Father, I—" Serena sat down upon the settee. There was so much she wanted to say, but couldn't. "This was meant to be a short trip. As it is, we've been here almost four weeks. I was quite looking forward to my life—that is, our life—back in London."

"I'm afraid that's impossible, poppet," he said, taking the place beside her. "There are graver issues at stake than I had at first surmised. And to drive that point home, the factions have resorted to more threatening tactics. Mr. Slayter, please show her the letter."

Malcolm held the letter out to Serena. She took it from his gloved hand and gave it a cursory glance.

"But clearly these people wish to convey their hostile intentions. Let us return to England. You can still serve our interests from home."

Malcolm squinted at her. "Does this letter no' frighten ye?"

Serena seemed to regard him for the first time. "Not in the least, Mr.—er—"

"Slayter," he provided.

"Mr. Slayter. It does, however, make me wonder

why my father would wish to remain here, even under the threat of such antagonism."

Earlington put a pale hand upon Serena's. "I have my duty."

"Your duty will not get done if you are dead," she said, bolting off the settee.

"With all due respect, miss," interrupted Malcolm, "the letter is not threatening him. It is threatening *ye*."

Serena flashed him a haughty look. "I appreciate your concern, Mr.—er—"

His lips pursed. "Slayter."

"Slayter, yes," she repeated in annoyance. "But you clearly do not understand my father's condition. He suffers from a weak heart. If any mischief befalls me, his heart will not be able to take the strain of it."

"Then perhaps ye ought to take his advice and return to England, where he knows ye'll be safe."

Serena grew irritated at his familiarity. "As I have explained to my father, it is out of the question. I cannot in good conscience leave him alone."

Earlington rose and stood beside the tall man. "Which is why Mr. Slayter is here. He will serve as your protector. He is skilled in battle, criminal detection, security, and high-risk fugitive pursuit, and he can properly defend you against anyone meaning to do you harm."

Serena's gaze dusted down the length of her presumed protector. His hardened expression proclaimed he had been in quite a few skirmishes already—and did not always emerge unscathed. His brow, cheek, and chin had tiny scars that contrasted whitely with his tanned complexion. The size and breadth of his imposing body made him look quite formidable, and she could only imagine the lethal skills he possessed. Certainly the type of figure that Serena would cross the road to avoid.

Her father continued. "He will be your constant companion, and will follow you wherever you go. Lord Askey assures me that Mr. Slayter is a man of honor and integrity, and can be trusted to accompany an unmarried lady. I don't wish to risk injury to your reputation, but given the level of the threat, it's imperative that he remain near you at all times."

The tall man turned to her father. "I'll speak to each of the servants of the kitchens, household, and stables to charge them with my new security measures. The doors to the house will be kept locked all along the day, and I'm to be informed immediately of any visitors. No servant will engage tradesmen without getting an aye from me first. If anyone from the outside is needed on the estate, I'm to know beforehand. I'll also make certain that no one accepts food or articles from people they don't know well, especially things meant for the family. Lord Askey tells me that the servants have been with the family for years, and they've shown themselves loyal, to a man. Dinna worry, Commissioner Marsh. In my care, yer daughter will be safe as mother's milk."

Serena swiped both hands down her face. "Father, this really isn't necessary. You mustn't take such petty threats to heart." She turned to the black-haired man. "I'm sorry that you were bothered—"

"Mr. Slayter."

Fire flashed in her eyes. "I was aware of that!"

A smirk touched his lips. "I believe in preparing for the worst."

Her hands pinned to her hips. "As I was about to say, there will be no need of your services. To his credit, my father is being overly protective. But I can't allow him to be fooled by these . . . juvenile pranks. My father will see you are adequately remunerated for your trouble. You may leave us now, with our thanks for your offered assistance."

He crossed his arms at his chest. "I'm no' going anywhere, Miss Marsh."

Her neck stiffened. "I beg your pardon?"

"Yer father is the one who's engaged me, and I will answer to no one but him. And the fact that ye make so little of the letter in yer hand leads me to think that ye're either very brave or very daft. Personally, I'm hoping it's the former. But yer casual attitude toward yer own safety—and yer father's duty—leads me to question my assessment."

Her eyes became round as saucers. "How dare you speak to me in so insulting a fashion! Father, discharge this man at once."

Ever the agent of appeasement, Earlington stepped between them. "Mr. Slayter, despite her delicate appearance, my daughter is a very strong woman. She has never been one to back down from a challenge, even as a little girl. I'm certain she realizes fully what is at stake. Nevertheless, I cannot take any chances with her safety." Earlington took Serena's hands in his. "Serena, my dear, I need you to please me in this matter. I know that having Mr. Slayter as a constant presence may be a slight inconvenience. But at least with a protector you will not be a prisoner of your rooms. As long as Mr. Slayter is with you, you may be at liberty to ride, take walks, and travel into the village. And if your desire is that my heart should be at peace, then please accept Mr. Slayter as your protector."

Serena looked into her father's concerned face, and the rigid reluctance in her posture softened. She sighed deeply.

But one glance at Mr. Slayter, whose expression was

just a shade too triumphant, and she stiffened once more.

"Mr. Slayter, I hope that you have a thoroughly unpleasant stay." She turned on her heel and stormed out of the room.

TEN

Serena closed the door to her bedroom and leaned her back against it. The nerve of that man! It was bad enough that she had to suffer more of this wretched country. But to do so in the intimate company of an impertinent and overbearing servant was more than she was willing to endure. She had to think of a way out of this predicament. Overwhelmed, she let her head fall back against the door.

The knock on the other side nearly tore a scream out of her.

"Who is it?"

"'Tis Caointiorn, miss."

Quinny! She'd forgotten that she'd asked to have a horse saddled. She opened the door.

The thin girl darted into the room like a mouse fleeing daylight. She began to burble something in Gaelic.

"What are you chuntering about, Quinny?"

"There's a grit ark o' a mon ootside, wi' the de'il's oon face, on he's heided straight fo' here."

Serena harrumphed, knowing immediately what put Quinny out of sorts. "*That* will be my new protector. I don't want him snagged upon my skirts any more than you do. We have to get rid of him somehow. If he comes here, tell him I'm indisposed."

"Please, miss." She cringed, as if Serena had asked her to walk through a house on fire. "A dinna ken hoo—"

A forceful knock made Quinny gasp.

Serena motioned to her to answer the door. Quinny wrung her hands upon her pinafore, shaking her head.

Serena rolled her eyes. "Who is it?"

"I'd tell ye, but ye'd probably forget the name."

Slayter! She turned to face the door, annoyance robbing her of the composure in her voice. "What do you want?"

"I'd like to come in."

"I don't want a protector. I thought I'd made myself perfectly clear."

"Aye. That ye did."

She puzzled over the uncertain victory. "Very well, then. Good day."

"But what ye want and what ye're going to get are two very different things, Miss Marsh."

"I *will not* have you giving me orders. Leave the environs of my rooms immediately."

The handle on the door shook as he tested it. "Ye'll open the door."

"I beg your pardon?"

"Miss Marsh, I'm warning ye. I must inspect yer rooms. Let me in or I shall break down this door."

Fury exploded inside her. She wasn't about to yell at him from inside her room like a cowering ninny. She wanted to yell at him face-to-face.

She turned the key in the lock and flung open the door. "How dare you speak to me in so impudent a manner! I will not—"

The words died in her mouth as he shouldered his way past her into the bedroom. Her mouth fell open, appalled at his insolence. She crossed her arms over her chest. "I hate to seem discourteous, but . . . actually, I don't. Get out!"

"By God, yer mouth alone is enough to keep assassins at bay."

She pursed her lips. "And you are becoming increasingly underfoot."

He cast a hard look at Quinny, who quaked in a corner. "Who's this?"

Serena stepped beside the maid. Next to Mr. Slayter, Quinny looked like a child. "Quinny serves as lady's companion to me."

"Ye'll have no more need of a companion. Ye've got me now."

She stuck her nose in the air. "It is highly improper for a lady to entertain gentlemen unchaperoned."

"Miss Marsh, ye're no' *entertaining* me. If ye want to entertain me, ye'll have to do a damn sight more than strut 'round like a persnickety dowager queen." He turned to Quinny. "What's yer name?"

"Caointiorn, sir," she replied meekly.

"Ye can go now, Caointiorn," he told her softly. "I'll be mustering the servants below stairs in an hour's time. Please be there when I do."

"Quinny, don't you dare move!" Serena told her. "Mr. Slayter, no one dismisses my servants but me. I'll thank you to remember your place."

Quinny's tremulous voice warbled behind her. "A'm sairy, miss. A feel no weel. A hae tae gang noo." She darted from the room so fast, Serena only caught a glimpse of her shadow upon the floor.

Serena sighed in frustration. Some chaperone Quinny turned out to be. It was yet another thing she should have brought with her into this backward country.

"Oh, hurry up and do what you must," she huffed.

"There are important things that require my attention."

He suppressed a smile and began an examination of her rooms. "Such as?"

"I'm planning my next column for the *Town Crier*." She arched an eyebrow. "I don't know if you know this, but I am a writer of some note. Have you heard of the 'Rage Page'?"

He cocked his head. "That's yers, then?"

She was pleasantly astonished. "You've heard of it?"

His green eyes shone. "No."

She rolled her eyes. "That hardly surprises me. Nothing of any importance happens here in the Highlands."

He chuckled as he scrutinized the windows. "Nothing? Do ye even know why yer father is here?"

Her back stiffened imperiously. "I'm perfectly attuned to the necessity of my father's mission, thank you. You don't need to lecture me on world events. I meant that culturally, Scotland leaves much to be desired. I've been here long enough to know that there is no need of a Society column in this country."

He opened the doors on her wardrobe, which equaled his height. "Mayhap it's because we've gossips aplenty without the need for another. Even a 'writer of note.'"

Serena walked over to her bed and sat down. His back was turned, and she stole a lingering glance at him. His black-clad figure dominated the room, filling its space. He had a most imposing physique, and briefly she wondered what such a man looked like without such second-rate clothes on. She stared at him for a few moments as he examined the corners of her room.

"Well?"

"Aye, quite well, thank ye."

She ground her teeth. "No. I meant are you finished yet?"

"Not yet." He strode over to her, his booted feet pounding upon the floor, and knelt right in front of her. She inched backward on the mattress, uncomfortable with his nearness. He got down on all fours and looked under the bed.

"Do ye entertain in here?" he asked.

"I beg your pardon?"

He straightened, and put a large hand on the mattress on either side of her. "Are ye in the habit of receiving gentlemen in yer rooms?" Black eyebrows flew up. "It's best that ye tell me now."

"Certainly not!" she responded. "What sort of a lady would I be?"

"Not the Scottish kind, to be sure."

Her chin jutted in affronted pride. "Mr. Slayter, since you've entered my rooms, you've insinuated that I was a virago, a busybody, and now a lightskirt. Do you have any more calumnies to launch at me?

His eyes sparkled in amusement. "No. That should do for now." Suddenly he leaned forward, his face only inches from her own, imprisoning her upon the bed. "But I'm still waiting for m'answer. Do ye have a secret lover, then?"

Serena looked away, an embarrassed blush pinking her cheeks. Lover? Yes, there had been a lover. Or more accurately, a Mistake. Even though it had happened a long time ago, the memory of that one night had never grown faint. A gentleman buck, confident and charming, had wooed her with thrilling exploits and honeyed words. Beautiful and charismatic he was, and it cost him very little effort to win her over. She let him get too close to her heart . . . and he took not only that, but her innocence as well. For as soon as she had given herself to him, he changed. No longer did he court and pursue; he criticized and disparaged. The man who had imprinted himself upon her and made her his own soon evaporated from her life. It was not a Mistake she would make twice.

Now here was a man who was getting too close already. His hips were barely an inch from her silk-draped knees, rousing a strange quickening that she found instantly appealing. To make matters worse, he was not as severe-looking as she'd first surmised. In point of fact, he was quite handsome—albeit in a gruff, Scottish sort of way. Deliciously masculine—even if somewhat barbaric—and her eyes traveled wistfully across the wide shoulders and dense torso.

"No lover," she replied.

"Good. 'Twould be a pity to break up a romance. For no man is going to get to ye while I'm around."

Serena inhaled sharply, considering the idea of being alone with this man. One thing she would have to admit—he was a dangerous-looking adversary. As large and strong a man as she'd ever seen. And yet there was that soft wave of his rook-black hair . . . and the thick lashes surrounding his emerald-colored eyes . . . and the small dent in the middle of his chin . . . and his lips, which had a beautiful, soft sheen to them. His height was an instantly fascinating feature, and a question mark hung in the air as to how much of him was proportionate to his size. Serena's thoughts began to traipse down a forbidden path. If he took it into his head to take advantage of her, Serena was not entirely certain she would object.

He stood up, depriving her of his presence. She swallowed hard, instantly missing the fortress of muscle that had surrounded her. He walked around her room, pounding his gloved fists upon the papered walls.

"Inspecting the structure for rot?" she asked, lacing the question with sarcasm.

He cast a sidewise glance at her. "I'm listening for hollowness. These old houses are full of false walls and trapdoors."

She shook her head. "I keep telling you. There is nothing to fear."

"I'm sorry ye think so."

He crouched down to inspect the lock on her door.

"Satisfied?" she said, a smug tone to her voice.

A crease deepened between his brows. "Something's not right."

"What do you mean?"

"There's a brass plaque on the outside of this door lock. The key fits into the lock only from the inside."

She harrumphed. "Why should it worry you that this door can only be locked from the inside? I have the only key; therefore, I am the only one who can unlock it."

"Hmm. Perhaps it is nothing."

"Seems your abilities have been subject to hyperbole."

He shot her an irritated look. Slowly, illumination dawned on his masculine features. "Or perhaps . . ."

He stood up and looked around the room. The emerald eyes scoured each wall, pausing over every inch of them, until finally they narrowed suspiciously on the wardrobe on the far side of her bed.

The massive cherrywood armoire stood in the middle of the long wall at the foot of her bed. It was weighted with all her garments and accessories. Nevertheless, he stood to one side of it, and began to push on it with all his might.

A sheen of perspiration broke out on his forehead as he grimaced with the effort. He strained against it until the monstrous wardrobe shifted with a heavy screech, revealing the wall behind it.

Serena jumped up and stood beside him. Hidden behind her wardrobe was a secret door that had been papered to blend in with the rest of her room. A small hole served as a doorknob, obscured by one of the larkspurs printed on the wallpaper. Malcolm pulled on it, and the panel creaked open.

A cobweb streamed from inside the darkened space, and Serena backed away in fright. The mere possibility of the presence of spiders made it a certainty that she would not follow him in there. She waited for him to emerge.

"What do you see in there?"

He came back out of the mouth of the doorway. "Looks like a lover's corridor."

"A what?"

He slapped his hands together, shaking the dust from his gloves. "Some old houses like this one used to be built with a secret passageway leading to a bedroom. It permitted the man of the house to sneak into a lady's room at night without being discovered. That brass plate on the outside of the door kept a curious wife or efficient housemaid from walking in on the couple while they were . . . together."

"Randy old sods!"

He smiled, revealing another hidden surprise . . . a row of beautiful white teeth. "Mayhap his attentions were not always unwelcome."

"Hmm," she grunted dubiously. "Well, where does this corridor lead?"

"I don't know. Probably a study or pantry. But I canna see the opposite door from here. There are crates and old furniture piled up in there. Looks as if the space hasn't been used in decades."

"Thank goodness for that. Otherwise, Lord Askey would have a lot to answer for. Imagine what a horrible experience to be asleep and have a strange man creeping into your room."

"All while giving the lady in the room a false sense of security." He looked down into her eyes. "Just as ye seem determined to feel."

"It isn't a false sense of security at all," she said defensively. She had already been proven wrong once. "There's no reason for alarm. I'm in no real danger."

"How can ye be so sure?"

She looked askance. "I just am."

Sarcasm dripped from his deep voice. "Well, as long as ye've thought it out carefully."

Her brows drew together. "I don't have to explain myself to you. I'm making a point."

"Ye're also missing one. All this time, ye've been sleeping in a room that a man might slip into to strangle ye as ye slept. I dinna call that 'safe.' "

"Well, he'd be welcome to try if he can push a five-ton armoire out of the way without waking me."

He shook his head. "Ye are bullheaded when ye want to be, aren't ye? Still," he said, glancing at the larkspur wallpaper, "I'm glad of the discovery. That room will make ideal sleeping quarters for me."

The thought of that made the blood drain from her face. "Do you mean to tell me you're going to sleep in that room?"

"Aye."

"With unfettered access into mine?"

"Aye."

"Where you can just march in anytime you like?"

"When necessary."

"What if I'm not dressed?"

A wicked smile cut across his face. "So much the better."

She didn't know whether to laugh in his face or slap it. "I'll not have it. This arrangement is not only an extreme affront to propriety, it will assuredly ruin my reputation. Whatever will people think?"

"They can think what they like. I'm no' after protecting yer good name. I'm after protecting yer hide."

"Mr. Slayter, this is completely out of the question. You will sleep in the servants' quarters, and you will come when I send for you."

He crossed his arms at his chest, forming an impenetrable wall. "Miss Marsh, perhaps yer predicament hasn't yet sunk in. Someone has threatened to kill ye. And where I come from, such threats are never made lightly. These are troubled times, and those who mean ye harm may avail themselves upon ye at any moment. Yer father is taking no chances with yer safety, and he's entrusted it to me. And will ye or nill ye, I will be master of my charge."

He wore the authority like his own skin. But she was not about to be bullied by a servant.

"Mr. Slayter, I do not take kindly to being insulted, nor do I care for being dominated like a colonial slave. You may have a duty to protect me, but I will not allow you to be my keeper." She sidled past him and through her bedroom door.

"Where are ye going?"

"To have Father flay some of your arrogant skin off."

ELEVEN

It felt as if the weight of the world were crushing him slowly.

Earlington sank into a chair by the open window, allowing the chill morning breeze to cool his fevered head. The world seemed so peaceful from the prospect of this window. The high wind blew a cloud across the sky, and the emerging sun made the rich green grass glow resplendently. Far off in the meadow, a scattering of sheep lazed, their gentle bleating the only sound for miles. This was a beautiful country, simple and natural.

And some people would never be happy unless soldiers' bodies bled the ground red.

He took a long draft from the glass of brandy in his hand. Drink was never a consolation for him, so he did it sparingly. But today, with the entire world set against him—and now his daughter, too—perhaps a drink would dispel the anxiety and help him think clearly.

"It's not doon there."

Earlington turned toward the voice and blinked. It came from the housekeeper, a thin woman with a thick shock of copper-colored hair.

"Pardon?"

"Whatever 'tis ye're looking for. Ye won't find it at the bottom of that glass."

Earlington ground his teeth. He knew that. But to be

upbraided by a servant was beyond intolerable. In England, no domestic would ever speak unless spoken to first. Nevertheless, in all the time he'd been here, it was probably the first time he had ever heard this woman speak at all.

The housekeeper was now oblivious to him, busying herself with clearing away the teacups upon a tray. What was her name?

"I don't usually drink—" Mrs. Walker? Mrs. Talker?

"Aye, that ye don't. All the more reason not to start noo."

Earlington suppressed his irritation at the woman's familiar manner, because despite the breach of propriety, what she had said was true.

He set down his glass upon the table beside his chair. "You're right, of course. Thank you."

She came over to pick it up. "Anyone can see ye're as tense as the skin on an Irish *bodhrán*. Another glass o' that and ye'd probably be making as much noise as that awful instrument."

He smiled. "I won't be having any more. Thank you for protecting my good name." He sank back into the chair and covered his eyes with one hand. Another breeze wafted in, gently cooling the skin on his face.

A few moments passed. Sensing no movement, he opened his eyes. The housekeeper was still standing beside his chair, the tray resting on her hip, watching him.

"So what's licked all the butter aff yer bread?"

He blinked in disbelief. It seemed something out of a dream to be having a conversation with this woman. For the first time, he took a long look at her. She was a handsome woman, and though she was well past forty, he could just glimpse the beauty she had been in her twenties. She had shocking blue eyes, as so many of her countrymen did, but hers were bold and much more perspicacious. Fine lines vined at the corners of her eyes and her cheeks had lost the plumpness of their youth, but her mouth was wide and sensual, a lovely feature for a woman of her advanced years.

"I'm just a bit preoccupied, that's all."

"Seems more like ye're a bit afeard."

It jarred him that she could read him so well. After dozens of years spent in politics, he was fairly certain he didn't exhibit his feelings to any perceivable measure. Yet her remark didn't seem meant to belittle. She appeared genuinely concerned. And he was genuinely overwrought.

"Yes. That, too." Having admitted his failing, he could no longer look her in the eye. His gaze fell to her hands, which were gnarled with work.

"Why?" she asked.

He sighed deeply. "Because I fear for your people. And for mine. I want an end to the rebellion. And the Council won't have it."

"Och. Ye mustn't froth yerself over those ruffians. Any twelve Highlanders and a bagpipe make a rebellion. They'll come 'round soon enough."

"No doubt, no doubt," he said with false cheer. "It's only the time from now to then that keeps my head in a knot. Things will improve soon. Thank you."

Despite his polite dismissal, the housekeeper didn't leave. Earlington marveled at her boldness.

"Ye're fashed for a great deal more than that, are ye not?"

Her voice was barely loud enough for him to hear. But his innermost being heard her loud and clear. Another human soul recognized the pain in him and wanted to soothe it.

"Yes, I am." His throat began to constrict as he real-

ized how much he wanted to unburden himself of the
awful, choking truth.

She lay the tray down on the tea table, crossed her
hands at her tummy, and waited in silence for him to
speak.

He sighed. "Throughout my entire life, my country
has been embroiled in war. When I was a boy, we were
at war with the American colonies. Then it was battle
with the Irish. Then war with the French. I can scarcely
remember a time when we were not fighting someone.
I went into politics with the express purpose of bringing peace to England. Perhaps it was only a pipe dream.
But I thought we could achieve that goal if only we
wanted it enough.

"So when I became minister plenipotentiary to the
United States in '11, I believed this was my opportunity
to show the world that Britain was not this horrible,
warmongering nation. I entered into negotiations with
President Madison, and I believed we had reached an
amicable solution between our governments. But I
failed to comprehend England's resolve. In the interest
of achieving peace, I compromised my directives . . .
conceded too many of our positions, perhaps. Within
less than a year, the king had me recalled, and the
United States declared war on Britain. I failed in my
official mission—and in my personal one." His voice
trailed off.

Her astute eyes scanned him. "And noo ye're afeard
ye're about to fail again?"

Earlington nodded slowly. "I don't want to go down
in history as the ambassador who begot wars instead of
ending them. It was my sincerest hope that I could
bring a peaceful solution to the unrest in Scotland.
Then I'd be remembered as the peacemaker I always
wanted to be."

It was her turn to sigh. "Seems to me that if the king truly wanted a peaceful solution, he'd have sent somebody else."

Earlington's eyes flew open. It was a hurtful thing to say. He was offended by her remark, especially after his uncharacteristic show of vulnerability. "I'm sorry?"

She shrugged. "Ye don't send a lame collie to herd the sheep. Yet here ye are, a man with a sick heart who's also sick at heart. Ye think ye've got something to prove, to the king and to yerself. I don't know if ye failed in America . . . might be that the king failed ye. Perhaps ye're the perfect man to send here if the king wanted to give the *appearance* of wanting peace."

His eyebrows drew together. "Are you saying that the Prince Regent *wants* me to fail in my commission?"

"I'm saying that he doesna expect ye to succeed. And if ye fail, the fault will then be with us, not him. Or ye."

Earlington's eyes danced around about the floor as he pondered the possibility. Could it be that this woman suspected a truth he didn't dare to believe? He knew that even now, troops gathered in the north of England to prepare for battling the insurrection. In case the talks failed, the general had told him. Maybe military action was being planned not *in case* he failed, but *after* it.

Earlington had wondered why he'd been chosen for this diplomatic mission. His failure in the colonies seven years ago distressed him greatly, and the heart seizure he suffered after his return had made him gravely ill. Parliament had been sympathetic, but he thought he might never be asked to return to foreign service. Until a few months ago, when trouble in Scotland started to brew.

The government could have sent anyone. The ambassador to Russia was available. So was the ambassador to Austria. Why, then, had they asked him to return to the service?

He hadn't questioned it. In truth, he had been so overjoyed at the opportunity to redeem himself that he hadn't bothered to ask why they would consider him. Yet even this woman, a household servant he didn't know, could see that despite his lofty title he was merely a pawn in a chess game with a predetermined winner.

His gaze flew back to the housekeeper's eyes. "You amaze me, Mrs.—"

A brief smile touched her eyes. "Ye can call me Gabby."

He grinned. The name hardly suited her, quiet as she had always been. She had been in his presence a number of times, and this was the first time she'd opened her mouth. Though when she did, a torrent of wisdom came pouring forth.

"Gabby. I had never considered it from that standpoint. Please do me the honor of sitting with me awhile, so that we may talk some more." He rose from his chair and motioned for her to sit.

She looked aghast. "I canna sit doon! With all the work there is to do? I'm behind as a cow's tail."

"Just for a moment. I would hear more of your perspectives."

She grabbed the tray from the table. "Nonsense. Idle words won't make the pot boil." Without another look back, she flitted out of the door.

He smiled at her retreating back. Though she'd just shed light on a matter of international relations, she clearly held household matters in greater esteem.

For the first time, disjointed concepts in his head began to fall into rightful place. Suddenly a plan of action formed in his thoughts. A cool breeze blew through the open window as he stood by it, and he felt a surge of something coil through him. Strength.

A knock at the door shook him from his thoughts. He hoped it was Gabby.

"Come."

Serena entered. "Father, I really must protest."

"Not now, poppet," he said. "There is an urgent matter I must attend to."

Malcolm appeared behind her and leaned a shoulder against the doorjamb.

"But Father, this *is* an urgent matter."

"What is it, Serena?"

"I can't abide this protector. Send him away."

Earlington went to the escritoire and scribbled something on a piece of paper. "I can't do that, poppet."

"But he wants to sleep in the room next to mine!"

"That's precisely where I want him."

"Yes, but inside the very walls?"

Malcolm cleared his throat. "I discovered a hidden passageway leading to Miss Marsh's bedchamber. It's no' been used in some time. But stationing myself in that corridor will give me a strategic advantage. This way, should an intruder make his way into Miss Marsh's room, no one will suspect her protector to burst in from the very wall."

Earlington pondered this carefully. "Make whatever arrangements you must to ensure my daughter's safety."

Serena shook her head. "But Father, you don't understand—"

"No, Serena. You don't understand. Mr. Slayter is your protector. I've hired him to keep you from harm. With the exceptions of the bath and the bedchamber, Slayter has been tasked by me to stand beside you at all times. Make full use of your abigail, but Slayter must also be present wherever you go. He is not a guest and he is not a servant. You don't need to entertain him, you don't need to govern him. You don't even need to talk to him. But you do have to put up with him. All right?"

"But Father—"

"Do it for me. Now I really must dash. I'll take Askey's carriage. You can take ours. Go into town. Go shopping with Zoe. And just pretend that Mr. Slayter isn't there." He gave her a kiss on the cheek.

Earlington felt empowered. His daughter was in good hands. Now he would make sure the Scottish people were in good hands, too.

TWELVE

As a chaperone, Quinny was about as useful as a bucket with a hole in the bottom. But Serena had no intention of spending the day alone with the indomitable Malcolm Slayter, so she went to kidnap Zoe. Zoe refused because she was scheduled to have a lesson with her French language master, a man on whom she had a hopeless crush. Only after Serena promised to accompany Zoe to the Saint Swithin's Day Festival the next day did Zoe agree.

The young girl was intrigued by the lover's corridor in Serena's room, so the two of them went back to her room to see it.

"Ooh!" exclaimed Zoe. "This is amazing! How on earth did you find it?"

Serena rolled her eyes, and pointed to Malcolm. "He found it."

Zoe blinked her widened eyes at him. "I've lived here nearly my whole life and never knew about this hidden room. How did you know it was here?"

Serena interrupted. "Perhaps he has intimate knowledge of such concealments. Ask him how many ladies' bedchambers he's infiltrated through such places."

Malcolm snickered. "Yer friend is as curious as a cat in a room full of mouse holes. But she'll no' get the gossip she seeks from me. Tell her that my affairs are none of hers."

Zoe seemed oblivious to their tense exchange. "Can I see where it leads?"

"It's rather dirty in there, miss. The servants are on the way up to muck it out."

"I don't mind," she said, seizing a candle.

"I do, miss," he said, gently taking the candle from her hand. "Besides, the passage is fair bursting with rubbish."

Serena whirled around. "You'll have to get used to being treated that way, Zoe. That is, unless you complain to your father about him. Maybe then he'll be discharged for good."

Zoe sat upon Serena's bed. "Could you see if there's a passageway like that into my bedroom?"

"I will. Tomorrow."

Two footmen came to the bedroom. Malcolm held a candle aloft and showed them into the dark corridor. Serena sat at her escritoire and watched as the two footmen began to cart away the crates and broken chairs that cluttered the secret passageway.

Zoe sat next to her, whispering something about how she would swoon with delight if her handsome French master came into her bedroom through such an opening. Serena only heard half of what Zoe was saying. Because at that moment, Malcolm Slayter took off his coat.

Never mind that no self-respecting gentleman would ever remove his coat in front of a lady he wasn't related to. Never mind that his shirtsleeves weren't voluminous, and they didn't even go all the way down to his wrists. The sleeves of his fitted shirt, made of coarse linen, ended at his elbows.

Serena stared at him over her embroidery hoop. The sight of his bare forearms sent a current of eroticism through her. Slightly furred and knotted with muscle, they fascinated her. She had never seen such a large man in semi-undress. He walked into the corridor and carried out a wooden chest so heavy that it required two footmen to take it from his gloved hands. Serena couldn't help but notice the swell of muscle at his shoulder and upper arms, stretching the rough-spun fabric. Definitely no London gentleman of her acquaintance looked like him. But then again, Malcolm Slayter was no gentleman. And they were far, far from London.

"You're from the Highlands, are you not?" Serena asked.

His green eyes jumped to her face. "Aye."

She bit her cheek. "I thought all Highlanders wore kilts."

"Aye. That we do."

"Why don't you wear one then?"

He wiped his damp temple on his sleeve. "That, I'm afraid, is yer doing."

"My doing?"

"Aye. I'm told that ladies . . . of the English persuasion . . . are too delicate to behold a man's bare legs."

"Who told you such a slanderous thing?"

He shrugged. "Common knowledge."

Serena harrumphed. "Well, you needn't put yourself out on my account. It takes a great deal more than a show of knees to offend someone like me."

He nodded in appreciation. "Judging by our less-than-cordial meeting, I think I may have discovered everything that offends someone like ye."

The words needled her. She didn't want to be thought of as a harridan. Truth be told, Malcolm Slayter was the most interesting thing that had happened since she'd arrived in Scotland.

"Is there a Mrs. Slayter?"

"Aye."

Her needle stilled. A sinking feeling went through her.

"That would have been my mum," he continued.

She rolled her eyes, but the gesture was coupled by a feeling of hope.

"I meant, are you married?"

"I know what ye meant."

But no explanation was forthcoming. There it was again, that impudence that challenged her authority over him. "Well?"

"That's private."

She laughed out loud. "You are standing in the middle of my bedroom in a state of undress intruding upon my every waking moment, and you're bothered by an innocuous question like 'Are you married?' " The irony of it made her laugh again.

He shook his head. "Yer father said ye don't have to speak to me. Feel free to avail yerself of that freedom."

Her laughs subsided to a chuckle. "Maybe I will."

"Good."

He turned to the last footman. "Please tell Mrs. Walker we've finished clearing this out."

Zoe jumped off her chair. "Can I see where it leads now?"

He flicked a smile at the girl. "Aye." His gaze swung over to Serena, challenge blazing in his eyes. "Ye can come, too. If ye dare."

Serena was not about to let him call her a coward. She set down her embroidery hoop and stood up. But first, she grabbed a shawl and threw it over her head. Spiders . . .

She followed closely behind him as he held the candle aloft. The flame flickered across the walls, blinking light upon what was essentially a drafty, unplastered corridor. Exposed planks and white mortar lined the walls, and a faint musty smell pervaded the passageway. She couldn't see herself sitting in this room for any length of time, let alone sleeping in it. He must be a brave soul indeed if he didn't mind bedding here.

Involuntarily, she clutched the back of his shirt. It was warm with him, and it gave off a scent that was very pleasing to her . . . like skin warmed by sunshine. Her fingers bounced upon the hardness of his back, and the intimacy of it was intensely pleasurable.

At the opening, the corridor took an immediate left turn, and they followed it for a distance. Here, the spiderwebs were plentiful, and they formed a canopy over her head. She squeezed in closer to him, using him as a shield.

Finally, the corridor ended at a spot where light shone through a door-shaped crack in the moldy beams. A sweep of his candle revealed a hook. He put a finger through it and pulled.

Light burst in upon them from the opposite side. They now stood behind six shelves aching with books, and they could see over them into the room.

"It's the library!" she breathed. "But I've never seen this doorway before." She picked up one of the books and turned it over in her hands. "How does one get through these shelves?"

He looked all around. "There has to be a hinge . . ." He pushed against the frame of the bookshelf, and it swung forward. The three of them stepped through the opening and found themselves standing in Lord Askey's library.

He swung into place the hinged door that doubled as the back panel of the oak bookshelves. Then he swung the hinged bookcase onto it. The doorway disappeared, leaving only what appeared to be a static bookshelf.

"Ingenious," he muttered, lifting the real books off the shelf. "No one would have suspected a thing."

"I wonder if Papa knows about this?" asked Zoe,

pulling open the bookshelf-door. "Oh, I can't wait to tell my friend Rebecca!"

"I must ask ye not to tell anyone outside this household about this hidden passageway," said Malcolm gently. "I myself will show it to yer father and the ambassador. The fewer people that know, the safer Miss Marsh will be."

Zoe smiled at him, her brown eyes turning their full allure his way. "If you insist."

Malcolm wagged a warning finger at Serena. "And don't ye be telling the world about it, either."

Serena bristled at the change in his demeanor with her. It was bad enough that there was no one in the whole of Scotland she held in any confidence. Now she was forced into an adversarial relationship with a man she didn't want to like . . . but did.

She adjusted her shawl around her shoulders and walked to the real door out of the library. "Get accustomed to stepping through that bookshelf to reach your bedchamber, for you won't be going through my bedroom door."

THIRTEEN

The clock downstairs chimed nine, reverberating through the empty house.

Serena put down the hairbrush. Gazing out of the window that was behind her mirrored dressing table, she sighed audibly. Light still filled the sky even though practically the entire household had gone to bed. This was what the Scots called "the gloaming"—the twilight time between sunset and dark. Outside, the sky had no moon and no stars—none of the beauty that night brings—but the sun had long since departed. It was a strange purgatory. All was suspended as day had given up, but nightfall refused to come.

Suspended. That was how she felt, too. Gone was the familiar life she had so enjoyed and reveled in, and still to come was . . . she knew not what.

A hollow knock startled her. It came from the wall at the foot of her bed, where her wardrobe had once been. On the other side of the larkspur wallpaper was the place Malcolm had made his bedchamber.

"Come in," she said on instinct, even though she was only in her dressing gown.

The secret door opened, and there stood Malcolm holding a candlestick aloft. "I've come to check ye're all right."

Despite their tense exchanges, she found herself glad

to see him. "Quite well, thank you." She said it before she could stop herself: "Would you care to come in?"

"Aye."

He had to dip his head to be able to walk through the six-foot doorway. But once he was inside, the candle-light from her bedside table brought a completely new look to his face. His weathered features softened, and his black hair came alive in shades of blue. He had on a cream-colored linen shirt and black trousers, but there was no cravat or coat on him. Also gone were his gloves. But more interesting were his eyes, which danced down her peignoir before riveting themselves to the floor. "I'll just check on the door. To make sure it's been locked properly."

His timidity beguiled her. "I assure you I've done so. But you may put your own mind at ease."

He went to the doorknob and tried it. Absently, he tucked the back of his shirt into his trousers.

"Do ye have everything ye need for the night?" he asked.

Not *everything*. "I believe so. And you? Are you comfortable behind the wall? It seems awfully cramped inside that little passageway."

"I've slept in worse places."

"Oh?"

"Hmm," he assented. "I once had to make bed inside four feet of snow just to stay out of the frigid Highland wind."

"What were you doing out in the wilds overnight?"

He cocked his head. "I have not always enjoyed the pleasure of a warm home."

"You mean you were a vagrant?"

He chuckled. "Ye make it sound as if it were a pro-fession. I'm no Gypsy, if that's what's in yer head. My father owned a vast tract of land, with many tenant farmers. But after he was . . . that is, I left home, I found myself a vagrant, as ye put it, for a short time."

Interesting, she thought. *This Mr. Slayter hails from a family of landowners.* "Why did you leave home?"

He was silent a few moments. "Circumstances."

"I see," she said, though she really did not. "Well, are you certain you wouldn't feel more comfortable in the bedchamber next door?"

"Sure I am that I would. But it would delay me coming to yer rescue. An intruder could always blockade yer door against me. Besides, as I said before, if an intruder did come in, the last thing he'd expect is someone coming through the wall. Surprise is key to victory."

Her eyes traveled down his long, lean legs. "And what's to keep you from surprising *me* during the night?" She found the idea shot a secret thrill through her.

He shook his head, spilling a lock of black hair down his forehead. A sidewise smile dimpled one cheek. "More sense than ye just showed in suggesting it."

An embarrassed flush heated her cheeks. She almost threw the hairbrush at him. "I-I only meant that I must rely on your honor to keep that door fully closed in the night. Because if I so much as catch you peeping into my rooms—"

His palms faced her in a defensive posture. "Sacred, I assure ye."

She should have been relieved to hear it, but she wasn't. In fact, it made her quite cross. She raked the hairbrush through her hair.

"I shall want an outing," she stated archly. "The Saint Swithin's Day Festival in Invergarry is tomorrow. Zoe and I will be attending. Make your preparations early, or we shall leave without you."

"I shall be ready. But make bet, ye'll no' be leaving without me." He turned on his heel and opened the secret door.

His high-handedness galled her. She was not about to let him leave with the last word, let alone the last command.

"You may take your leave now. But first, fetch me the milk."

It stopped him in his tracks. "Eh?"

She didn't even look at him, instead peering into the mirror. "The tray on the table beside the bed. Fetch it to me."

Out of the corner of her eye, she sensed him go to the night table and collect the pot of warm cocoa. Dutifully, he placed it on the dressing table.

But he didn't move.

After a few tense seconds, she couldn't stand it anymore. She looked up into his face. Amusement danced in his eyes.

"Shall I pour it, too, milady?"

This was worse. Now he was laughing at her expense. She should have slapped the mischievous grin off his face. But truth be told, she was mesmerized by the handsomeness of his features when something pleased him.

"You may."

His eyes became mere slits as he studied her, and she grew uncomfortable under his penetrating gaze. His hips were mere inches from her head. But he did as she asked. He righted the overturned teacup, and placed it in the saucer. Her gaze feathered down his arm as he picked up the teapot. It looked like a toy in his large hand. Briefly she wondered what such a large hand would feel against her cheek, her shoulder, her breast. Her own hand would be swallowed up in one of his. As the cocoa filled the cup, twin tendrils of steam swirled upward, like two people waltzing. What a treat it would be to dance with a man as large as this. She gazed at his heavily muscled forearm. How heavenly it would feel against her back!

As her gaze drew downward, she saw something shocking.

The skin on the back of his hand was hideously distorted.

Impulsively, she grasped him by the wrist, making him spill the cocoa onto the saucer. "What's happened to your hand?"

He jerked it away and set down the teapot. "It is nothing."

"Show it to me at once!"

His lips thinned. He flattened his hand on the table before her.

She leaned the candle closer. Sliced across his hand was a most horrible scar. It covered the whole of the back of his right hand, the skin lifting whitely in the shape of what appeared to be an *S*.

"Is this why you never appear before us without gloves?"

"Aye. I don't allow anyone to see my burn."

"That's no burn. It's a—a *brand*."

His jaw tensed. He could not meet her eyes. For the first time since she'd met him, he registered something she'd never seen before. Shame.

Her forehead twisted. "Who did that to you?"

"No one. It was a long time ago. Leave it be."

"Did you do something wrong?"

"I said leave it be, woman!" He seized his candlestick, nearly extinguishing the small flame, and ducked through the opening into the passageway.

The air fairly pulsed with the fury of his departure.

She hadn't just touched upon a sensitive nerve . . . she had stomped all over it.

She expelled a heavy sigh. There was so much Malcolm wouldn't speak of, so much she wanted to know. But his lips were a vault, and he himself a fortress. Perhaps a softer touch was needed.

She lay her head upon the pillow, wondering what horrible chain of events had led to that scar upon his hand. What did the *S* stand for? *Slaughterer*? *Slave*? *Sexual Deviant*?

As she considered the array of crimes that her protector might have been guilty of, she realized that life in Scotland had just become a lot more fascinating.

FOURTEEN

Slaighteur.

It was a word that screamed at Malcolm every cursed day of his life. No matter where he went or how he tried to hide it, they always found out.

Damn his folly for not putting on his gloves before going into Serena's room. Now there would be questions. Suspicions. Fears.

He sensed, rather than looked at, the scar that broadcast his secret. It was as obvious and palpable as a third arm. He stood before the small mirror that rested on the bare interior framing of the wall. Even when the gloves were on, the word seemed imprinted on his face.

Slaighteur.

Twenty years had passed since the awful day of his family's massacre, and it still pained him as if it were yesterday. For years, he wondered what had become of the wee ones who'd been kidnapped. Even now, he subsisted on the tenuous hope that they were still alive, growing older and less familiar with each passing year. If they were alive, then like him they were forbidden to carry their real name. Like him, they were now only *slaighteur*—knaves.

Refusal to stand with the clan in battle was treasonous. A villainous act that was punishable by expulsion from the clan. Not just you, but your whole family. It was the Highland way. And just to make sure that any chieftain you swore loyalty to knew about your cowardice, the sign of *slaighteur* would tell the story that your shame refused to.

He dipped his hand in the basin and splashed the cold water onto his face, hoping in vain to wash away the memory of his little siblings cowering together in the corner, their little hands blistering from the awful branding. Their innocent eyes watching the slaughter of their entire family. Wrenched from their homes. God alone knew what further torments had lain ahead for them. He choked on the horror.

The pang of regret in his gut stabbed at him. He would never forgive himself for surviving, for escaping. Or for failing to protect them.

His thoughts turned to the woman on the other side of the plaster wall, and he shook his head.

There was a woman who warranted his protection. He knew the dangers she was up against, even if she didn't recognize them. That note wasn't just a warning, it was a prediction. Malcolm was aware of how serious these rebels were. He'd already been sent to catch three such rebels, including Jock McInnes. These men were beyond the point of talking about their grievances . . . they were after instilling terror, and they didn't care how many innocents died in the process.

Serena Marsh. He had to admire her courage. Even after the threat of mutilation and death, she refused to back down or be driven into hiding. It may have been foolhardy, but it was bold. Worthy of a Highland woman.

God, what an iron-willed lass. He had to smile. All that pluck in the heart of one so fair. She always fought him like a cat on its back, four sets of sharp claws ready to do damage. For the hundredth time, he imagined what it would be like to have all that hiss and spit in his bed. To have each of those milky limbs wrapped around his body. Every time she shouted some imperious command at him, he felt like silencing her sensual mouth with a forceful kiss. Every time she behaved dismissively, he felt the urge to make her moan for him all the more.

And he was just the man to do it. Just the man to turn her hisses into kisses, her scratching to caressing. Because he understood her. He knew that underneath all that bravado, there was someone desperately in need of protecting. He could read it in her eyes. She had been hurt, and she would let no man get within ten feet of her heart. Treating men like a spoiled child treats its playthings . . . enjoying them for a time and then leaving them lying around just as soon as she tires of them. It was safe for Serena to keep her distance, because if the toy came to life and left her, she would be devastated. Again.

Malcolm shrugged off his shirt and lay on top of the narrow cot in the passageway. He was involving himself too deeply in this assignment. It was not his job to fix Serena Marsh. It was his job to protect her. In fact, it suited him well that she would not let men get close. It made his job easier. She had little enough regard for the peril in which she stood. The less attention she drew, the better.

He draped his forearm over his eyes to concentrate on the security measures for tomorrow's outing. Point by point he went over the best strategy to get her safely to Invergarry, to protect her while out in the open, and to see her safely home. And as he finally began to drift off, one thought kept resurfacing.

Was he trying so hard to keep her from the enemy, or just to keep her for himself?

FIFTEEN

That very midnight, near Invergarry, nearly a hundred men met on a remote field, their torches blazing. As they drew together from all directions, their lit torches looked like an explosion happening in reverse.

In the dark, their differing tartans looked much the same. It was just as well, since they were there for a common purpose.

"Tomorrow's the Games, lads," said Guinnein Kinross, heartily shaking hands with a MacLaren. "Hope ye're ready for a Kinross thrashing."

"Still think ye're a match for the MacDonnels, Kinross?" interrupted a MacDonnel man. "Or did last year's Games not convince ye?"

Brandubh McCullough planted his flaming torch in the wet ground. "There will not be a contest among us this year, men," he said. "Tomorrow we play to a different aim altogether."

The firelight played on the underside of Brandubh McCullough's face, giving his handsome features a ghoulish appearance. "We've thrown down the gauntlet to the English. They know we'll not be paying their tax. By now that Marsh fellow, the one they sent to tell us to draw off, will have sent word to Parliament. England will be readying her troops. And when they step foot on Scottish soil, I want us to be ready.

"By my reckoning, there will be twenty-seven clans at the Games tomorrow. Not all of them sympathize with our cause. The heads of fifteen of those clans live in English pockets, and speak with English tongues. That leaves twelve of us to carry the protests of the people into battle.

"Tomorrow, our men will not be there for trophies and rewards. Our men will be there for training. Tomorrow, we'll be perfecting our battle skills. Our weapons of war will be the clachneart, the caber, and the pitchfork. I want us to be fit and strong and fast. Forget the piping and the dancing. Yer people will be training at swordplay and wrestling and tug o' war. Because that, gentlemen, is what we'll be preparing for. A war."

A shout erupted from the gathering.

MacLaren shook McCullough's hand. "Don't ye worry, son. There is no' an Englishman alive that can take one of my lads. We've been waiting for this day since my grandfather was a boy. The time has come for us to stand up to the tyranny of the Protestant king. Scotland will be bullied no longer. What do ye say to that, lads?"

Another shout erupted from the men as they stabbed their torches into the night air.

Brandubh McCullough took up his torch from the damp earth. "Scottish home rule, gentlemen. That is the real trophy. Tomorrow, we train champions!"

Their collective shouts split the night.

And when the men finally dispersed, their outgoing torches formed an explosion in the right direction.

SIXTEEN

The day dawned gloomy and forbidding. Gray clouds blanketed the sky, bringing the heavens even closer to the earth.

Serena gazed out through the dining room window. It seemed there was always something around to dampen her mood. Today, aptly, it was the rain.

"You're cross," remarked Earlington over the breakfast dishes.

"Can you blame me? Look at the weather. The one day that there's going to be a fair, and the weather turns anything but."

"Hardly seems fair."

Serena cracked a smile. "It isn't funny, Father. This is a brand-new frock." She ran her fingers along the delicate embellishments of her neckline, a detail she had ordered specially. Tiny green leaves were sewn along the yellow muslin, above the ribboned waist, and along the hem. It was a beautiful walking dress, and she knew that it would turn Malcolm's head when he saw it.

"I wouldn't worry overmuch. The sky should clear up soon."

She set aside the bowl of oatmeal that she had quickly learned to despise, and spread some strawberry preserves on a piece of toast instead. She was upset that she hadn't bothered to pack her yellow parasol when she left England. Certainly, the green parasol she brought down would match, but it was such a waste to ruin the breathtaking effect of the entire costume. Still, this was Scotland—she doubted anyone would even notice the departure from perfection, let alone bemoan it.

Zoe bounced in. "Are you still eating? Hurry up! Invergarry is still over an hour away. I don't want to miss any of the Games."

Truth be told, neither did Serena. This rustic fair that she had scoffed at had turned out to be the high point of her stay. She put down her toast, kissed her father on the cheek, and followed Zoe to the front door.

Their town coach was already waiting in the driveway. A groom stood holding the horses while a footman opened the carriage door. But something was missing.

"Where's Mr. Slayter?" asked Zoe.

A thread of irritation snaked through her as the girl read her thoughts. All Serena knew was that Malcolm had not yet seen her in her new dress. "I don't know."

"Shouldn't someone go find him?"

Serena perched a hand on her hip. "It is his job to follow me around, not I him."

Zoe sighed. "Would you like me to run upstairs and call him down?"

"No need of that," Serena drawled. "Just draw a pentagram on the floor and shout 'I summon thee.' That should do the trick."

Zoe giggled. "Come now, Serena. I can see that you don't dislike Mr. Slayter as much as you pretend. In fact, I would go so far as to say that you feel for him what I feel for Monsieur Leveque."

"Don't be absurd, Zoe. I feel nothing warmer than indifference to him. To either of them."

Just then they spotted a horse and rider galloping down the path toward the house. Even from the distance, she could tell it was Malcolm—he was a man of singular size. But as the distance closed between them, she noticed something altogether different about him: his clothing. The man was wearing a kilt. A black one.

The horse skidded to a halt on the gravel behind the carriage. Malcolm threw one leg over its giant neck and slid to the ground. Serena caught a glimpse of a long, muscled leg, all the way up to the thigh, before the folds of his kilt draped back down to his knee.

Her heart began to flutter. Here she was, expecting to be upset at him, but all she could do was marvel at the change he presented. Until now, he had dressed in coat and trousers, even a cravat—clothes befitting an Englishman. The man standing before her now was completely alien to her. A coarse white linen shirt, a black woolen kilt, a black plaid draped over a wide shoulder, and a sporran made from brown hide resting between his legs. A head-to-toe Highlander.

He patted down the horse, soothing the great animal as she caught her breath. He gave instructions to the groom, who led the animal away. Finally, he turned his attention to Serena and Zoe, who stood in the doorway.

"Mornin'," he said, touching a finger to his forehead.

Serena cocked an eyebrow. "Where, may I ask, have you been?"

He gave her a sidewise glance as he checked the harness on the two horses pulling the carriage. "Canvassing your path."

"Canvassing it? For what?"

"Making certain it was strewn with rose petals. What do ye think, woman? I was checking it for brigands. Highwaymen. Cutthroats. Assassins."

Finally, he turned around and gave her the full measure of his attention. He leaned against the horse and crossed his arms at his chest. Audaciously, he looked her up and down, which gave Serena satisfaction . . . and a secret thrill.

"Ye look fetching," he said. "Ye both do," he added with a nod to Zoe.

Against her will, Serena blushed. "Thank you," she replied with as much archness as she could muster.

"Planning to find a champion at the Games?"

"Perhaps. Does that make you jealous?"

He cocked a smile. "Just stay out of trouble. That's all I ask."

It was not the answer she had hoped for. As if to echo her ire, a distant rumbling in the sky was followed by a spittle of rain. Serena ducked back farther into the doorway, opening her green parasol and raising it heavenward. Malcolm, on the other hand, was completely indifferent to the rain, the drops adhering his shirt to his body.

A look of consternation crossed Serena's face. "Perhaps we should postpone our trip until the weather clears."

"No!" cried Zoe piteously.

Malcolm shook his head. "Just a smirr of rain. Come over to the carriage with ye."

The skies opened up, and the rain turned into a downpour in a matter of seconds. She gave her lace parasol a distrustful glance. The decorative accoutrement was useless.

"Even a sheep bleats in complaint when it rains. It's not my fault if you haven't its sense."

Zoe tugged on Serena's sleeve. "If we make a mad dash, we won't get too wet."

"No, Zoe. These are new shoes."

Malcolm stamped over to her. "Och, woman, ye do get yeself into a state over naught." He took the parasol from her and set it on the floor. He slipped the plaid from his shoulder and, unfolding it, wrapped her in the wide swath. It was a thick wool cloth, resistant to the dampness.

"Thank you, Mr. Slayter, but I'm afraid—" The next thing she knew, she was bent forward over his shoulder like a sack of barley.

He carried her in that ignoble manner all the way to the carriage, and tossed her through the open doorway. She clambered to the seat just as Zoe ran inside, and Malcolm ensconced himself on the opposite seat.

She stared at him, her mouth open in affronted pride.

"No thanks necessary," he said. "It's reward enough that yer shoes are still dry." A knock on the carriage roof signaled to the driver that they were ready, and with a lurch they were off.

In the seat opposite her, Malcolm ran a hand through his wet hair, which spiked chaotically. He seemed entirely unaffected by the rain on his skin. She, on the other hand, found the look of it on him quite irresistible. As he adjusted the plaid back in place over his shoulder, Serena stole a long look at him. Rainwater glistened on his face, giving his complexion a bronze sheen. His eyelashes became tiny black daggers as they fanned across his wet cheek. The damp shirt turned invisible now that it stuck to his chest and arms. For the first time, Serena could see the well-defined bicep that mounded over the crook of his arm, and the thick pads of muscle on his chest. He was a stallion of a man, all hard curves and beautiful lines. A rivulet of rainwater fell from the hollow of his throat, and Serena watched as it slowly caressed the valley of his chest and disappeared behind the open shirt.

Serena looked away. The vistas of rolling hills and lush greenery became nothing more than a languid blur as her thoughts wandered to the man in the opposite seat. Her skin still tingled from where he had handled her. Breathlessly, she began to imagine what such a man would feel like wrapped around her entire body. To feel those knotted forearms wrapped around her waist, that hard chest pressed against her exposed breasts, those lean hips spreading her thighs . . .

She pulled a frilled kerchief out of her reticule and dabbed it upon her reddening cheeks. How heavenly it would be not to have to be so strong, so proper anymore. If she could cease to be Serena Marsh, the ambassador's daughter, and just be Serena, an ordinary woman? Maybe then she would be able to give vent to the desires that consumed her.

Malcolm sat back in the seat and peered out of the window. What a mystery he was to her. He was always *present,* but never *there.* Close at hand, but inaccessible. Beautiful to look at, but unavailable to the rest of her senses.

If only he would touch her first, then perhaps it would be easier to reciprocate. But he never made any overtures toward her. After he'd checked her room last night, he'd never come back in, even though she'd secretly hoped he would. It was almost painful knowing that his bed was so close, his nearness tempting her like a forbidden sweet. There, through that secret door in her bedroom, slept a healthy, gorgeous man. If she had dared to go to his room to steal a kiss, no one would ever find out.

And yet, she was forced to wonder if he would even welcome her attentions. Malcolm was the most inscrutable man she'd ever met, and even when she could read him, he seemed so hard and unyielding. The only time she'd seen him less than self-assured was the moment she discovered the brand on his hand. That scar seemed to be his private shame, his Achilles' heel. The thing that made him most human.

"Your gloves are wet," she ventured. "Perhaps you ought to remove them to let them dry."

He shot her a warning look. "No' the now."

"Oh, I'm sorry. I'd forgotten about your scar."

Zoe's ears perked. "You have a scar?"

"Aye."

"May I see it?" she asked.

"No."

Zoe blushed. "That was rude of me, wasn't it?"

His eyes bore into Serena's. "No ruder than Miss Marsh was for bringing it up."

Serena stiffened. "I was only trying to pass the time."

"Find some other topic of conversation."

She wanted *him* to be the topic of conversation. "Very well, then. I'm glad to see you've finally decided to identify yourself with the costume of your heritage."

"Costume of my—? Ye mean the kilt?"

"Of course. And the—" She pointed to the black cloth pinned to his shirt.

"The fly plaid?" He chuckled. "This is no' a costume of heritage. It's a very practical garment."

"In what way?"

"It kept the rain off yer backside, didn't it?"

Zoe giggled. Serena flicked her a withering glance.

"Nevertheless, it is a costume, just as my dress is a costume. Does one wear anything under that?"

A twinkle in his eye signaled his amusement. "Mayhap ye'd like a wee keek?"

Serena felt a blush zooming up her neck. The answer to that question was embarrassingly *yes*. "Hmm. Thanks all the same, but I fear that, in the words of William Shakespeare, it may be 'much ado about nothing.' "

There it was again. That smile. It transformed his dangerous face into something quite delectable, dripping with sexual charm.

"Please yerself."

She'd love to, but he was making it very hard. She would have to find a way to make *him* very hard. Who knew . . . perhaps her next column would be all about *his* column.

SEVENTEEN

As they left Fort Augustus, a band of silver edged the dark thundercloud, until finally the storm cleared altogether. The carriage rumbled past the shore of Loch Uanagan, beside the rough hinterland of Newtown, and along the green pastures at Aberchalder. It was a rich tapestry of landscapes, and despite Serena's initial dislike of the stark country, she had to admire its wonders.

Invergarry was a little more than a scattering of homesteads at the foot of thick forest. But in one large pasture, hundreds of people gathered. Colorful flags flapped in the high breeze, and tents and tables skirted a huge playing field. The music of flutes and drums added a decided twinkle to the chill air. Even from her carriage, Serena could smell meats roasting on spits.

Zoe was fairly bouncing in the carriage, and for once Serena shared her enthusiasm. It was a festive scene, full of unusual scents and sights, and Serena could hardly wait to explore them. Unmindful of ladylike decorum, she opened her own door.

A gloved hand pulled her in again.

"Remember what I said," Malcolm remarked. "Never leave my sight. Understood?"

Irritated, she jerked her arm away. She was unaccustomed to being around brusque men—at least, men who didn't worship her beauty and charm. "Very well.

Just make sure to keep your distance, or people will think we're friends."

Arm in arm, Serena and Zoe hurried along the edge of the playing field. Everywhere she turned, there was something fascinating to look at. To one side, vendors were noisily selling fabrics, bread, ale, and livestock. To the other, people crowded around the competitions. Out of the corner of her eye, Serena saw something fly into the air. Grabbing Zoe's hand, she yanked her in that direction.

They joined the gathering that circled a group of men who took turns pitchforking a heavy jute sack and tossing it backward over their heads in an attempt to make it fly high over a horizontal bar between two standards. Judging by the strain of the effort, it was not an easy task.

Adjacent to this game was another in which a man clutched a heavy rock to his neck, then spun around and around before he released it, tossing it as far as he could. Serena watched in amazement at the distance these thick, burly men could make the unwieldy rock fly.

A cheer erupted behind her, and Serena pulled Zoe toward it. By this time, Serena's beautiful yellow slippers were smeared with wet mud, but she didn't really care. On this playing field, a beefy man hoisted up a slender, twenty-foot-long tree trunk by its end between his clasped hands and cradled it against his shoulder. The man pulled all sorts of grimaces as the heavy trunk swayed in the air and he struggled to keep it from falling over. Once he gained its balance, he ran with it, heaved it up and over, and the tree trunk fell end-over-end. The crowd cheered, signaling a successful throw.

This seemed to be the most difficult game, and Serena was enthralled. The competitions all centered on common objects—rocks, logs, heavy hammers—but the difficulty of the tasks made them fascinating. Back home, the most strenuous competitive game gentlemen engaged in was horse racing, or perhaps even the odd game of court tennis. Never had she witnessed a sport that required such feats of pure brute strength. And all by thickly muscled men wearing what her own countrymen disparagingly called "skirts."

She turned around, and there, behind her, was Malcolm. His eagle eyes were scanning the crowds, keeping a watchful eye on the people who surrounded her. He, too, wore a "skirt," but she'd be hard-pressed to find someone less feminine. A man like him would never fit in in English Society.

Truth be told, he didn't seem to fit in among all these other Scots, either. There was something otherworldly about him, as if he was caught between two civilizations, ill-fitting in both. For one thing, whereas everyone at the gathering was wearing their colorful tartans, his was but black. For another, there were those brown leather gloves he never removed, hiding that brand that he never showed. She was itching to know what he had done to deserve such a punishment.

"These certainly are peculiar games," she said, loud enough for Malcolm to hear behind her. "I'm not certain I understand the rules of this one."

She could sense Malcolm step in a little closer behind her.

"This is known as the caber toss. The man who tosses the caber so that it lands straight ahead, in the twelve o'clock position, wins."

"That's what I mean. There's no thought involved, no . . . strategy. It's all about whoever is strongest." She couldn't resist turning around and glancing at his body.

"There's a time for chess, and a time for wrestling. Think of this as the latter."

"Will you not play, Mr. Slayter?"

"Aye. Love a good game of chess."

"No, I mean here, now. Tossing that . . . caber."

Malcolm shook his head. "No' the now."

"Why not?" She'd give anything to see him use those incredible muscles she'd glimpsed under his rain-soaked shirt earlier.

"If I'm in there," he said, pointing to the field, "then who will be out here protecting ye?"

She turned around and faced him full-on. "Must you be at my side at every moment? My goodness! If you were a Roman soldier, I swear your name would be Ubiquitus!"

He tried to suppress a grin. "This is a competition among clans. I canna participate."

"Why not? What exactly is your clan, Mr. Slayter?"

He looked away. "I'm sure ye've not heard of it."

She narrowed her eyes at him. "No clan wears a black tartan. From whom do you hail?"

"I am a Highlander. Nothing more."

"Why will you not name your clan?"

There was a warning in his eyes. "Turn around, Miss Marsh. Ye're missing the competition."

He drifted back into the crowd. It was a growing frustration that she could not see into his life. But she thought it best to leave that line of questioning for another time. "I'm hungry, Zoe. Let's go get something to eat."

Malcolm followed them to a wooden cart where a stocky lady with thick arms had arranged three baskets of pastries that gave off a delicious aroma.

"Mutton pies, biggest size," she sang, showing the spaces in her mouth where her teeth used to be.

"What's this one here?" Serena asked, eyeing the flaky triangles that were fairly bursting with filling.

"Mincemeat bridie, hot and tidy." She picked up two and handed one to each of them in a cloth.

"Would you care for one?" Serena asked Malcolm.

"No' the now," he said.

Serena dropped two coins into the woman's hand and took a bite of the pastry. Instantly she sank into a realm of pleasure. The beef-and-currant filling was warm and flavorful, and the buttery pastry added just the right touch of crispness. It was common food, eaten by common people, but right now, to Serena, it was heaven in her mouth.

"Serena, can we go see the collies?" Zoe said between mouthfuls. "I love to see the dogs do tricks."

"Sounds delightful," Serena replied halfheartedly, "but I see a fortune-teller's tent over there. Let's get our palms read!"

Malcolm snorted derisively. "Don't tell me ye believe in that nonsense."

Serena didn't particularly, but it was enticing entertainment nonetheless. "And if I did?"

"I credit ye with more sense than that, Miss Marsh. No one can see into the future. Those so-called fortune-tellers are nothing more than tricksters who like to prey on over-anxious people desperate for answers." Malcolm looked into her face, his expression hanging between bemusement and concern. "Are ye such a person?"

She hated to admit it, even to herself. But no one could answer the questions that plagued her. Would she ever return to London and the life she had left behind? Had her readers forgotten her or stopped caring about her column? Would she ever find a man who would love her for who she was?

"Very well, Zoe. Let's go see the collies."

There was a separate encampment where the livestock

was kept. It was a place for horse and cattle trading, which some people were doing with overly loud voices. But there was also a large paddock in which herders were competing to see how fast their border collies could steer a small flock of sheep into a pen.

Serena and Zoe stood behind the fencepost to watch the competition. But watching a dog bark at some confused sheep as they got corralled into a small pen had a natural time span of enjoyment for Serena. She peeked behind her to get a glance at Malcolm.

He was gone.

She whirled around to look for him. He was usually about ten feet behind her, just far enough to give her some space but close enough to step into a fray. Now he was nowhere to be found.

Finally she spotted someone who looked like him inside a rudimentary aviary. She came closer to inspect. It was Malcolm, and perched on his forearm was a falcon whose eyes were covered by a soft leather hood. Malcolm stroked the bird's chest gently, his lips puckered as he cooed softly at the animal. Watching a man like Malcolm act so tenderly incited a feeling of yearning in her—and it was something she was not accustomed to feeling.

Then, adding insult to injury, a young woman came up alongside him. She was a brown-haired girl with freckles all over her face who apparently owned the aviary. As Malcolm softly caressed the bird, the young woman seemed to be pointing out the animal's unique characteristics.

But to Serena's practiced eye, the freckled woman was clearly offering more than just birds of prey. The woman's eyes raked Malcolm up and down, her gaze settling on the very features that Serena herself had been appreciating during the carriage ride. The woman's hand touched Malcolm's gloved hand, then his arm, and finally came to rest on his chest. Though crude and unrefined, her efforts at allurement were not lost on Malcolm. He took his eyes off the bird, looked down at her . . . and smiled!

Serena inhaled sharply, and it fanned an inexplicable flame of jealousy within her. She didn't even recognize the expression that Malcolm gave that woman. It was Malcolm's face at its handsomest . . . and it was for someone else.

In a fit of pique, she stormed off. *Let him try and find me,* she fumed. Served him right if he became well and truly worried when he went to look for her and she was not there. Here she was strategizing how best to grace him with her attentions, and instead he bestowed his own on some stupid bird of prey—two of them!

Almost as if by intention, her steps led her to the fortune-teller's tent. Outside, there were two ladies talking. Both had auburn hair, but one was about double the girth of the other.

"I'm here to see the fortune-teller."

The rounder one spoke up. "An' ye've found her. Step inside, love."

She held open the flap of the tent for Serena. It was dark inside, but it smelled like a garden. Hanging from each corner of the tent were bundles of lavender, rapeseed, and heather drying.

"Can you really see into the future?" Serena asked as she perched herself on a milking stool.

The heavy woman sat opposite her on another stool, her legs open immodestly. "Aye. All my life. An' the babe that grows inside me has made the power even keener. The name's Alice. What's yer name?"

"Serena."

"Serena," she repeated, as she lifted a kettle off of a

fire that burned on the ground. "Tuppence is the price of yer fortune. An' e'en if ye don't care for it, then ye'll still have had a nice cup of tea."

Serena handed over the coin and took the cup that Alice held out.

"Drink doon yer tea, but leave a sip in the cup."

She blew a wisp of steam away, and slowly drank the hot liquid. Inside the rustic earthenware cup was very fine China tea. The tea leaves swam inside the cup, tickling her lips. When just a drop of the liquid remained, she went to hand the cup back to Alice.

Alice held her hand up. "I'm no' to touch it yet. Swirl it aboot and chuck it over on the ground. Then let me see what gets left behind."

Serena did so. Inside the cup, a dredging of wilted tea leaves spotted the cup.

"Noo then, let's see where yer fortune lies." Alice opened her eyes widely as she turned the cup around and around in her hands. She breathed deeply, letting the images in the residue float up to her eyes.

"Ye've come from afar."

Serena rolled her eyes. She would have thought that was obvious.

"But there's a lang way yet fer ye to go."

Her eyebrows drew together. "North? Or south?"

Alice shook her head. "I canna tell. But ye'll cover a great distance afore ye're home."

Serena pursed her lips. She hoped it was the distance from here back to London. "What else do you see?"

Alice looked full-faced at Serena. "There's great danger ahead."

Serena's forehead creased. She grabbed Alice's arm to look into the cup herself. "What sort of danger?"

"Evil men with evil intentions."

Serena's heart sank. "What would anyone want with me?"

Alice's blue eyes peered into the cup. "I canna see that. But I can tell that the struggle will be difficult. Ye'll need all the help ye can get to overcome it."

Serena pulled away. Inside her, reason warred with fear. Silently, she argued that there was no such thing as seeing into the future. But she was far from home, and her father was embroiled in a battle to stop a nation from turning against itself. Doubt crept in.

"Is my father in peril?"

Uncertainly, Alice shook her head. "I see a sword or an arrow. But I canna tell if it be man or woman 'tis pointed at." Alice put her hand on Serena's. "But here's a good portent. Love awaits ye. And where there's love, evil flees."

"Love? From whom?"

"A good man, I see. He has the mark on him."

Her thoughts flew to Malcolm. "Mark? What mark?"

"Here," Alice said, pointing to a glob. "See the horse's head? That signifies yer man. An' see above its head? 'Tis the mark of a cross. It means that sacrifice is not unknown to him. 'Tis a good man that has that mark. And there's a crown nearby. That means he's a man with a title."

It was not Malcolm after all. Serena couldn't ignore the feeling of disappointment. She tried to convince herself to be pleased by the prediction. In her future lay a nobleman who was also a *noble man*. And though she was attracted to Malcolm—he was a fine-looking man, after all—the idea that she'd find love with such a rough and common person was absurd.

And yet she couldn't ignore that unwelcome feeling that tugged at her heart. Regret.

"Ye're a fortunate woman," said Alice. "When ye find him, cleave to him."

"I will," she said cheerlessly. "Thank you." Serena stood, and then helped the pregnant Alice to her feet. She bid the woman outside the tent a good day, and wandered back toward the field.

Alice's words weighed heavily upon Serena. She found herself dissecting and deliberating the predictions Alice had made, wondering at the shadowy man in her future who was *not* Malcolm.

Finally, in utter self-mockery, she shook her head free of the misplaced importance. Serena was no ignorant, unsophisticated peasant who would easily succumb to a fortune-teller's musings. She was an educated, cosmopolitan woman who well understood the charlatanism of fortune-telling. Alice and her friend were probably snickering to themselves that *they* had just taken a small fortune off *her*. No doubt Alice "foretold" the same thing to all who were gullible enough to listen—a hint of danger and a promise of a prince's love for young ladies; a prediction of virility, long life, and monetary success for the men. Serena was disgusted with herself for giving it any credence whatsoever.

Before she knew it, her distracted wandering had led her onto unfamiliar grounds. Here, there was another competition happening. Men stood in a circle watching two men with wooden swords swing at each other. At first glance, the clacking noise of the counterfeit weapons gave the scene the appearance of actors rehearsing for a play . . . until their blood and bruises convinced her it was all too real.

One of the men didn't parry quickly enough, and his opponent's wooden sword hit him across the forehead—hard. The blow spun the man's head, sending him sprawling to the ground.

A shout erupted from the circle, and the winner raised his arms in triumph. The loser stood up on shaky legs, a gash across his forehead bleeding.

Serena was horrified. This was nothing like the other games, which tested strength, speed, and balance. This game was all about might, violence, and brutality.

She turned to leave, but the heel of her slipper got caught in the mud. Losing her balance, she fell to her knees.

She swore under her breath. Awkwardly, she clambered back to her feet. Her shoes were now fully covered in mud, which also streaked the front of her beautiful yellow dress. She tried to wipe the smudges away, but the muck on her palms only spread the stains even more.

"Damn and blast!" she cried out.

A voice came from behind her. "That's no way for a lady to talk."

Anger coiled within her. She spun around to give the disrespectful man a piece of her mind, but was met with a frightening sight. Twelve kilted men, bloodied and bruised, stood in front of her.

Her eyes drifted from man to man. Never before had she faced a gang of such dangerous-looking men. She felt like a gazelle cornered by a pride of lions.

"I beg your pardon?"

"And well ye should," said Brandubh McCullough, "and that of every other Scottish child who goes hungry so ye could dress like a bloody queen."

"Who are you?"

"My name will mean nothing on yer ears. But yer name, Miss Marsh, is like venom in ours."

Fear gave her voice a distorted edge. "How do you know my name?"

"I know who ye are. And I know who yer father is.

The Crown's marionette. A nanny for hire sent to mollify the unruly Scots with a sweet from the king's table."

Serena had no idea who the man was, but his rage against her father seemed to transcend all reason. The skirl of bagpipes, loud and shrill, would surely drown out her screams. She turned to walk away.

"Where d'ye think ye're going?" he growled as he grabbed her by the wrist. "I'm not through talking with ye."

"Let me go!" she cried, twisting her wrist in his unyielding grasp. Dozens of horrible visions of rape flashed across her mind.

"Come here. I've a message ye can take home to yer father!"

She screamed, her heart willing for Malcolm. If only she hadn't walked away from him. If only he were there right behind her.

A rock whizzed over Serena and clocked the man on the side of his head. He turned around, cradling his wound, but he never released his hold on Serena.

The next few seconds were a blur of motion. Malcolm ran out of the trees, barreling into one surprised man. As he fell backward, Malcolm rolled over him, and kicked another man's feet from under him. He jumped up and swung a clenched fist at a third. The burly man ducked, and swung at Malcolm. The blow caught Malcolm on the cheek, but he returned a punch to the man's face. Just then, one of them jumped on Malcolm from the back, immobilizing his arms. The burly man landed two punches on Malcolm's face and one in his gut, making him gasp for breath. When he came in for a fourth, Malcolm kicked the man in the stomach, sending him reeling. Deftly, he stomped on the foot of the one who held him captive, but he refused to let go. So Malcolm tossed his head back into the man's face, breaking his nose. He grabbed the man who'd fallen to the ground, lifting him by his hair, and then twisted his arm high behind his back. From the waistband of his kilt, he slid out a dagger and held it to the man's testicles.

"Sweet Jesus," gasped the man. "Don't do it."

"Ye're wasting yer breath on me," rasped Malcolm into his ear. "Plead with yer friend over there to let the girl go."

"Brandubh, do as the man says," he said, panic warbling his voice.

Malcolm's eyes homed in on Brandubh's. There was a fierceness to them that shocked Serena, and she desperately hoped it had the same effect on her captor.

Brandubh made no movement, save to squeeze his hold on Serena.

"What's it to be, friend?" said Malcolm. "I'll trade ye this man's ballocks for the girl. And by the look of things, ye'd better hurry. They're shrinking so fast there'll be nothing left to cut off."

"Hold on, man," Brandubh said. "Ye don't have the way of it. I mean her no harm. Do ye know who this girl is? It's her da who's bringing with him England's decrees that Scotland will be yoked forever with the new taxes. We've got a message for him as well."

"She's got nothing to do with yer quarrel. Let her go."

The corners of Brandubh's mouth turned down as he squeezed Serena's arms. "Ye're making a lot of demands for one in so compromised a position."

"I'll no' ask again. Ye can walk away from the girl, or you can limp away from the girl."

Brandubh's eyes narrowed on Malcolm's kilt. "What clan are ye? Ah, ye're *slaighteur,* aren't ye?"

A thundercloud passed across Malcolm's face.

"Aye, ye are. I always wondered if I'd ever run into

yer kind. No wonder ye won't take a stand with yer own countrymen. A coward bastard from a coward clan."

Serena's breath came in rough gasps. Malcolm tightened his grip on the dagger. The man he held captive cringed.

"Come along, man," said Brandubh. "There are hundreds of our countrymen about. Our *patriotic* countrymen. A single call, and ye're done for."

"That may be, friend. But this man will pay for my defeat with his balls."

The man was sweating profusely. "For the love of God, Brandubh. Let her go."

Slowly, Brandubh trained his gaze on Serena. "Tell yer father that Scotland is tired of hearing English commands. Tell him that her children are weary of being given promises instead of food. Tell him that the next time we have to state our grievances, 'twill be with claymores and muskets in our hands." Brandubh let her go.

Malcolm waited until Serena was behind him. Then he released the man's arm and shoved him forward.

"If ye lay hold of this woman just once more," he said, pointing his dagger at Brandubh, "the last pleasant thing ye'll feel is the gentle whisper on yer hair from my blade before it slices yer ear clean off."

Malcolm didn't sheath his weapon until they were out of the clearing and back into the competition field. "Are ye all right?"

"Yes, I'm fine," she said.

"Are ye sure?" Worry was etched all over his face.

"Quite sure," she replied, her fear finally ebbing now that she was with him.

He looked her all over, as if to reassure himself. "Yer dress. It's stained. Did they make ye kneel before them? Oh, my God. They didn't—"

She put his hand on his arm. "I fell over. They didn't hurt me."

"Ye're certain?"

She smiled. "I'm fine." Truth be told, she was more than fine. The look of genuine concern on his face, and the heroic way in which he'd come to her rescue, made her feel exuberant.

Relief washed over his face. She could almost kiss him for that. Seemed her little lesson brought out the side of him she wanted to see.

"Come along," he said, tugging her by the arm. "We're leaving."

"Where's Zoe?"

"Waiting in the carriage. *As I told her to.*"

It was hard to keep up with his long stride. She had to practically trot to keep pace. He didn't seem to be escorting her as much as hauling her.

And he didn't slow down until they had reached the carriage. As he said, Zoe was already inside the coach, and her young face peeked out from the open carriage window.

"Where did you go, Serena?" asked Zoe.

"To the fortune-teller's."

"Without me?" she cried petulantly.

"Without the both of us, apparently." Malcolm pulled Serena away from the carriage door. "Ye . . . up onto the roof. I want a word in private."

Serena seldom rode on the seats atop the town coach, even though they were designed for riding in fine weather. But Malcolm gave her no other option. He climbed up after her and barked a command at the driver. In a trice the carriage pitched forward, and they were off at full gallop.

He took the seat next to Serena. Even through his sun-kissed complexion, Malcolm's bruised cheek began

to color ferociously. He hugged his side, where the burly
man had swung a meaty fist into his gut.

"Thank you, Mr. Slayter. I don't know what would
have happened—"

His anger cut her sentence off. "Why did ye walk away
from me?"

She had no intention of confessing her jealousy over
him. "That doesn't matter."

"It bloody well does matter! 'One rule,' I said. 'Never
leave my sight,' I said. And what did ye do?"

She stiffened. "Then your sight wasn't on me, was it?"

The fierceness intensified in his eyes. "Ye put yer
own life in danger. To say nothing of mine!"

Serena crossed her arms defensively. "No one asked
you to intercede."

"Ye're willful, disobedient, foolhardy, inconsiderate—"

"Don't vent your spleen on me."

"—and it's high time ye learned a lesson." He seized
her by the arm and yanked her across his lap.

She fell facedown, her hips folded over a muscled,
kilted thigh. Stunned, she tried to lift herself up, but a
hand on her back held her down fast.

Her modesty and pride were at once outraged, and
she opened her mouth to speak the anger that surged
within her. But before she could utter a sound, another
noise reached her ears that chased away all words.

Whap! His open hand connected on her upturned
posterior, ripping an outraged gasp from her mouth.

"Ow!" she cried out as another fierce smack landed on
her behind. No one had ever physically chastised her
before . . . not her father or her nanny or her governesses.
It was mortifying, outrageous, scandalous. "How dare
you lay a hand on me!"

But alarm replaced fury as she realized he was not

going to stop. Again and again, his large hand swatted her backside, spreading hot pain across her rump.

Panic laced her voice. "Let me go!" But she may as well have been shouting at the green landscape that rushed past.

With one elbow on the leather carriage seat and one hand on his hair-dappled shin, Serena tried valiantly to push herself off his lap. But Malcolm had wrapped his muscled arm around her waist, rendering all her bucking and wriggling useless. She turned the air blue with swear words, threatening all sorts of retribution at him. But nothing succeeded in freeing her from his hold.

"Please, I'll give you whatever you want," she cried. Where commands and threats failed, bribery might work. "Just stop!"

He did not relent.

But soon she felt more than pain . . . she also felt remorse. She had treated him shabbily, and as a result he had been treated harshly by the men on that field. She had put both their lives in peril, and though they had both walked away from the skirmish, only she had come away unscathed. If he had left her to her own devices—if he had not cared enough to rescue her— she would not have been so lucky.

"I'm sorry," she shouted out.

Finally, his hand stilled.

She scrambled off his lap and backed as far away from him as she could, panting. Now free, her first inclination was to rebuke him harshly. But the look on his face—as fearsome as any firearm—made her rethink that course of action.

Malcolm leaned an elbow on his knee, the one she'd been bent over just a moment before. "I am willing to endure a beating for ye. I am even prepared to accept the fact that protecting ye may cost me my life. But I will *not* allow ye to casually sell it away from me. Ye can play the high and mighty mistress to yer heart's content . . . but not to me. While I'm yer protector, ye will do as I say do. Because if I say it, it'll be because I'm after protecting both our lives. Now, should there be a next time to all of this, the drawers are coming down. Is that clear to ye?"

Serena's chest caved. She nodded, pouting piteously.

"Good. Then lesson learned."

EIGHTEEN

The carriage ride back to Fort Augustus seemed to last a lifetime. Her bottom felt as if it were being pricked by thousands of tiny pins, and she wondered if the stinging would ever stop. The mere possibility of another such chastisement turned her heart to water.

Earlier, here in this carriage, she had made a silent wish that Malcolm would touch her in a very intimate way. She had even fantasized about being on Malcolm's lap. She just never thought it'd be facedown.

The carriage rolled up to Copperleaf Manor as her father's carriage came to a halt in the driveway. Serena practically leapt off the perch and flew into his arms.

"Father! I'm so happy to see you!"

He put his arms around her. "Serena, I didn't expect you back from the Games so soon. Why are your clothes in such a state?" He glanced at Malcolm, and the blood drained from his face. "What's happened?

"There was an incident, sir," Malcolm said.

"Are you all right?" he asked Serena.

"Yes . . . and no."

"Come inside, all of you."

He hugged Serena tightly. Tears of self-pity threatened to spill over the rims of her eyes, but she held them back.

As they arrived at the drawing room, Earlington

called for some brandy. Overwrought, he displayed an uncharacteristic show of emotion. "Are you hurt, Serena?"

Serena glanced at Malcolm. "Not exactly."

Earlington turned to Malcolm. "Slayter, tell me what's happened."

"Yer daughter was beset by a group of men. They knew who she was. They knew who ye were."

"Dear God. What did they do to you, Serena?"

"Nothing, Father. Truly. They just frightened me, that's all."

"Who were these men?"

Gingerly, Malcolm rubbed his face. "I couldna get all their names. But one of them they called Brandubh." He described all that had happened in the clearing.

Earlington's nostrils fanned open, but he said nothing.

"He also said that the next time they had to state their grievances, 'twould be with weapons drawn."

"What happened to your face, Slayter?"

Malcolm hesitated, so Serena spoke up. "He fought them off, Father." Despite Malcolm's insult to her person, she had to state the truth. "He . . . saved me from them."

Malcolm shrugged. "I used my hard head to split their knuckles for them."

Earlington's expression unclenched. "I'm much obliged to you, Slayter," he said, shaking Malcolm's hand. "Much obliged. You've earned a place in my family."

For the first time, Serena saw a crack in Malcolm's stern countenance. His green eyes blinked in astonishment, and his mouth dropped open. It was the look of a starving man who's just been offered a feast. "Thank ye, sir."

"The thought of losing my daughter to those men . . . I can only thank God you were there." He put a hand on Malcolm's shoulder. "You're a hired man no longer, Slayter. Join us at the dinner table. We want you to. Don't we, Serena?"

Her wounded pride protested. "But Father, he—" Serena still felt keenly the soreness where Malcolm had thrashed her. "Mr. Slayter took me atop the carriage and—" She was embarrassed to tell her father that Malcolm had acted like a father to her. But more than that, she was needled by the sudden feeling that if she crushed her father's esteem in Malcolm, she would be depriving both men of something wonderful. "Yes, Mr. Slayter must join us at the dinner table."

Earlington kissed her on the forehead. "I want you both to know that I will take care of this. No further harm shall come to you. I promise. Go and get washed up. We'll discuss this at dinner."

Once the two of them had retired, Earlington sank into a chair. The dizziness was getting worse. Every challenge— and every failure—brought another ache in his chest.

So many things to fear, so many things to regret. The negotiations had broken down, and talks had ceased. First the factions had resorted to intimidation, and now violence. A physical threat against his family was enough for any other ambassador to return to his own country and let the government finally declare war. Everything he had learned in politics told him to leave Scotland and turn the people over to their own foolish devices. But his instinct told him differently. Earlington knew that if the king sent in the troops, the ensuing conflict would profit them nothing. It would be a war with no winners. England and Scotland were like two halves of the same body trying to destroy each other. If one died, so would the other.

He was at an impasse, and he needed help from

someone wiser than he. Only one person in the world
came to mind.

He got up from his chair and went in search of Gabby
Walker.

He questioned a passing maid, who told him that
Mrs. Walker could be found in the vegetable garden. With long, purposeful strides, he charged to the
kitchens.

Light burst in upon him when he threw open the
kitchen door to the gardens. The smell of herbs warming in the sunlight greeted him. He made his way down
the rows of leeks, potatoes, and carrots.

When he finally found her, she was kneeling on all
fours at the end of a bed of turnips. Her sleeves were
rolled up to her elbows, and brown mud caked her
arms. The afternoon sun sliced across her face, giving
her skin a rosy hue, and illuminated a flurry of tiny
gnats that swirled in a cloud behind her. A plain brown
bonnet covered her head, but he could still see way-
ward ginger curls bouncing against her cheek.

The sight of her made him forget why he was there.
There was a loveliness about her simplicity that he
found instantly appealing. She was wholly unlike the
debonair woman who was his first wife. When he had
married Lady June Harrison, it was a match made in
heaven. The lady had breeding and wealth, and there
never was a finer hostess in all the world. Gabby, on the
other hand, was not beautiful, nor was she elegant . . .
but her earthiness roused a desire in him that he found
difficult to tame.

His shadow along the ground announced his arrival.

"Ambassador?" she said, squinting in the sun. "Whatever are ye doing oot in the kitchen garden?"

"Looking for you, actually."

She wiped her hands on her pinafore. "Oh? What may I do for ye?"

Gazing down at her kneeling before him, her rosy freckles and dazzling blue eyes looking up at him, he suppressed a truthful answer. "Er . . ." He raced for an answer. "Salve. Mr. Slayter's been in a brawl, and he's suffered a few bruises. It's nothing serious, but I was wondering if you had any remedy that would help him in that regard."

"I see," she said, an answer that quickly made Earlington nervous. Gabby was a woman who saw a great deal more than most, even the things he didn't want her to see. "I'll get Caointiorn to take him some cream of calendula."

"Yes." Earlington wrung his hands, his gaze bouncing around the garden.

"Will that be all, sir?"

He couldn't look her in the eye. "I was wondering . . . that is, if you're not too busy . . . if you would be so kind . . . could you talk with me awhile?"

Gabby nodded slowly. "Aye. But ye may as well make yerself useful. Take that spade and help me dig these holes."

A bemused frown crossed Earlington's face. He had had in mind a quiet chat over a cup of tea. But he was fascinated by the prospect of the fresh adventure, so he shrugged out of his coat and laid it on a nearby shrub. He took the spade from a milk pail full of gardening tools and began to burrow into the ground.

"Aboot four inches deep, mind, and wide enough for yer hand to fit."

He set about digging holes in the soft, moist earth. Although his trousers grew damp at the knees, he actually found pleasure in working the cool soil with his bare hands.

Gabby was silent, and he could sense that she was waiting for him to speak. But he found it difficult to put his feeling to words.

"Er, I'm afraid I'm not very good at this."

She handed him a different spade. "Little by little, as the cat eats the fish."

He shook his head. "No. I mean talking with you."

"Aye. I ken what ye mean."

"Oh." There it was, that feeling that she could understand well beyond that which was plain. "You see, I've been very concerned about the negotiations. They're not going as I'd hoped. The factions have split, and the ones with revolutionary sympathies are taking control. The English Parliament is perfectly prepared to go to battle with Scotland, and the Scottish Council is daring them to. It seems the only one who is after peace is me."

"Aye."

"And now I've awakened a great swarm of enemies. The opposition has not only threatened my daughter, but actually accosted her. I'm afraid that any attempt to negotiate a peace with Scotland will not only endanger what's left of my family, but will be to no avail whatsoever. I even made a promise to keep my daughter safe, a promise I'm not confident I can keep."

"Aye."

"And to top it all off, I'm so angry at those men for laying their hands on her. I actually started to think a spate of war might do those stubborn Scots some good. They robbed me of my impartiality and turned me against them, when all I really wanted to do was restore their faith in union and bring about goodwill on both sides."

"Aye."

Despite his problems, he had to chuckle at Gabby. "Do you always talk this much?"

She smiled. "Aye." She lifted a wisp of hair from her cheek. "If the Good Lord had meant for us to be doing more bletherin' than listening, he would hae given us two mouths instead of two ears."

Earlington smiled. "Perhaps you're right. However, I would appreciate even half a mouthful right now. I'd like to know your thoughts."

"Why should a man of yer importance be after asking someone like me?"

He shrugged. "Call it seeking the wealth of wise counsel. King Solomon was widely believed to be the wisest man who ever lived, and even though he needed wise counsel the least, he wrote about its value the most."

Gabby handed him a bowl full of peeled garlic cloves. "Drop one of these in all of the holes, then push the soil back in."

"What's it for?" he said, puzzling over the bowl.

"The garlic will dispel the wee beasties that'll be after m'neeps."

He shrugged, but did as she asked. "What do you think I should do?"

Gabby swiped a smudge of mud off her nose with her sleeve. "I think ye should dig a small trench with yer finger, like so, all along this row."

Earlington sighed, running his finger along the dirt. "Not meaning to be rude, but—"

"And place one of these turnip seeds aboot two inches apart all doon the row."

He took the seed pouch from her dirt-smeared hand, and pulled one of the tiny seeds out. He dropped one onto the soil, then another and another. "There. Two inches apart."

"Noo cover it up with the rest of the soil. Just like that. Well done. And give it a sprinkle of water to moisten the topsoil."

Earlington took the watering can and upturned it all along the row of turnip seeds they'd just planted.

Gabby stood up, and shook the dirt from her hands.

"You're leaving?" asked Earlington, setting down the watering can.

"Aye. I'll be off to fetch the balm for Mr. Slayter."

"Wait . . ." Earlington's eyebrows drew together. "What am I to do?"

Gabby looked down at him, her face transforming into something serene. "All we can do is sow the seed. It's up to the Good Lord to make it take root. Isn't that right, sir?"

Her eyes held a world of meaning. She was transmitting a message in a language Earlington was just beginning to understand, and he began to see dimly what she was saying. All he could do was sow the seeds of peace. It was not his responsibility to make the peace grow. "Yes, of course," he agreed softly. "Still, there are those who would destroy what we've so carefully sown."

"Och, the wee beasties! They're oot there. Probably waiting till oor backs are turned to come and snatch oor crops away. A healthy drop of the garlic should ward off the attackers for a time, no?"

Earlington clambered to his feet. *Malcolm?* "For a time, perhaps. But any preventive measure wears away when there are too many to overpower it."

She shrugged and picked up her pail. " 'Tis a chance we have to take. Do it, and there's a good chance we will eat. Do it not, and we shall certainly starve."

No more speaking in riddles. "And what of the hate? How do I combat the hate that is growing within me?"

Gabby sighed deeply. "Anger is more hurtful to ye than the wrong that caused it. Let it go. Ye've too good a heart to let it be poisoned by the deeds of evil men.

Remember the ones who have no voice in the matter. They're the ones ye're doing all this for."

Earlington smiled at her. What an amazing woman. He stepped up to her and pressed a kiss on her cheek.

The lady blushed to the color of her hair. Her entire demeanor changed, and once more he caught a glimpse of the innocent young girl long gone from the wise eyes.

"Sir! What would the other servants think if they saw?"

"They'd realize what a treasure you are."

NINETEEN

Serena sat at her vanity desk, slowly brushing out the wet strands of her long blond hair. Her bath had left her scented of English roses, and her afternoon tea was still warm in its cup. Her muddied dress lay in a heap on the floor like a shed skin, and her elegant evening clothes were laid out on the bed. Though everything had returned to its normal routine, nothing was as it had been. And at the heart of the transformation was the man who lay just beyond that secret door . . .

The memories of the eventful day swirled about her like a snow flurry. The sheen of the rainwater on Malcolm's skin; the feel of his hand on her wrist in the carriage; the elation at his arrival on the battlefield; the mortifying sensation of being chastised like a schoolgirl. The remorse at putting his life in danger.

A soft knock sounded on her bedroom door, bringing her daydreaming to a screeching halt. "Miss? It's Caointoirn, miss."

"Come in, Quinny."

The petite maid ventured in. "I've come to do yer hair."

For the first time, the prospect of pinning her hair up in an elegant coif depressed her. "Very well," she said with a sigh.

"I've brought some salve for Mr. Slayter. Would it be

all right if I go through here rather than the library door, miss?" She nodded in the direction of the secret passageway, a place where Serena's thoughts had been just moments before.

Serena glanced at the brown glass bottle and white cloth, and an idea came to her. "No. Leave it with me, Quinny. I'll take it in to him. Come back later. You can do my hair then."

"Very well, miss."

Medicines. How she hated them. They were a reminder of how imperfect the world was . . . and how mortal. Her father was reduced to taking powders and restoratives every day, each of them foul and unpleasant, in an effort to extend his life. The thought that she was the cause of Malcolm's need for them needled her with guilt.

She tightened the dressing gown around her and knocked on the secret door.

A moment passed. And then the door swung open.

The sight of him took her breath away. He was back to trousers, but he didn't have on a stitch of clothing above them, displaying a torso that seemed sculpted from gold. His chest was smooth, like marble statues of old, with just a smattering of hair down the middle. Muscles fanned out from his neck and connected with two chiseled shoulders. Odd scars told a tale of a tortured life.

A look at his face brought a fresh stab of guilt. His cheek had purpled, and now she could see a tiny cut on his lower lip.

"I-I've some salve for you."

He looked her up and down. There was no judgment in his expression, only a reserved air. "Thank ye," he said, holding out his hand.

Ill at ease, she clutched the bottle tighter. "May I come in?" she heard herself ask. There were dozens of reasons why it was a mistake to suggest it. Impropriety, indecency, shame . . . spiders. She put all those out of her head as she stepped over his threshold.

For the first time, she got a close look at the chamber he now used as a bedroom. The walls were bare of plaster, and he used the interior wood framing as shelves. A few books, probably borrowed from Lord Askey's library, lined one shelf, and a comb and razor lay on another. A narrow bed, certainly too short for a man of his height, edged the wall separating them. On the framing above his pillow lay his pistol holster and daggers. The smell of antique wood and mold permeated the room. It was surely a misery having to live here. And yet he put himself through it willingly. For her.

"Let me help you apply it," she said.

"I can manage."

"No. I want to. It's . . . the least I can do."

His frown softened, but only a little. "Very well."

She glanced nervously at his semi-nude body. "Show me what pains you."

He raised his right hand before her eyes, palm downward. The knuckles were discolored, and a tear sliced through the middle knuckle. She couldn't look him in the eye, lest he see how remorseful she felt.

She opened up the bottle and poured some of the grassy-smelling liquid onto the cloth. She placed her hand beneath his to sustain it, and gingerly dabbed at the broken skin. The branding scar on the back of his hand was visible to her now, and she drank in each of the ugly details with her eyes.

"Is that better?"

"Aye." His expression had gentled, and he regarded her thoughtfully. "Thank ye."

"What else pains you?"

He raised his left elbow up to reveal a dark bruise on his rib cage. "I can't take a breath without remembering the face of the bastard that gave me that."

She sighed, and moistened the rag once more. He winced a little as she applied the unguent, so she took her time. He had a lovely warm smell to him. His abdomen was strong and sturdy, each muscle well defined. Too late she considered how wonderful it would have been if she had thought to apply the medicine with her fingers rather than a cloth.

"And your cheek?" she asked.

"Aye. It throbs a good deal."

He was too tall for her to get to it comfortably. "Please sit down."

He perched himself on the edge of the bed, and she wedged herself between his open legs. The hair at his temples was still wet from washing. She lifted the damp cloth and dabbed it on the swell of his cheek. It was an ugly bruise, discoloring and deforming his otherwise handsome face. Another pang of guilt damned her. That mark was a direct result of a deformity in her own character. If it hadn't been for her, none of this would have happened to him. She glanced into his eyes, which were looking straight at her.

Her tattered pride was unable to contain her true emotions any longer. "I'm so sorry for getting you into all this trouble."

"So am I."

His agreement stung. "I shouldn't have stormed off as I did. Never mind that I left Zoe unchaperoned, which on its own was a thoughtless thing to do. But to put you in harm's way was inconsiderate and foolish . . . and cruel."

He closed his eyes, revealing silky white lids above

thick black lashes. "Apology accepted. Glad I am to know that ye'll not be doing it again."

But there was more that she had to say. "You stood up for me. Not many men would have done what you did, especially after the way I'd treated you. I'm really very grateful. And I just . . . wanted to . . ."

Everything in her being told her not to do it, but she refused to listen. She put her hands on his bare shoulders, and brought her lips to his.

It was a gentle kiss, nothing more, bestowed upon him while he sat before her. His lips were soft and warm, yet surprised by the affection. But then he wrapped his thick arms around her as he stood up, and suddenly, she was engulfed by him. His head descended over hers, and he returned the kiss, transformed into a passionate thing.

His lips smoothed over hers, igniting her body. She closed her eyes as she inhaled the soap-and-water smell of him. Wrapped in a blanket made of skin and flesh, Serena hummed in contentment. The kiss of gratitude had become a kiss of need, and he was quick to give her what she demanded. She could taste the salty-sweet blood from the cut on his lip, and it roused a carnal desire that she could not subdue.

The feel of his bare skin under her hands reawakened her passion for a man. But this was so very different from her first love affair. Back then, that one fumbling tryst was born of a need to win a man's love, and a curious desire to be pleasured. This embrace was compelled by her need to show Malcolm Slayter her own feelings, and a desperate longing to pleasure him.

But his kisses were like nothing she'd ever known. No practiced techniques, no contrived approach. At first, his mouth opened softly to her, his response to her as guarded as a wild animal. But when he tasted her desire for him, the truth of his own yearnings broke forth. His kisses were foreign and strange, but artless—as if his whole heart expressed itself through his kisses.

A crease formed between his thick black eyebrows as his kiss deepened. She felt his fingers spread into her still-damp hair, gently directing her in the dance of his possessive kiss. A familiar hunger pulsed in her feminine opening, desperate to be fed by his flesh.

How glorious that his body connected with hers at every point! Their legs touched, their hips pressed against the other's body, her breasts were flattened against the ridges of his abdomen. A rush of eroticism flowed inside her.

Her arousal must have provoked his own, for she began to feel a thickening against her belly. And just as it started, he pulled away.

His hands gripped her shoulders and held them at bay. "I canna carry on."

She could not disengage from that paralyzing bliss. "What?"

He fought to catch his breath. "Yer da has entrusted ye to me. I canna betray that."

She had never resented her father until just that moment. "But . . ."

"Ye should go back now," he said, jerking his head toward the secret door. "Before I forget myself."

It was precisely the thing she wanted to do . . . forget herself. Forget Society with its fashions and foibles, forget the need for ease and eminence, forget the pursuit of ostentation and adoration. Above it all, she desired the colossal simplicity of just her . . . and just him.

He bent his head over her hand, and kissed it tenderly. She found herself shaking her head. She wanted to lie down on the too-small bed and let him open her dressing gown. To let him kiss her breasts. To give her willing hands the freedom to possess every part of his body. She wanted more . . .

A lingering look from his emerald-colored eyes told her he wanted more, too. But it also begged her to help him be strong.

Disoriented by the thrumming inside her, she let him lead her back to the doorway in the wall. But when she stepped through it, the room no longer felt like hers. She gave a last look toward Malcolm, and slowly, he shut the door between them.

She stood against her bed for some time, reassessing her surroundings. The vanity with its ornate brushes and hairpins; the wardrobe bursting with the best of London's fashions; the elegant bedspread covering a down-filled mattress—all the accoutrements of a lady—looked like mere toys in a child's playpen.

And she had very quickly outgrown them.

TWENTY

For the first time, Malcolm Slayter felt like a true gentleman.

He was headed into a formal dinner with an ambassador and the lord and lady of the manor. And on his arm was Serena Marsh.

For once, he was walking not behind her, but beside her. And she was only too happy to have him there.

He glanced down at her. She looked exquisite in a white gown with blue flowers sewn into it.

Serena smiled back at him. What a charmer she was. More beautiful than any woman he'd ever met. Those sapphire eyes of hers could silently convey a thousand emotions. It had taken an eternity to get his body under control after he escorted her to her room. All he could think about were those plump lips, opening to him like petals in full bloom. He could taste them still. But the most magical part of it was that *she* had kissed *him*.

He inhaled deeply, his chest filling with pride. He had changed in her eyes. She didn't see him as just her protector now, or even as her servant. His reflection in her eyes had become one of a man. A gentleman, even. A gentleman suitor.

He liked that thought. Even Ambassador Marsh had told him that he was as good as part of the family.

Family. The word was so unfamiliar to him, and yet deep in his heart, beneath the years and the calluses, he still remembered what it felt like. It had been two decades since he had felt the joy of his own loving family. The happy memory of it was still there—not quite obliterated by the terrifying day he last saw them alive.

Still, there was something else that worried him. As a protector and a fugitive hunter, he lived by a series of rules—foremost of which was never to become emotionally entangled. It clouded the judgment and made one react with the heart instead of the head, which was the first step in getting oneself or someone else killed. The growing closeness with the Marshes would make him less effective at his job . . . and make Serena more vulnerable.

"So there's the hero I've heard so much about!" said Lord Askey jovially when Malcolm stepped into the parlor. "Marsh told me what happened today. My boy, you deserve a drink."

"Thank ye, sir," he said, taking the glass of golden-colored whiskey.

"How are you, my dear?" Lord Askey asked Serena. "I trust you weren't hurt by the experience?"

"No, Lord Askey. I'm quite well."

"Thanks to Slayter here. Looks like they took a croquet mallet to his face."

Lady Rachel Askey threaded her hand around Malcolm's elbow. "Come, Mr. Slayter. Sit next to me. I want to hear every detail of your misadventure."

Malcolm shifted uncomfortably. "Surely not, my lady. It's not fit for ladies to hear."

Serena cleared her throat. "I suppose it's fine for ladies to experience?"

Malcolm smiled sheepishly. "Ye've got the better of me there. Well, it seems that these men were trying to frighten Miss Marsh. I just persuaded them to rethink their plans." Briefly he touched upon the events of the afternoon.

"Honestly, Mr. Slayter," admonished Serena, "you're about as open as a vault. If the incident had been a newspaper article, your account of it would have consisted of the headline." Serena described everything in detail that had happened once she encountered the group of men.

"One against so many!" remarked Lady Askey. "Mr. Slayter, weren't you frightened?"

Malcolm shrugged. "I suppose so."

"But that you should leap into the midst of those ruffians without a care . . . how did you do it?"

"I had to." He glanced at Serena. "I wanted to."

There it was again . . . a remark from Serena's vocal eyes. She smiled back at him.

"Enough, Rachel," admonished Lord Askey. "You don't ask a hero to recount his own heroics. Let's into dinner, Slayter. I can see that Marsh here has a few significant questions to put to you."

To Malcolm's disappointment, Lady Askey had placed Serena opposite him at the table. Though it was the proper thing to do, Malcolm had looked forward to having Serena's new warmth nearby. Still, Lady Askey had put him in a place of honor, just to her right, and that made him feel appreciated.

Malcolm looked with confusion at all of the glasses and pieces of cutlery. A bowl of soup was placed before him, and he had to hunt among the spoons for what looked like a proper utensil.

Earlington spread his linen napkin across his lap.

"Tell me, Mr. Slayter, did you recognize any of the men who attacked you?"

"No, sir. But I did recognize a few of the tartans. There were two MacDonnels, a Ferguson, and a McInnes, but the others I couldna make out. I only wish I knew what they were doing so far from the rest of the Games."

"I know what they were doing," said Earlington, his veal soup untouched. "They were preparing for war."

Serena went cold. "War?"

"I'm afraid so. Negotiations have been faltering. Each side remains entrenched in its positions. The Scots are suing for various freedoms, chief among them to maintain their own judicial system, and a complete liberation from taxation."

Askey sighed. "That's preposterous. No taxation? How do they expect to support the cost of the military, the monarchy? All British subjects must pay taxes. And the less said about their own judicial system, the better. Those clans you mentioned are a monarchy unto themselves, some of them no better than bands of street toughs. What laws can exist among such people?"

Malcolm rubbed the brand on the back of his hand, which he kept hidden under the table. "I canna argue with that."

"It is to the Scots' benefit to live as free men under a single British Crown, rather than under chiefs who impose their own laws."

"But there's more to their quarrel," Earlington continued. "They want a republic. They want to secede from Great Britain altogether."

"You mean like America?" Askey cried.

"That is what I'm hearing."

"I don't understand it," Rachel added. "Scotland has

been part of Great Britain for over a hundred
Why should they want to succeed now?"

"*Secede,* my dear," her husband corrected, w.
light chuckle. "But the question is a valid one. Why
separation? Why now? And for the love of God, how?
Scotland is, as far as nations go, the poor relation.
She'll never make it on her own."

Earlington shook his head. "It is a small minority that
disagrees with you, but a vocal one. The Scots have
moved beyond the negotiation stage. Bills are plastered
all over Glasgow rallying support for a Scottish government. The Scots are acquiring weapons, provisions. It
appears as though they are establishing a more aggres-
sive posture."

"Why can't the Scots be more like the Welsh?" Serena quipped, the music in her voice trying to lighten
the mood. "You never hear a peep from the Welsh."

Malcolm chuckled and wiped his mouth with his napkin. "Scots have never been supple at the knee. Even
within our own clans, it is difficult for us to be servile."
He turned to Ambassador Marsh. "I must ask ye—are
there any terms under which the Prince Regent will allow a self-governing Scottish nation? Is there any chance
at all that Scotland may in fact become independent?"

Earlington responded without pause. "None. The
British Empire will not be divided. The Prince Regent
has been very clear on this point—he will not have his
government subverted. He has told me in no uncertain
terms that he will suppress the insurrection, even if he
must obliterate his Scottish subjects to do it."

Silence filled the room as they looked around the
room at one another.

Askey set down his glass, and his voice became
grave. "*Si vis pacem, para bellum.* If you seek peace,
prepare for war."

Earlington spoke in soft, even tones and measured words. "I'm afraid so. My desire and my most fervent wish, therefore, is for the Scots to crave peace as much as I do."

Being the only Scotsman in the room, Malcolm felt the weight of the outcome of this conflict shift to his own kind.

"Sir, if I may say so, the common folk are no' in favor of war. It's true there's a new patriotism among the Scots. But they're content to sing songs in the pubs and tell old stories. They don't want to be disloyal to the Crown. But they must do what the chiefs tell them to."

Earlington nodded. "I know that. The Council won't listen to reason, preferring an ill-conceived rebellion to any reconciliation. But I am not unmindful of the truth of their grievances. I know that the new tax will be a terrible burden on the poorest of the Scots people. Therein lies my problem. What does one do when both sides have an equal claim on justice? When both sides to an argument are in and of themselves justified? Right is not always an absolute. Do we allow the man to choose which laws he obeys, leading to chaos? Or do we enforce his loyalty at the expense of his blood?"

Askey put down his glass. "Judas on the one hand and Pilate on the other."

"Precisely," Earlington responded, his forehead creasing in despair. "And I don't mind confessing that I just don't know what to do."

"Father?" Serena put her hand on top of her father's.

Earlington gripped her hand. "I know I am in a position of leadership, but that doesn't mean I have all the answers. I know where I would go, but not how to get there."

Malcolm regarded Ambassador Marsh thoughtfully. The older man may not have had all the answers, but he had extreme clarity in the midst of so much uncertainty, and that was something he knew the people would want.

"I can see ye've a desire to bring peace to this country. Yer vision is a noble one, sir, and as a Scotsman, I would follow it to the death."

"Thank you, Mr. Slayter. It only remains for me to convince the man who accosted Serena. His vision is the only one the nobles are following."

Serena swallowed hard. "You know who he was, Father?"

"Yes. The one you heard called Brandubh . . . his name is Brandubh McCullough."

Malcolm felt a surge of ire course through his blood. "So that was Brandubh McCullough. I know the name well. McCullough stands in line to inherit the chiefdom of one of the wealthiest clans in Scotland. His father, the current chief, is on his deathbed, and most think that Brandubh will succeed him."

"That's right," concurred Earlington. "You might say he's the Scottish equivalent of the Prince Regent. He's convinced of the Council of Scotland's ability to self-govern, and is vociferously recommending that no one pay any more taxes or duties to the Crown."

"Let me guess," said Malcolm. "He's telling the chiefs to bring the revenue into his treasury instead."

"Why, yes. That is what our intelligence is telling us. That he is using the money to secretly acquire arms from foreign governments. How did you know?"

"Yer man McCullough is not just a rebel, sir. Given half a chance, he'll become a tyrant."

"What do you mean?"

"I know this man McCullough. I've heard he's a glutton for power and money. I think he's after more than just rebellion. I think he wants to rule the country."

"How do you know all this?"

Malcolm thought back to what Will Dundas had told him at the Thorn & Thistle. By their third glass of whiskey, Will had whispered to Malcolm that it was in his favor to join the revolt. Anyone who fought for the revolution and helped name Brandubh McCullough the leader of the new republic would be rewarded with land and animals. "Word gets around."

The wrinkles in Earlington's face deepened, making him look haggard. "Then I fear now more than ever for the Scottish people. For when such a villain is elevated . . ."

"Father," admonished Serena, "what have you always told me about fear? You are forever on about not fearing imagined dangers. Please don't trouble yourself now with the uncertainties the future holds."

Earlington smiled wanly at her. "You're right, of course. As was I in saying it," he chuckled. "However, it is my duty now to see that my imagined fears don't become real ones." He turned to Malcolm. "Mr. Slayter, I ask you to be exceedingly vigilant. I am concerned that McCullough's tactics may become increasingly violent. He will hire scoundrels, ruffians, men with no code. If my daughter were to fall into their clutches, they know that I would say anything, do anything, to get her back. But the Crown will not be coerced by rebels. Do you take my meaning?"

Malcolm did, loud and clear. McCullough believed he could bend the will of Parliament if he kidnapped Serena. But Ambassador Marsh was telling him that if

Serena were ever to be captured, she would be considered the first of many losses to come.

Malcolm glanced at Serena.

A man didn't exist who could take her away from him.

TWENTY-ONE

Though it was nigh on nine o'clock, the gloaming was not yet over. The sky was swathed in a hundred shades of blue and purple, as if the heavens were lit only by candlelight. A chill air wet the night.

Serena clutched her wrap tighter around her shoulders as she took a stroll around the gardens with Rachel Askey. She stole a glance at Malcolm, who trailed a few paces behind them.

It had been two weeks since the Saint Swithin's Day Festival, and during that time Malcolm had spent a great deal of time with her father. Earlington had found a surprise treasure in all of Malcolm's knowledge of the clans in general, and of Brandubh McCullough in particular. But Serena missed having him around most of the day, and she relished the opportunity to step outside the house, even for something as simple as a walk, just to be able to reclaim him.

Rachel rearranged the blanket around the sleeping child in her arms. "There, my wee rabbit. Mother missed you at dinner."

Smiling, Serena glanced down at the baby, who raised a tiny fist to her face. The baby had Rachel's strawberry curls, but Lord Askey's plump cheeks. "She's a sweeting. And such a quiet babe, too."

"Aye. Hardly ever cries when I hold her. Nanny Muire-all is a blessing to have around—she was my nanny, too—but she likes to sing to the baby, and between you and me, she sounds like a cat caught in a roomful of rocking chairs."

Serena laughed. "My nanny sang about as sweetly as a wooden bell. And she smelled of old woman."

Rachel laughed. "Oh, aye. She does that and all!"

They dipped their heads as they passed under a low-hanging branch. "You're so attached to your baby, Rachel. I know we're about the same age, but I wonder if I'll be nearly as devoted a mother as you are."

"Certainly you will! It's inevitable."

"I'm not so sure. In London's set, I'll wager most of the ladies hardly even see their children most of the day. Some of them go days or even weeks without sending for them."

Rachel looked aghast. "Sending for them? You make them sound like they were servants."

Serena shrugged. It seemed to be the way of things.

Rachel pouted down into the baby's face. "Oh! I can hardly stand to be apart from Annabella, even for the length of a meal. Don't women in London love their children?"

"It's not a question of not loving them. Among the *ton,* children are meant to be seen and not heard. It's just not very fashionable to have your children about all the time." Even as Serena said this, she could fathom the absolute stupidity of the fashion.

"Well, count me unfashionable. Imagine keeping my own daughter out of sight and out of mind! I don't think I could do it. What do they do when their children cry?"

Serena reflected on it. Whenever she'd gone to someone's home to call, she'd rarely seen children in the company of her hosts. Sometimes they'd be presented to her, usually just to parade their clothes or their manners, and then they'd disappear with the governess. She hadn't ever questioned it. Until now.

"Gosh, I don't really know."

"Well, I can't speak for the ladies in the southern kingdom, but we here in the north handle things a bit differently. I know that when I hear my babe cry . . . my insides ache. No matter what I'm doing, I must go to her. Everything natural within me yearns to soothe her and care for her."

As if to test the theory, the infant Annabella began to fidget and then snuffled out a fussy cry.

"There, there, rabbit. Don't you fret." Rachel shifted the child to her shoulder. "I'll just go back inside and lay her abed."

Serena glanced at Malcolm, who stood with his hands crossed behind his back. "Er, I'll come inside in just a moment. I'd like to take a turn around the rhododendrons first."

Rachel's gaze followed Serena's, and she smiled surreptitiously. "Don't be too long, now. It's turning chilly."

Not where she was standing, Serena thought. Whenever Malcolm was around, she felt decidedly warm all over.

Serena turned and walked deeper into the garden. Everything was steeped in shadow, the whole world in silhouette. But she could still smell the fragrance of the night-blooming flowers drifting to her on the ever-cooling breezes. A centuries-old wall, part of it in ruins, edged the formal garden. Behind it, invisible from the house, the wall was overgrown with shrubs and ivy, and it was there Serena was headed.

A warm, husky voice caressed her from behind. "I'd like to see ye with a bairn in yer arms."

She flicked him a mischievous grin. "And one in my belly, no doubt," she said as she plucked a pink bloom.

"Aye. And that."

Serena hid her smile in the rhododendron blossom. "And in this tender picture of domesticity, do you also see me with a husband?"

"No."

She spun around to face him. "What?"

Even in the dearth of light, a sparkle glinted in his eye. "I imagine ye'd already sliced him to shards with yer tongue."

She rolled her eyes and continued walking. "I can see now that protectors are a lot like children," she tossed over her shoulder. "They, too, are meant to be seen and not heard."

Malcolm sighed. "Serena, Serena. Feathers on the one side and thorns on the other."

"Are you going to continue to make belligerent remarks?"

"I speak as I find."

"That's the trouble with you. In England, a lady can tell a man anything, and the gentleman's code would compel him to believe it . . . or at least pretend to. It would do you good to be more circumspect."

He laughed. "And leave myself defenseless to yer verbal fencing? No."

"Verbal fencing? You make me sound like I should be wearing a suit of armor."

"Ye've already got one of those. And a mace and shield. I can lob words at ye all I want, but they'll just fall away like rocks against a turret wall."

She pursed her lips in mock anger. "Is my father paying extra for all this abuse or is it part of your service?"

"I like to think of it as a gratuity."

Serena had to chuckle. She pulled the gossamer mantle closer around her shoulders, a gesture that was not lost on him.

"And I canna help but notice that ye still haven't learnt anything about Highland dress."

"How do you mean?" she responded, secretly tickled by the way he rolled his *R*'s. Not *dress,* but *drrress.* "I'll have you know this is quite *au courant.*"

"Whatever ye call it, it is going to cause yer death of cold." He slipped off his coat, revealing a white shirt and a leather holster fastened around his chest, and draped the warm garment upon her shoulders. "When will ye learn to see things with yer own eyes and not through the eyes of others?"

"Well, how could anyone have anticipated such cold weather in the middle of summer? These temperatures are fit only for Highland cattle. Or Highlanders."

He smirked, and it made his eyes go quite boyish. "Are you equating me to a Highland coo?"

Serena shook her head. "That's *cow,* not *coo.*"

"And now ye're making fun of my English."

"Ha! That's a far cry from English."

He laughed then. "By God, Serena, ye would ha' made a good plague on Egypt."

She proceeded imperiously ahead of him down the path. "And that's another thing. I must remark that you are becoming entirely too casual. For the second time, you have used my given name."

"Aye. So I did."

"Do you find it proper that you should become so informal?"

"It's one thing to become familiar. It's another to take liberties."

"Is there a difference?"

Serena gasped as his hand gripped her elbow and

spun her around. She found herself pressed against his
battle-honed body, his arm holding her tightly against
him. Her eyes snapped to his face.

"Let me show you." His voice was gravelly with heat.

His head descended slowly, and his lips pressed
upon her cheek. Soft and warm on her wind-chilled
cheek, she wanted to bathe in that one kiss.

"*That* is getting familiar. And *this*," he whispered,
placing a hot kiss on her exposed neck, "is taking liberties."

His steamy breath on her neck sent shivers of pleasure skipping down her spine. She closed her eyes. Just
underneath his lips, her heated blood delivered the
erotic sensation throughout her body.

He slipped the coat from her shoulders, and it fell to
the ground. Slowly, his mouth trailed down to her
chest, the kisses dripping upon her like warm rain. As
he did so, his hips curved into her imprisoned body,
multiplying the heavenly sensations. Surely he was
well past taking liberties . . . he was also taking her
will to resist.

"Malcolm," she breathed, but wasn't certain what
she wanted to say. Except that she liked the sound it
made coming from her mouth.

He straightened, his silky hair caressing her cheek. A
callused hand stroked the place on her neck that his lips
had just savored. Tender and rough. She desired more.

Malcolm's lips pressed against her mouth. His lips
were soft and smooth, a stark contrast with the emerging roughness on his face. So delightful. She returned
the affection, their lips sliding gently upon one another.

He began a slow descent to a crouch, and she held
their unbroken kiss as his head lowered. His open hands
glided down her back and over her bottom cheeks,
squeezing their roundness. She gasped in surprise at

how quickly her body responded. Her nether regions came alive at his touch, igniting each of her feminine parts. Her hands gripped his biceps in protest, but she didn't want to stop him. And when he straightened against her, his own passion was aroused.

In the gathering darkness, she gave her other senses free rein to explore. She slid her hands up to his shoulders, reveling in the dense muscle under her fingertips. It swelled and tightened, like the sinews of a running stallion, as his hands explored the rest of her. Behind his neck, her fingers threaded through the glossy waves of his thick hair. It felt soft and strong between her fingers, like rushing water. Everything about him reminded her of something wild and untamable, and the farther along she let herself get, the more dangerous she knew it would become.

A hand slid under her arm and spun her toward the wall. She braced herself against the ancient stones, the ivy leaves crunching between her fingers. The rose-colored poplin at her shoulder edged by the dark pink ribbon collapsed in his clawed fingers as he drew it down.

A hot tongue laved at the exposed flesh of her shoulder, sending ripples throughout her body. Her breath came out in raw gasps as a large hand cupped her right breast, still imprisoned in the fabric of her dress. Her nipple tightened, rising into the warmth of his open palm. Instinctively, her back arched, pushing her bottom into the rock-hard bulge in his trousers.

Both hands now squeezed her breasts, stoking her passion as well as his. Her hands flew to her breasts and flattened upon his own. She could feel the two hands now, one smooth and veined, the other scored and welted. But oh, what magic was in them that made her want to feel forever connected to him! His imperfections made him perfect for her.

He crouched low and she felt his fingers against her stockinged legs. The gentle pressure of his palm against the curve of her calf sparked a flame in her womanly parts that made her moan. .

Higher his hand climbed. His callused flesh snagged at the fabric of her stockings as his hand brushed upward—across her knee, along the crest of her garter, and between her naked thighs.

The feeling of so rough a thing on her soft skin awakened a hunger long forgotten. Malcolm's touch aroused more than her ardor—it also aroused her affection. The scars that were left upon her heart when her first and only lover cast her aside were changing, shifting . . . healing.

A gentle finger probed and pushed apart the folds of her whetted womanhood. A thousand pleasant things flashed through Serena's fevered mind, but there was one warning voice loudly complaining. She had made the mistake of giving herself once to a man, and it had ended in disaster. *Don't do this again, not with this man. He's too special to lose.*

The shame of her secret was still fresh, as daily she hoped no one would find out that she had acted like a wanton. But now the man with the disfigured hand was inside her, and he was about to learn that she was scarred down there, too. Her virginity was gone, replaced by the smoothness that belonged only to she who was married.

His hand stilled, and her heart stopped. Facing away from him, she was relieved not to be able to see the expression on his face. She had expected to have this confrontation on her wedding night, and she would have an answer ready by then. But she hadn't expected to need that answer tonight.

She tensed, bracing for an appalled pronouncement— or worse, a snide remark. But nothing came.

Instead she felt his fingers begin a slow back-and-forth motion. She expelled her breath, unaware she had been holding it. Had he even noticed she was no longer pure? It didn't matter, she realized. Whether she had given herself to another man or just to Malcolm right now, she was no longer an innocent.

As the pleasurable sensation grew, she allowed herself the delicious oblivion of putting her shame out of her mind. Languorously, she rested her head back against his shoulder, allowing him greater ease in pleasuring her. The delirium grew as the sensation intensified. She rocked her body against the organ of his hand, her bottom bouncing against his thighs. His own arousal had grown—she could feel it—and it also cried for release. But right now, he wanted her pleasure, and she was prepared to give it to him.

His fingertip made a tight circle against one side of her nub, heating it to beyond tolerance. The pain-pleasure increased, and she grasped his hand, partly to still, partly to guide. But as he cocooned her from behind, he seemed to know precisely what would bring her to release. His hand kneaded her breast harder through her bodice, and she felt enveloped in a sheath of eroticism. His lips nibbled on the spot just beneath her earlobe, sending her spiraling toward a weakening surrender. The place between her legs that was now joined to his hand became hotter, tighter, more insistent—until her pleasure exploded in a blinding burst.

She pulsated onto him for several moments, her hands squeezing his forearms involuntarily. She emerged from the orgasm to find him kissing her tenderly on her cheek. Contentment flooded her, and she turned in his arms.

She snaked her arms around his neck and gave him a kiss of pure delight. He breathed in the kiss, his chest swelling to enormity.

She'd give him anything at that moment, so grateful was she. His acceptance, his selflessness, his gentleness, his desire for her . . . she felt beholden almost, and wanted to give him the same experience.

But Malcolm broke off the kiss. He stiffened and pulled away.

Worry quaked within her. Had she displeased him? Repulsed him? Was she about to lose this man's respect and regard? *Please, dear God, not again.*

His gaze focused on a spot beyond her, his ears perking. His eyes bristled with danger.

"Malcolm?"

He looked down at her and put a finger on her mouth, warning her to be quiet.

He reached over and pulled his pistol from the holster. She had no idea what had alerted him, nor even what threat he perceived. Night had stolen upon them, and she couldn't see a thing under the moonless sky. But whatever it was, in a flash Malcolm had transformed from a lover into a warrior. He shoved her behind him, his weapon leading ahead of them.

His breath made no sound as he crept along the wall like a predator. Terrified, she clutched the back of his shirt, the invisible fear making her own breath falter. Though her heartbeat hammered in her chest, she tried to be as quiet as he was as he advanced toward the end of the wall.

Then she heard it. A faint rustling. Then earth-muffled footsteps, moving in quickly. The sounds seemed to come from everywhere and nowhere. In panic, Serena scanned around her, every shadow a potential assassin. Her every instinct was to run from the danger. Yet

Malcolm was advancing toward it. She swallowed her horror and followed him.

The footsteps—a man's—drew closer and closer. Malcolm stopped before the end of the wall and stretched out his weapon, waiting. A shape walked by, and Malcolm cocked his pistol.

Just as the barrel of Malcolm's pistol touched the back of the man's head, the unknown assailant froze in his tracks.

"Ye can either kneel down, or be shot down. Which is it to be?"

Instinctively, the man raised his arms. "Slayter, it's me, Marsh."

Serena unclenched and ran toward him. "Father!"

Malcolm exhaled and uncocked his weapon. "Ambassador. I thought ye were an enemy."

Earlington embraced his daughter. "You were so long in returning from your walk, I came looking for you. I thought something had happened to you both."

"I'm so sorry, Father. It was my fault. I wanted a long walk to clear my head. I just . . . lost count of the hour."

"I'm just happy you're all right. My mind began to imagine the worst."

"Quite understandable, sir," Malcolm said, relief straining his voice. "In future, I will give ye a report on Serena's planned comings and goings."

Serena glanced at Malcolm. She couldn't help but chuckle at his unintentional double entendre.

"What's so funny, poppet?" asked her father.

"Nothing, Father. I'm just happy you weren't hurt."

Earlington chuckled weakly. "I wasn't. But with Mr. Slayter around, I pity the man who comes at you from behind."

Her nervous laughter intensified. She reached for Malcolm's hand. "I pity him, too."

Embarrassed, he squeezed her hand. "Serena," muttered Malcolm, a warning clear in his tone. "We should be getting indoors. Now."

"Certainly, Malcolm," she replied, unable to stop giggling. "Whatever you say. I know I'm in good hands with you."

He narrowed his eyes on her as she walked past him, arm in arm with her father back toward the house.

TWENTY-TWO

The morning room glowed with the light of a rare sunny day. The cerulean wallpaper reflected the color of the cloudless sky, and sunbeams fell upon the landscape paintings hanging on the walls.

Zoe sat on a settee in her pretty pink frock. Promenading across the squares of light cast upon the rug from the windows was her French master, Monsieur Leveque.

Or as Zoe liked to call him when she fantasized about their wedding, *Luc.*

Monsieur Leveque—Luc—was reading a passage from Molière's *L'École des Femmes,* a comic play that clearly brought him a great deal of pleasure. He laughed as he conveyed the madcap machinations of Arnolphe, a man in his forties, in trying to marry a girl of seventeen because he desired, above all, a virtuous wife. Luc acted out each part, and Zoe was having a great deal of fun watching him.

He was, in fact, a good actor, and his fresh masculine beauty would be welcome on any stage. He wore his hair in the style of the day, his mahogany curls feathering forward around his face. His tan tailcoat hugged his slender frame, and his white cravat was modestly arranged under his cleft chin. His eyes were the same emerald green as Mr. Slayter's, though not nearly as fierce. In fact, they were gentle, playful eyes, and when they looked at her, her heart skipped a beat.

Luc had the pale, smooth skin common to French people, with generous lips and an aquiline nose. He looked younger than his twenty-three years, but it didn't matter to Zoe how old he was. She wanted to marry him.

It was a blessing that her governess, Miss Tracey Archibald, did not speak French. Even though she was always present when Luc gave her lessons, she could not understand a word they said. It allowed Zoe and Luc to have the most delightful conversations. Luc spoke to her not as if she were a child, but as a woman, and she was immensely grateful to him for it. He told her all about his fruitless search for a wife—in French, of course—and Zoe dreamed of becoming that woman for him. She even practiced writing her married name . . . Zoe Leveque. She signed it with such a lovely flourish, she hoped it would one day become her own.

It didn't matter that he had made no overtures . . . yet. She understood that he was trying to establish himself as a dramatist. He loved the theater, and—being equally proficient in English and in French—he dreamed of seeing one of his plays produced in either language. He spoke often of his literary models, William Shakespeare and Pierre Beaumarchais, and he dreamed of being as famous as they.

Zoe was counting down the days until his birthday. She had been feverishly embroidering a sweetheart pillow, and she couldn't wait to give it to him. It was fate that their birthdays fell in the same month. He would turn twenty-four on the first of September, and two weeks later she would turn fifteen. Past the age of consent.

She clapped as he came to the end of the first act. *"Bravo,* Monsieur Leveque. *Très génial."*

"Merci bien," he replied, effecting a curt bow and smiling sheepishly at her. *"Avez-vous tout compris?"*

"Parfaitement. Vous avez donné une exécution magnifique."

There it was again, that fresh, honest smile that made her feel as if she were the only one in the world he would share it with. *Please, Luc, just one kiss! I will be yours forever!* His lovely eyes danced across her face, with those long lashes that were too beautiful to belong to a grown man. Bashfully, she smiled, her breathing suspended in expectation of a look, a whisper, a peck—anything that would tell her that he loved her as much as she him.

Suddenly, a rap at the front door echoed across the entrance hall, turning Luc's head. *Zut!* Zoe grumbled to herself. A pox on whoever it was for breaking this spell!

"Allow me," he said to Miss Archibald, who sat nearest the door. Luc rose and went to answer it.

Zoe pouted until Luc escorted the visitor to the morning room.

"Monsieur . . . eu . . . Weston," Luc began, his French accent lifting her spirits, "may I prezent La-dee Zoe, and her governess, Miss Arsh-ee-ball. Make yourself comfortab'. I will return with Monsieur Slayter."

Zoe curtsied before the guest. Mr. Weston was a handsome man, with a bright sparkle in his brown eyes. His sandy hair was lovely, and his finely tailored navy-colored coat exuded a fragrance of sandalwood.

"Good morning, ladies. Please forgive my unexpected visit."

"Mr. Weston," said Zoe, "won't you sit down?"

"Thank you, no. I've come all the way from London, and after four days in that wretched carriage, I'm quite relieved to be able to stretch my legs."

"We have some guests with us from London. Ambassador Marsh and his daughter, Serena. Do you know them?"

Mr. Weston smiled. "I have the honor of knowing them both. I know Miss Marsh quite well, in fact. I was hoping to be able to see her. Is she in?"

"That depends," Malcolm's voice rumbled from the doorway. "May I ask the nature of yer business?"

Mr. Weston turned to face him and extended his hand. "Yes. I'm her publisher, Archer Weston. I've had a letter from her. I hope I didn't arrive at an inopportune time."

"Archer?" Serena's voice carried from down the hall. In a moment she shouldered past Malcolm. "Oh, Archer, I'm so glad to see you!" Serena wrapped Archer in a firm embrace, and only Zoe seemed to notice the thunderous look that stormed over Malcolm's face. "What brings you here?"

Archer smiled and pulled a lettersheet from his coat pocket. "Your *crie de cœur.* You sounded quite despondent. I came as soon as I could, firmly resolved to cheer you up. Here . . . I've brought you a little gift." Archer handed her a parcel wrapped in brown paper.

Serena put a hand on his face. "What a dear man you are! Oh, I missed you so! I can't tell you how much it's gladdened my heart to see you. Why didn't you tell me you were coming so I could have it to hope for? Archer, have you met Lady Zoe? This is her governess, Miss Archibald. And this is Malcolm Slayter—" Serena was startled by the look on Malcolm's face. Though tightly leashed, his anger was palpable. "—my . . . protector."

It hit her full force. To call him her protector now presumed a great deal. At that moment, it seemed as if it was she who needed protection from him. Her expressions of affection toward Archer had earned her a lightning bolt of jealousy from Malcolm.

"Protector, you say?" remarked Archer. "Has it come to that?"

Malcolm looked him up and down. "I'm afraid so. And before I can allow ye to converse with Miss Marsh, I must ask ye to submit to a private interview. If ye please, sir?"

He waved a stiff hand toward the library. For a moment Serena was afraid for Archer's welfare.

"If you wish it." Archer took some hesitant steps ahead of Malcolm, who closed the door behind them.

Serena mouthed a silent prayer. Foolish, foolish girl! In light of her and Malcolm's growing fondness, she had been too effusive with Archer. She had to tread more carefully.

"Zoe, would you mind continuing your French lessons in your father's study? I'd be very grateful."

"Who is that man, Serena? Is Mr. Weston your suitor?"

"In a manner of speaking."

"But I thought you said that you and Mr. Slayter were—"

Serena interrupted her. "If you leave right now, I promise to tell you everything."

Zoe smiled. "He must be quite special to perturb you so. You look like the cat that swallowed the canary."

"Don't be ridiculous. I'm just happy to see an old friend."

"Papa used to tell me that a guilty conscience needs no accuser. And you, Serena, are standing amid a cloud of yellow feathers."

Serena pursed her lips and whispered a warning. "Go on, you insolent brat, or I'll tell Monsieur Leveque that you were the one who stole his gloves. I wonder what he would think of you if he knew you slept with them under your pillow."

"Very well, I'm going. But I want to hear more. Mr. Slayter looked as if he was fit to kill someone."

"Leave it to me. I'll get him to calm down."

Zoe turned around in the doorway. "When you do, you must let the vicar know. It'll be the first time we've had a miracle at Copperleaf."

A miracle was indeed what she needed. Serena sat in the airy room, perspiration sheeting her brow. She'd had no intention of giving away her feelings for Archer, especially not in front of Malcolm. Malcolm had been kind to her, and their recent tryst was unforgettable. But she had been so long away from home, and Archer represented many aspects of the life she left in London. Perhaps she had been just a trifle too demonstrative. She waited for the door to the library to open, fidgeting as if she had a corset full of toast crumbs.

Finally, Archer emerged tugging on his coat. Annoyance marred his features.

"I say, what goes on here? I've just ridden six hundred miles to see you, and I'm greeted by a behemoth of a servant who paws at me searching for weapons that I don't carry."

"I'm sorry, Archer," she said, with snap of her eyes to Malcolm. "Precautions are being taken."

"Why, for heaven's sake?"

"It's a tangled story. I'll ring for tea."

Archer adjusted his cravat. "Well, does he have to be here? With us?"

Serena glanced at Malcolm. His carefully tethered anger was reaching its limit. She spoke in gentle tones.

"Malcolm, would you kindly wait outside?"

"I'm afraid I canna. Yer father is not here at the moment."

"Archer is an old friend from London. I'd like to reacquaint myself with him and hear of home. It's perfectly all right."

"I can be assured of it if I remain here with ye."

"It may be a tick or two south of proper, but there's no need of you to serve as abigail. Archer is a perfect gentleman."

His gaze slithered to her face. "My presence is compelled by duty. And I feel an obligation to remind ye that a lady *such as yerself* should not be permitted to be alone with a man." His tone reeked of a hidden meaning, and she knew exactly what he was getting at.

Fury rose to her cheeks. "*Mister* Slayter," she began in her most imperious tone, "I do not appreciate the insult to the propriety of either myself or Mr. Weston. Your presence is *not* required in this salon. You will wait outside until you are summoned."

Her dismissive attitude seemed to have stung both his pride and his heart.

"For once, *Miss* Marsh, I am only too happy to comply." He turned on his heel and slammed the door behind him.

That infernal woman!

Blood thundered in his ears as he stormed off to the solitude of the stables. The stable yard was silent except for the birds chirruping in the pear trees, but if his anger were a sound, it would shake the very hills.

Inside the stable, the pungent smell of animal assaulted his nose. He walked his horse, Old Man, out of the stall and tethered him in the stable yard.

By God, he had half a mind to quit this assignment, and let the devil take his own daughter back. He grabbed a boar's-hair brush and dragged it through Old Man's long grizzled mane.

He didn't understand that exasperating creature Serena. They spent half the time in each other's arms, and the other half at each other's throats. Just when he thought she had come to really appreciate his devotion to her, she turned and embraced that . . . that . . . English fop!

The horse craned his neck in Malcolm's direction and neighed in protest.

Malcolm stilled his brush. "Sorry, Old Man. Dinna mean to take it out on ye."

A piece of straw crunched behind him. Instinctively, he turned in the direction of the sound, his hand ready to access any of the four weapons that he had at his disposal.

"Who did ye mean to take it oot on?"

It was Gabby Walker, the housekeeper.

Malcolm untensed. "Just bletherin' to my horse."

"Shouldna wonder why. He seems to have more sense than ye do."

Malcolm's eyebrows met as he looked down at the copper-headed woman. "Eh?"

Gabby advanced to the horse and caressed its neck. "The beastie forgives yer rough treatment because he knows ye mean him no harm. Ye would be wise to do as much with Miss Marsh."

"How did ye—" Zoe must have told Gabby about Archer Weston's arrival; little wonder, that. But how did she know—

Gabby put a hand on his arm. "Any woman who's had a sweetheart can see the coddlin' ye have for her. Biting and scratching is Scots folk's wooing."

Malcolm sighed in frustration as he leaned on Old Man. "I must've been mad to take up with a Sassenach wench."

Gabby shrugged as she caressed the horse's ears. "Thoroughbreds may be better than quarterhorses, but what's the difference if ye're going to ride them the same?"

Malcolm exhaled a confused breath. "There's a limit to what I will take. As soon as that woman saw her rich London friend, she fell into his arms."

"A wealthy man's wooing need seldom be a long one."

"It's not his money she'll be after. She's got money of her own. It's his . . . his . . . God knows what she sees in him!"

Gabby grunted in assent. "What does she see in ye, then?"

He turned the question over in his mind before his defenses shot up around him. "Whatever it was, she'll see it no longer. I'm through trying to win her over."

She cast him an amused look. "Is *that* what ye've been doing?" Gabby shook her head, the ginger curls bouncing against her cheek. "Ye've a strange idea of courtship, Mr. Slayter."

Malcolm waved his arms, punctuating his words. "And what am I supposed to do? Quote yards and yards of romantic poetry? Sing her songs? Bring her flowers and sweets like a lovesick schoolboy?"

"Hardly that. A town lady like Miss Marsh has probably had her fill of flowers and sweets. If ye want to get on the right side of Miss Marsh, ye've got to *show* her how ye feel. Not in a way that any man can do, and certainly not in words." Gabby picked a pear up off the ground.

"How do I do that?"

She cleaned the pear off with her apron before starting back for the house. "That's for ye to figure oot. Try asking the horse."

It was a royal mess.

After listening to Archer rant about being searched and interrogated upon arrival like a common criminal,

Serena had to endure stories of how her audience had grown annoyed over her absence from the column these many weeks. Some ladies had even started writing letters about parties they'd been to in an attempt to replace Serena as the writer of her own column. Archer admitted he had seriously considered opening up the "Rage Page" for submissions, making Serena feel even more dejected. And when Archer tried to kiss her, it failed to give her the spark she had always felt with him, even when he announced his intention to speak to her father about pursuing a courtship. Instead, her mind wandered to a certain irate Scot, whom she thought was just outside the door but instead had disappeared altogether.

She finally left Archer in the hands of the housekeeper, who had preceded him up the stairs to show him his room. Her fight with Malcolm and her disenchantment with Archer made Serena feel stuck like an insect in amber, and she decided to go see the only man who ever gave her wise advice.

"Come in," said Earlington from inside his bedroom.

Serena opened the door and witnessed her father swallowing the tonic meant to steady the beating of his heart. She bit her lip in consternation as he made a pinched face. "How you are feeling, Father?"

"Well, Serena, well. I can feel my heart grow stronger with each passing day. As long as I take my infusion of digitalis, I shall be fine. It's only when I don't take it that I'm in trouble." An aftertaste made him grimace once more. "Ugh. The cinnamon water adds a taste, but it's still as bitter as venom."

"Will there come a day when you don't have to take it anymore?"

He shrugged. "That's for the doctor to say." He patted a place on the bed beside him. "How are you, poppet? I haven't seen you all day."

She flounced on the bed beside him. "Father, I'd like to press a question to you, and I'd like your honest counsel. What would you say if I told you that I was beginning to feel a certain . . . tenderness . . . toward a gentleman?"

Earlington smiled widely. "This wouldn't by any chance have to do with a certain visitor who's just arrived?"

Serena smiled sheepishly. "In part."

He put a hand on her own. "I've always thought well of Archer Weston. He's a decent chap, good mind . . . he's not titled, but you know that I've never been an adherent to those sorts of outdated modalities. The Americans are forward-thinking in that respect. Not a lord or lady among them, and their matches are just fine." He lowered his head to look up into her face. "That *is* who you meant, isn't it?"

Serena shifted uncomfortably. "Yes. That is . . . no. Well, what do you think of Mr. Slayter?"

Earlington retracted his hand, the significance of which was not lost on Serena. "I like Mr. Slayter just fine. But isn't he a bit too . . . rough around the edges for someone like you?"

She had opened the door to those doubts, and now they assaulted her on every side. "I suppose so. As far as appearances are concerned. But I do feel something for him."

Earlington cocked his head. "I expect it's gratitude—he did rescue you from a horrible situation—and he also protects you every day. But you need to remember, Serena, that it is his job. It is what he is being paid to do. Besides, he is a Scotsman, and . . ." His frown deepened. "I know he's a good man—and he's been helping me considerably in strategizing how to deal with Brandubh McCullough. But I'm not certain that he's the type of man that I would want for you. I don't mind that you enjoy a friendship with Mr. Slayter, but if you begin to lose your heart to him—"

A lengthy pause prompted her to speak. "Father, you left that sentence hanging in the air."

"I know," he replied with a futile shrug. "I can't finish the sentiment. I have an entire slew of paternal platitudes, but leveling them at you would make me feel like a hypocrite. You see, poppet, Mrs. Walker and I have been enjoying a friendship as well."

Serena shook her head in confusion. "Mrs. Walker, the housekeeper? The woman who barely talks except to speak in proverbs?"

Earlington grinned. "She's a very wise woman. And I feel a certain tenderness for her, too."

Serena felt similar reservations about her father falling for, of all things, a Scottish housekeeper. But since she'd met Malcolm, so many things had changed. "Does she make you happy?"

"Yes, she does." He stood and went to the window. "I don't know, poppet. Old age encroaches upon you swiftly. It's rather like the first day of snow. One day you wake up, and everything is white. And then your health starts to go, and then your profession, and you start to feel about as useless as rain on the ocean." Earlington turned to face her. "This simple, beautiful woman came to me and told me to doubt my doubts and believe my beliefs. Somehow, she reminded me that who I was is who I still am. And that has made all the difference to me."

Serena bowed her head. It was the opposite with her. Malcolm had made her see that who she was *is not* who she is now—and she quite liked it that way. But

Archer had brought with him a memory of the familiar Serena, and she put on that persona like a comfortable gown, even though it felt out of fashion. And there was that fear, too, of her heart being wounded all over again. She could not let Malcolm—or any man—do that to her.

Earlington approached her. "And what of the genteel ruffian, Malcolm Slayter? Does he make you happy?"

"He did. But now, I don't know."

"Has the relationship turned sour?"

"No, it started sour. Now it's just turned into an un-mitigated shambles." Serena stood up and hugged her father. "Why does love have to hurt so?"

"Oh, poppet. Love doesn't hurt. People hurt. The love we bear them doesn't change."

Serena grinned jadedly. "Is that the wisdom of the ancients?"

He shrugged. "It's the best I can do. I'm not as good at it as Gabby is."

TWENTY-THREE

Scottish weather was nothing if not mercurial. As evening approached, the Highlands had tired of the beautiful cloudless skies. Gray clouds gathered from the east, blotting out the light of the setting sun. In no time, a storm exploded over Copperleaf Manor, blackening the prospect from the windows.

The prospect over the dinner table had been just as stormy. While Archer regaled them with stories of the most scandalous murders, political events, and *on-dits,* Malcolm ate his dinner in stony silence. Even a chuckle at Archer's witty comments would earn Serena a thunderous look from Malcolm. She was happiest when her father took the lead in the conversation, relating the growing civil unrest in Scotland since they'd arrived. In true journalistic fashion, Archer asked many questions, and Serena was wise enough to keep her mouth closed.

Sitting in her bedchamber that evening, Serena considered the man who slept just beyond the flowered wallpaper. Thunder rattled the windowpanes, and still she believed there was far more turbulence inside her room than outside the house.

Malcolm had been dutiful in following her at all times, but she wished more than anything for distance between them. They had had only one exchange since their argument that morning, and it occurred shortly after the gentlemen retired to the library for port and cigars. He cornered her in the hall before she joined Rachel and Zoe in the sitting room.

"Just tell me one thing," he had said. "Was Archer Weston one of yer lovers?"

A shamed blush zoomed up her face. It was clear now that he knew her to be a sullied woman.

She swallowed hard before she answered. Her voice was barely above a whisper. "There has been only one."

"And was it he?"

The truth somehow made her feel like a reprobate. "No. It was not Archer."

"Good. Because if it had been, I would have—" His jaw tightened and his fist curled, but he didn't finish that sentence.

The rest of the evening dragged by, and she was glad when everyone decided to retire. Now, sitting in her room, her cocoa growing cold in the pot, she wished Malcolm would come through the secret door and give her a chance to explain, or at least to claim her for his own. But as the clock on the mantel struck midnight, Serena began to believe that the wild Scot was just too untamable for her. Perhaps it was best, after all, to embrace Archer Weston as a possible suitor instead.

There was no reason for her to feel downcast. She liked Archer, and they were ideally suited to each other. Even her father thought so. But somehow, the idea of a lifetime without Malcolm filled her with utter desolation. Still, perhaps it was better for her to return to her familiar life in London, and Malcolm to remain where he belonged—in the Highlands.

Her father should be told. In light of their earlier conversation, she would have to inform him that she had changed her mind about choosing Malcolm. She sighed. Better sooner than later. If Archer decided to talk to her father over breakfast to ask permission to court her, she didn't want her father to give Archer the impression that she was not open to his suit. As she put on her dressing gown and slippers, she thought about how she would tell her father that she would choose Archer. But somehow, the words didn't seem to come.

She walked down the long hall toward Earlington's bedchamber, and knocked on the door. There was no answer.

Poor man. The hour was late, and he had been tired. He was probably fast asleep. She shook her head, and decided she'd better wait until the morning to talk to him.

But as she started back toward her room, a powerful sense of foreboding slammed against her. Silence from a sickly man portends all sorts of disaster. She had to make sure he was all right.

She returned to the door and knocked a little louder. "Father? Are you awake?"

Nothing.

She tried the doorknob, and it turned. But the door wouldn't open.

"Father?" Her voice grew alarmed as she shoved against it with all her might. Something on the floor inside the room kept the door from opening.

One more push opened the door enough for her to get through. She sidled through the jammed doorway, and nearly tripped over the body on the floor.

"Oh, no!" she cried as she knelt down beside the form. "Dear God, please don't take him yet!"

But it was not her father's body after all. It was his mattress.

"Father!" she cried while looking around the room,

trying her best to see in the utter darkness. She groped her way to the night table, upon which stood a candle. With trembling fingers, she searched for the tinderbox and lit the candle.

A soft glow radiated from the single wick, but it was enough to see by. There had been a scuffle. The doors to his wardrobe were open, his writing desk was over-turned, and the ewer and basin lay in pieces on the floor. The window was wide open, and rain fell inward onto the carpet. But her father was gone.

Serena screamed.

Within seconds Malcolm came to the door. He rammed his shoulder against the obstructed door, over-turning the mattress.

He took her in his arms and looked her up and down. "Are ye hurt?"

Tears were streaming from her eyes. "My father . . . he's gone!"

Malcolm's eyes tore around the room. He flew to the open window and shoved his head through the pelting rain. "There's a ladder wedged up below the window."

Serena crumbled in a heap to the floor, sobs racking her body.

Malcolm raced to her side. He righted the desk chair and placed Serena upon it. "Look at me, Serena. Look at me!" He gazed intently into her watery eyes. "We will find him. I swear it."

Serena met his gaze, and she seized the tenuous hope he offered her. She couldn't speak, so she nodded instead.

Within minutes, the entire household was roused. Malcolm assembled the male servants and organized a search party. Mrs. Walker sat Serena down in the hall and wrapped a shawl and an encouraging arm around her.

Lord Askey scratched out a note to the local magistrate. He then penned a letter to the Prince Regent. Rachel shepherded Zoe and the infant Annabella into the nursery, and reinforced the windows and doors.

Armed with guns and lanterns, the search party headed out the door. Although the heavy rain would have obliterated any tracks and the darkness of night hindered their sight, they set out to cover the surrounding acreage as best they could. Malcolm ordered his horse saddled, strapped on his holster, and headed for the door.

Archer stopped him at the doorway, outside the curtain of rain. "Mr. Slayter! Shouldn't I go with you?"

Malcolm turned his horse around. "Here," he said, tossing him a second pistol from the waistband of his trews. "Use it to protect Miss Marsh. That's yer job now. If anything happens to her . . ." Roiling thunder echoed behind him. "Turn the weapon on yerself."

He dug his heels into Old Man's flanks, and was off.

"It's gone two in the morning, miss." Gabby picked up Serena's untouched glass of whiskey from the dining room table. "Go back to bed. I'll wake ye when the men return."

Archer put a reassuring hand on hers. "Mrs. Walker is right, Serena. Get some rest."

Serena put her elbows on the dining room table and buried her forehead in her hands. Her hands trembled. "I'll sleep when my father is safe and sound back in his own bed."

"As ye wish." Gabby went back to the window and looked out into the empty night.

A few moments later, Serena heard a stifled sob from Gabby's direction.

"Mrs. Walker?" Serena went to stand beside her. "Are you weeping?"

The copper-haired lady wiped her face with the end of her pinafore. "I canna help it. The thoughts that go through m'head frighten me."

Serena embraced the slender lady. "I fear for him, too. God only knows what those abductors have done to him. Just the shock alone . . . he has a weak heart." Though she had already soaked two handkerchiefs, she felt tears welling up all over again.

"But he has a good heart, miss. His work canna be for naught. I firmly believe that he that's born to be hanged will never be drowned."

"What?" Serena looked aghast.

"It's just a saying . . . yer father is a great man, and he will yet do great things. He is not fated to be done for in this way."

Serena wanted to believe the distraught housekeeper. But she was too afraid of the present circumstances to put on a false bravado. Serena handed her the glass of whiskey.

Gabby downed it in one swallow. "'Tis good to dread the worst, as the old Scots saying goes, for the best will be all the more welcome."

Serena nodded. "Agreed. But let's have no more talk of hanging or drowning, shall we? Let's consider how we shall celebrate when he is returned."

A few moments later, they heard the front door open. Serena and Gabby flew to the hall with soaring expectations. But the look on the men's faces told a sadder tale.

One by one, the servants lumbered in, soaked to the skin and dragging their weapons behind them. Rain puddled on the floor from their clothes, and mud smeared their tracks. Malcolm was the last to come through the door, his woolen shirt plastered to his skin, and his hair dripping down his face.

He walked up to Serena. "We can do nothing more

tonight. The darkness deceives us, and the rain keeps extinguishing our lanterns. We'll set out again at daylight."

Her heart turned into a gaping hole. She wanted to say thank you to Malcolm for all he had done, but all she could manage was a sob. Malcolm took her into his arms and embraced her tightly.

The freezing rainwater from his clothes soaked into the front of her dress, but she didn't care one bit. Nothing could erase the heartache she felt, but Malcolm's soothing presence was like a sanctuary from the pain.

Archer came up behind her.

Malcolm exhaled deeply, Serena still clinging to him. "Thank ye, Mr. Weston. I'll look after her tonight. You go and get some sleep. There will be much to do in the morning."

Numbly, Serena let Malcolm walk her to her room. He sat her on the bed, lit a candle, took off her slippers, and lay her down on the bed. Tenderly, he stroked her hair before slipping through his secret door.

Serena lay awake on her bed for several minutes. Her whole world had been shattered, and she had no idea how to piece it back together again. But when Malcolm walked out of the room, he left a void she could not bear.

"Malcolm?" she whispered.

The secret door opened, and Malcolm was standing in her room. He had changed to dry trousers, and had shuffled off his wet shirt.

She sat up in bed, wanting to say something but completely unable to. Silently, he padded over to her bed, lay down next to her, and enfolded her in his bare arms until they both fell into a restless sleep.

TWENTY-FOUR

Serena awoke with a start.

The room was awash in pink and lavender as the dawning sun penetrated the lace-edged curtains. All was quiet and still.

She exhaled in relief. She'd had a horrible nightmare that her father had been abducted. Rolling over in her bed, she closed her heavy eyelids against the syrupy memory, and loosened the constricting ribbon on her dressing gown before she let herself doze off once more.

Her dressing gown? She bolted upright, still clutching the silver-embroidered garment, and realized with growing terror that it had been no dream.

She looked around the empty bed. Malcolm! He had been here. But now he, too, was gone.

She flew to the secret door and flung it open. His bed was empty.

In a sleepy stupor, Serena raced to her father's room.

There was Malcolm on his knees, studying the broken window.

She didn't know which to register—relief at seeing Malcolm, or horror at witnessing the state of the room.

"I think I can piece together what happened here last night," he said, straightening to his feet. He was fully dressed in his black tailcoat and trews, and his white cravat was hastily tied. "Let me show ye."

He held out a broad hand, and she placed hers in it. It was warm and dry, and enfolded her trembling one completely. He pulled her to the window.

"As near as I can surmise, there were probably four of them. Two of them came up the ladder, and two remained below. They waited for the ambassador to fall asleep." He picked up a piece of glass from the floor. "They must have used a club wrapped in a plaid, or an elbow—something covered in cloth—to break the lower window pane."

He held the shard up for her inspection. A few threads of wool were snagged on the jagged edge.

Malcolm pointed at the window hasp. "That's how they were able to release the catch to let themselves in."

Serena's gaze crossed from the window to the bed. "Did my father not hear the window break?"

"I don't believe so. The crash might have coincided with a peal of thunder, or he was too heavy in sleep. At any rate, two men came in and . . ." He went to the bedstead, grabbed a pillow, and mimicked the gesture of covering a man's face with it. ". . . muffled his cries with the pillow. See here? The pillow is still damp on both sides—from the man's rain-soaked hand, and from yer father's open mouth."

Serena whimpered.

"After waking him, I think they would have put a kerchief in his mouth to keep him from sounding an alarm, and flipped him over to tie his hands behind his back. Nothing was taken from the room, so it would seem they brought everything they needed. It was planned meticulously."

"Oh, my poor papa."

"And brave. He didna go with them meekly." Malcolm walked over to the upturned mattress on the floor. "The ambassador put up a fierce struggle. I think he grabbed the mattress behind him when they tried to lift him. I also think he pushed one of them onto the writing desk, for it was overturned. They seized him and dragged him to the window, where he continued to fend them off. But as ye can see"—Malcolm closed the wardrobe door, and Serena saw a crack in the wood webbing up from its center—"they slammed him up against the wardrobe. Once, maybe twice. This must have been how they were finally able to subdue him."

Serena covered her mouth with her hand. In addition to the shock to his heart, her father was also probably injured.

"His shoes are here, his suits are here. They took him away dressed only in his sleeping gown."

Hauled away from his bed in the middle of a rainstorm—frightened, injured, and undressed. Anger replaced dread. "Who took him?"

He crossed his arms at his chest. "Hired toughs. I'm certain of it. I found his diplomatic case on the floor beside the overturned desk. If they had been any smarter as to what they were about, they would have taken this case, which contained all his papers. What I canna understand is why they dinna leave a note."

"A note?"

"A ransom note. A man like yer father would ha' commanded a king's ransom. Or they might have left a note like the one they taunted yer father with when they threatened to kill ye. It stands to reason that they would brag about stealing the ambassador right from under our noses. But I searched everywhere for a note and didna find one."

Serena buried her face in her hand, and swallowed

hard before she asked the question that had beleaguered her all night. "Do you think they are going to kill him?"

Malcolm put his hands on his hips and let his gaze fall to the carpet. "I don't know. But one thing I do know. The people who ordered the kidnapping would be foolish to do so. He's worth more to the cause alive than dead."

"The cause." Serena's nose went skinny. "So you think it's the rebels who've done this terrible thing?"

Malcolm nodded his head. "It's been tickling my wrinkles all morning. But I'll wager my last pound that Brandubh McCullough either is behind this or knows about it."

Slowly, resolve solidified inside Serena. Anger and fear dissolved, and courage took its place. "Then that is where I shall start." She walked out.

"Where are ye going?" he called out to her, but she did not answer. Malcolm followed her back to her room.

Serena pulled a valise from the floor of her wardrobe, and opened it upon the bed.

"What do ye think ye're doing?" he asked.

"I'm going to get my father back."

Malcolm had the gall to chuckle. "Ye?"

Serena ignored him, and continued to layer clothes in the small case.

He crossed his arms and leaned a shoulder against the doorjamb. "And which army do ye have at yer disposal? In the first place, wherever they've taken him, I can assure ye 'twill be heavily guarded. In the second place, the McCulloughs have holdings throughout the Highlands. Ye've no idea where to start. And in the third—"

"You don't have to give me reasons not to go. I can think of dozens on my own. What I need is for you to draw me a map to all the places you think they might have taken him. I shall take it from there." She marched back to her father's room.

Malcolm followed her there. "Serena, I ken that ye're frightened, and that ye want your father back safely. But the worst thing ye can do is to go off half-cocked. Stay here at Copperleaf. As soon as General Wallingford arrives, he'll send troops out to cover the ground—"

"It could be days, weeks even, before the army is dispatched. My father doesn't have that kind of time." Serena rifled through her father's drawers until she found it. She cradled the brown bottle with the cork topper in her hands, and drew her thumb across the printed word on the label—DIGITALIS. "I may not be able to rescue him. But I might be able to bring him this."

"His medicine?"

She shook her head. "It's not just his medicine. It's his lifeblood." She wrapped the bottle carefully in one of her father's cravats. "I know the rebels took my father to force the Regent's hand to do their bidding. Equally, I know that once the rebels have gotten what they want, they will have no need of him, and they may kill him. But if he doesn't take his medicine, he will be dead anyway. The king's army may be sent to rescue him, but they may not get to him in time. I cannot let my father's heart give out. Not while I have breath in my own body."

"Ye can't go after him. There are too many dangers. The Highlands are no place for an Englishwoman."

"I don't care about myself."

"Ye don't have to. It's my job to look after ye."

She whirled upon him. "It *was* your job. With my father gone, you work for no one. You may go."

"I'm no' going anywhere. And neither are ye."

Serena recognized the resoluteness in his voice. Malcolm had considerable authority and will, and the physical strength and weaponry to enforce it. Moreover, he had the respect of the staff, and no one would dare countermand him, even for her. Lord Askey himself would support him in assuring her safety. She hadn't a single shred of power to stand up to him. If Malcolm ordered her to stay at the manor, then that was what would happen. Whether she liked it or not.

But there was one way—and only one way—she could wriggle out from under his protection. She marched downstairs in search of Archer.

She found him in the dining room, about to sit down to a rudimentary and hastily prepared breakfast with Lord Askey.

"Archer," she said, halting him from sitting in his chair.

"Serena," he responded, half surprised. Although there were dark shadows underneath his eyes and his hairstyle was slightly rumpled, he looked almost regal in his immaculately pressed green tailcoat and fawn breeches. "Good morning. How are you feel—"

"Propose to me."

Confusion marred his brow. "I beg your pardon?"

"Ask me to marry you."

Archer looked at Lord Askey in utter bewilderment. Serena was aware what a bizarre sight she must have presented—in a state of *dishabille*, her hair uncoiffed, and spouting strange propositions. But she could not let fear of eccentricity deter her.

"Archer, I want us to become engaged. This moment."

Lord Askey's expression had lost its customary jollity. "Serena, you've had a very trying night. I know you're distraught, but this is hardly the time to—"

"Lord Askey, I appreciate your sympathy, but I assure you that I have full control of both my faculties and my decisions. Archer?"

Archer's nervous glance bounced between Lord Askey and Malcolm, who remained in the doorway behind Serena. "Shouldn't I consult your father first? That is, when he is found?"

"I don't need Father's blessing. I'm already twenty-five. Ask me, Archer. I'll say yes."

"Very well. Serena, will you marry me?"

"Yes."

He gave her a nervous smile and took her hands in his. "Darling, that's wonderful. You've made me very happy. A bit surprised, of course, but quite pleased."

Serena squeezed Archer's hands firmly. "Now. As my betrothed, and in the absence of my father, you are in your rights to discharge Malcolm Slayter."

She hazarded a glance at Malcolm. He was leaning against the doorjamb, his arms crossed at his chest. His gaze had fallen to the floor, and a muscle twitched in his cheek. But now he leveled such a look at her from beneath hooded brows that it forced her to look away.

"But why? He is your protector, and in light of what's just happened—"

"*You* are my protector now, Archer."

"I see. Are you certain that's what you want?"

"I've just said it's what I want."

"Very well. Mr. Slayter, it appears your services are no longer wanted."

Malcolm said nothing. He remained right where he was.

Serena was relieved that Malcolm didn't quarrel about it. "Good. Now that's done, please pack your bags. I'd like us to set out to look for my father."

"Ah."

"I will have Father's town coach readied, and we can start out immediately. I'll ask Mrs. Walker to prepare us something, and we can eat it on the way."

She started for the door, but Archer held her back. "Darling, I've got a better idea. Come with me to London. You'll be safe there."

"No, Archer. We've got to find my father. There isn't a moment to lose."

"Serena, please. We must let the authorities handle this. Your father wouldn't want you dashing off in search of him, not when war's about to break in Scotland. No, I think it best if you come with me to London."

She looked at him as if he were mad. "Archer, this is important to me. I must find him. He needs me."

"There are other ways we can help. Look at this." He handed Serena a few sheets of paper. "I wrote it last night. It'll lead the next issue of the paper."

Serena read the headline at the top of the page.

BRITISH AMBASSADOR ABDUCTED
FEARED KILLED BY SCOTTISH REBELS

"I need to run this as soon as possible. The public has to know what is going on. We'll create a public outcry so loud that the rebels will have to surrender your father."

"Do you really think he's dead?"

"Of course not, darling! But we have to alarm the public in order to move the hand of government."

Serena's brows knit together as she skimmed over the hastily written article. "Archer, you make it sound like a foregone conclusion that he'll never be rescued. I need your help to make sure that none of these things will happen. I need you to help me change the news, not fulfill it."

An uneasy look came over his features. "Serena, I would do anything for you. You know that. But this is my job. I'm an editor of a newspaper, and this is news that has happened right before my eyes. I have a duty to inform the public."

She shook her head. "But the trail to my father will grow cold, Archer." *As will my love for you.*

"Perhaps it's best if we let Mr. Slayter find him. He is a fugitive hunter, after all. That's what he's best at. I'll pay him handsomely. Come back to London with me, Serena. I'll take care of all the rest." He held out his hand.

She gazed at his upturned hand. It was soft and smooth, a gentleman's hand. Everything she had been taught to believe told her that her hand belonged in his. But everything she felt in her heart screamed that it didn't. She knew that if she put herself in Archer's hands, she would eventually slip right through those silky palms.

"No, Archer." She placed the sheets of paper in his outstretched hand. "Go. Publish your headline. Speak to the world. And forgive me for forcing your proposal. I . . . am not myself." It was a fact that she was accepting with growing certainty.

Silently, she made her way back to her room. She sat down on the edge of the bed, cradling the wrapped bottle in her lap.

Malcolm appeared in her doorway. "I'm sorry." He saw her wipe a tear from her cheek. "He's a fool. And a yawning bore. I never liked him."

"That's only because you're an excellent judge of character."

Malcolm cocked his head. "The fool is right, though. Ye would be safer in London."

"If I hadn't wanted to go to London so badly, my father wouldn't be in the mess that he's in."

"Eh?"

She squeezed the wrapped bottle. "It's my fault he's gone, Malcolm. I caused it. That threatening letter? 'Sing a song of sixpence,' like the nursery rhyme?"

"Aye?"

A lump formed in her throat as she formed her next words. "I wrote it."

Malcolm's mouth fell open. "Ye? Why?"

"Because I wanted to go home. I wanted our familiar lives back. I thought that if Father believed my life was in danger, he would take us both back to London. But I hadn't considered the possibility that he'd engage someone like you to protect me. I tried telling you, over and over again, that my life was in no danger. But his was! Don't you see? All this time, my father was the target, and no one was protecting him."

Malcolm sat down next to her on the bed. "'Twas a selfish thing to do, Serena."

"I know."

"But 'tis yer good fortune it was me who was engaged. If anybody can find yer father, I can."

Her moist eyes snapped up to his. "Do you mean that? You'll come with me?"

He sighed. "My place is with ye. And where ye go, there I'll be."

"Oh, Malcolm!" She threw her arms around his neck.

"No' Malcolm," he said, returning the embrace with a halfhearted smile. "The name is Ubiquitus."

TWENTY-FIVE

Darkness.

Flashes of sound broke through Earlington's nothingness. He stirred, and pain pounded out a staccato in his head. The ache made him wince, but he forced his eyes to open.

He found himself lying inside of a crate. His knees were wedged up against the wooden sides, and his arms were bound behind him. He lay on his right side, rendering his right arm completely numb. Around his head, damp straw lay scattered upon the wooden planks.

From inside the confined space, he heard the turning of carriage wheels. Daylight seeped in between the wooden planks, creating prison bars of sunbeams. He shimmied as close as he could to see out.

The crate appeared to be mounted on the back of a dogcart or trap, and he saw the hills hurtling past the carriage. He heard men's voices, but he couldn't make out how many there were or what they were saying.

Within minutes, the carriage came to a halt. He heard the sound of wrenching as the lid of the crate, which had been nailed shut, was pried open. The sun exploded in his face, and he winced. Two pairs of hands lifted him forcefully from the box, and set him on unsteady legs.

"Wake up, Your 'Ighness. Ride's over now."

It was a gutter-class English accent. His eyes adjusted on the man's face. The man's hair was matted to his head, and his leathery skin was pockmarked. It was the same man he'd seen last night, the one who'd tried to smother him with his own pillow.

"Who are you?" Earlington demanded, the effort of his voice creating a throbbing pain throughout his head.

The man smiled, revealing places where his teeth used to be. "I'm your coachman, sir!" he mocked. "And it is my duty to make sure you're delivered safe an' sound to your final destination." He turned to the other man, who had hopped back onto the driver's seat. "Right. You can take that coffin back, now. Not too far, mind. We may need it later."

Earlington spun around and looked with horror at the crate out of which he'd just emerged. It was, indeed, a pauper's coffin. A small stain of blood was left behind where his head used to be.

"Come with me, Your Majesty." The man grabbed Earlington around his elbow and dragged him toward what looked to be an ancient castle fort or garrison. The Englishman hollered through the portcullis. A kilted man appeared behind the iron grille.

The kilted man was in his seventies. A thin white beard, at least a foot long, drizzled onto his shirt. "Is that him?"

"Yep. This 'ere's your prize." He stretched out his hand. "And now I'd like mine."

The old man looked Earlington up and down. He signaled to someone in the room above the portcullis, and slowly, the heavy barrier was lifted. "I have your purse of monies inside the bailey. Take the ambassador to the stronghold. Then we'll settle accounts." The old man handed the Englishman a ring of keys.

"Right you are." The Englishman pushed Earlington through a courtyard with an ancient cobbled floor. They entered through a doorway at the foot of the keep, and turned down a set of narrow stone stairs that had been worn smooth from use. They passed through an iron gate and stopped in front of a heavy oak door. He fitted the key in the lock; with a rusty complaint, the mechanism turned.

The Englishman shoved him through the door. The air inside the cell was fetid, and a ghastly smell emanated from what appeared to be a bucket for human waste in the corner. A single small opening served as a window, and it was high above the floor. Against another wall, a cot strung with rope was the only piece of furniture. The floor was nearly black with use, and ground in between the flagstones were things he thought best not to contemplate.

"Kneel down for me, sir."

Fear shot through him. God only knew what indecency this man had in store for him. His abductor was not a tall man nor a brawny one, but he had the compact strength of a man of violence, and the inclination to use it.

"Why?"

He leaned in and his breath came out in putrid puffs. "You're going to be knighted."

Hesitantly, Earlington sank to his knees. His nightdress was still damp, and it clung to his skin in places.

The Englishman pulled out a knife from a sheath in his belt. The blood drained from Earlington's face. The Englishman went around behind him, and Earlington held his breath.

The Englishman lifted up his bound wrists, forcing Earlington to bend forward. Earlington grimaced. But the man only sliced at the rope that bound his wrists together. When his hands were freed, Earlington's elbows and shoulders screamed from the cramping. He wanted to rub the deep ligatures in his wrists, but his hands wouldn't respond properly.

His captor sheathed his weapon and headed for the door.

"You're English," remarked Earlington.

The man chuckled. "Right you are. Glad I'm not being confused with one of these skirt-wearing, thistle-assed barbarians."

"If you don't like them, why would you ally with them? Can't you see that having me abducted is a prelude to war? A war with your own countrymen?"

The man spit on the floor. "Listen 'ere. I don't give a squeaky fart about politics. Run 'em all through, that's what I say. It's the only way to get rid of this Scottish vermin once and for all."

"Then why would you help them by abducting me?"

His back straightened. "Because Your Lordship is worth two hundred knicker. And their money is just the right color for me."

"But there is money to be had in England, too. A man with your skills is highly wanted—"

The man broke out into hollow laughter. "Oh, they want me all right. They want me dead. I'm not a soldier. I'm a criminal. And England has become too hot to hold me."

Earlington held up his hands. "Listen to me. I'm in the middle of peace talks with the Scots. If you set me free, or at least tell someone that I am being kept here, I will make sure that you are not only pardoned, but rewarded for your patriotism."

The man put his hands on his knees to bring his face on a level with Earlington's. "If you want my advice, milord, forget talks of peace. The only peace these savages understand is the pieces they hack each other to."

He turned around and walked out. The heavy door thudded shut, and the lock ground closed.

Earlington clambered to the cot. He was now just the chess piece that had stood in front of the king, the final chess piece to be toppled before war broke out.

But now he was here, useless, leaving his daughter vulnerable and exposed. He wrung his hands. Had they taken her, too? Or, worse—he shuddered to contemplate—had she been killed? The mystery of it was almost worse than the fact.

He buried his face in his hands in self-recrimination. Why hadn't he taken her back to London, where she would have been safe? Why had he been so concerned about these people that it blinded him to the needs of his own daughter?

Serena, he thought, *if you're still alive, please head to safety.*

TWENTY-SIX

The household returned from a daybreak search of the grounds with no evidence of Earlington Marsh or his captors.

Malcolm changed to his black kilt and plaid, and began to load up the ambassador's town coach. The boot took a large basket of provisions provided by Mrs. Walker, a valise of Serena's, one for himself, and a small case containing some clothes for Serena's father.

Serena came out of the house. For once, she carried no parasol and wore no bonnet. She was dressed in a simple blue printed muslin dress, with a matching spencer and sensible shoes. Her long blond hair was pinned up, but hastily so. Malcolm couldn't help reckoning that even in plain clothes and a slapdash hairstyle, Serena was a vision of loveliness. In fact, he liked the look of her even more.

Malcolm attempted to ensconce her inside the coach, but she would have none of it, insisting instead on riding beside him in the driver's seat. With a flick of the reins, Malcolm urged the pair of grays forward.

"Which of Brandubh McCullough's holdings will we try first, Malcolm?"

While her intention to search for her father was ill conceived and ill advised, Malcolm would give it this much credit: The two of them alone stood a greater chance of finding the ambassador than did an entire army of British redcoats marching through the Highlands.

"None of them . . . yet. It won't do to go off in the hunt for a needle in an entire field of haystacks. I think we should first narrow down our search to a single haystack."

"How are we going to do that?"

"I have a friend who lives near Cannich. If anyone knows where yer father's been taken, McLeish does. And what's more, he'd tell me."

"Why?"

"Let's just say that I'd be paying him in his own coin. McLeish is not yer typical Scotsman. He sort of dances upon the fringe of society, if ye take my meaning."

"A criminal, you mean?"

"Aye. But I wouldna use that word in front of him. He's . . . had his hand in a colorful array of clandestine activities."

Serena shook her head. "You keep company with strange sorts."

"I keep company with all sorts of sorts. Even saucy, crabbit scolds like ye." He cast her a smug look.

She gave him a sidewise glance. "*Quel drôle.* Was that the pinnacle of your wit?"

His smiling eyes looked back out over the horses' heads. A steady wind pushed onto the coach, and Serena lifted the collar of her blue velvet spencer.

"How long will it take to get there, do you think?"

"Depends on the length of our horses' legs. But we should be arriving in Cannich by nightfall."

Malcolm felt Serena tuck in against him for warmth, wrapping her arm through his elbow, and it filled him with a dense happiness. It was such a rare sensation for him. Her touch aroused more than just his desire. It also aroused his heart.

"I'll be so happy when my father is found." She laid her head on his shoulder as she gazed out at the countryside. "He doesn't deserve what's been done to him here. It was he who tried to get me to appreciate Scotland. A place of extremes, he called it. When it's cold, it's freezing. When it rains, it's a deluge. And when it's beautiful, it is sublimely so."

He chased her gaze toward the horizon. The narrow one-carriage road was intermittently canopied by copper and silver beeches, and sunlight slid through the branches, dappling their path. On one side of the rutted road, the landscape mounded upward toward green hills, which were crowned with layers of fir trees. A clear-water burn ran along the other side of the road. The cool air was perfumed with the green scent of grass and trees, and the grating caw of crows could be heard in the distance.

"It is beautiful." *And so are you,* he wanted to say. The mosaic landscapes of his homeland were all reminiscent of Serena. The thick yellow gorse reminded Malcolm of Serena's vivid blond hair, the thistle in bloom reminded him of her regal beauty and prickly nature, and even the vast yellow fields of rapeseed called to mind visions of them both engaged in ruthless lust . . .

"Perhaps I have been too shortsighted after all," she said. "With all its beauty of architecture and formal gardens, there is nothing in all of London to match the simple majesty of this scenery."

The mere mention of London brought forth an angry sigh from Malcolm. He'd never been to that city, but he already hated it because it threatened to take her away. "And yet ye miss it."

"I must admit, yes. There was an uncompromising elegance about my life there. Did you know that in my home, there are twenty-five sets of dishes? You could stay a whole month and never eat off the same dishes twice."

He doubted he'd ever get the chance to see for himself. The likelihood of Serena Marsh asking Malcolm Slayter to stay at her home in London was practically nonexistent. "Seems an awful waste, if ye ask me. Ye only need one."

Serena grew pensive. "Perhaps you're right. Perhaps it is ostentatious. It's the thing, you see. One feels compelled to exhibit one's wealth. Seems ludicrous now. I wouldn't trade my father's well-being for all the place settings in Great Britain." She sighed. "London has a way of making you feel as though you're more important somehow. Here, though, you are forced to see yourself as you truly are." Her voice trailed off.

"And Archer Weston? How did he see ye?"

Her hand in the crook of his elbow stiffened. He turned to look at her, and her countenance had fallen.

"I suppose I was yet another one of those glittering fantasies that vanish once you peer too closely." She sighed, lost in contemplation. "It's a great pity, really. I found Archer to be very different from most of the gentlemen I know. For a start, he's a man of intellect, not of leisure. He's the first man I'd met who seemed like he could actually change the world if he wanted to. And we were excellent friends. But try as I might, I couldn't make him love me."

"*Make* him love ye? Why should ye have to try? Either someone loves ye or they do no'."

"It's not that simple. Men see women through the eyes of other men. They're very competitive creatures. A man wants a woman on his arm who will be the envy of all the men in the room. He revels in the triumph of having acquired her."

"That's no' a very flattering picture of us."

"An accurate one, nonetheless. Archer is simply one of those men who needs to feel as if he's somehow *achieved* a woman." Serena looked down at her lap. "But this morning, it became evident that I could never be that prize for him. I always suspected that his profession was more of a religion to him, but when he chose the publication of his headlines over helping me find my father, I knew I had failed. I was simply not charming enough, nor popular enough, nor pretty enough to get him to fall in love with me."

Malcolm was silent for a few moments as he tried to stem the flow of anger. "That's the biggest load of havers I've ever heard. Serena, those things are just trappings. Charm is misleading. Popularity wanes. And even yer beauty will one day fade. What remains is what is the true prize. Ye. Just ye. And that ought to be enough for any man." He placed his hand on her face. "And if that peacock of a suitor of yers can't see that, then . . . yer Archer missed the mark."

She chuckled halfheartedly at his offhand quip. "One thing I do know. Archer and his words, they're . . . invisible. But your presence here with me, now, when I needed someone the most . . . this is very real." She placed a gloved hand on top of his.

Mrs. Walker's advice came floating back to him. *If ye want to get on the right side of Miss Marsh, ye've got to show her how ye feel. Not in a way that any man can do, and certainly not in words.* Did Serena understand the depth of his feelings for her?

"Ye've got yer besom ways about ye, Serena Marsh. But I care for ye. Just the way ye are."

Sunlight sparkled on the tiny droplets forming in her moist eyes. "You do?"

He smiled. "Aye." He bowed his head, touching his lips to hers. So soft, so open. He swept in for another kiss, this one longer, deeper. He closed his eyes to savor the sensation of her lips caressing his. God, what heaven this was, to be kissed by such a woman. It fed something deep within him, as the first drops of rain on parched soil. Serena responded by caressing the hair at the back of his head, which invoked a thread of pleasure that wended all the way down to the area between his legs.

He let his mouth trail down to her alabaster neck. Her skin smelled of rose, jasmine, and lavender, and he inhaled deeply the soft, feminine scent. He kissed the V at the base of her throat, and his lips sensed her heart beat faster. She made a sound, a pleading mewl. She had slipped a hand from its glove and threaded her fingers through his hair. The sensation of her nails on his scalp sparked a powerful hunger for her.

Suddenly the carriage lurched, and he and Serena were shaken from their embrace. The carriage stopped dead.

"What was that?" asked Serena, straightening in the seat.

He didn't know. He looked around for the reins, which he'd let slip from his hand. Finally, he spotted them on the floor of the carriage. But just as he reached down to pick them up, the carriage tilted sideways.

Serena shrieked, and so did one of the horses. One of the wheels had rolled onto loose ground that now began to collapse. Malcolm looked beyond Serena seated beside him and was chilled at the sickening sight.

The carriage was tipping down a deep ravine.

And below, the steep rocky slope crumbled into the churning water.

Instinctively, Malcolm latched onto Serena. Fear was in her eyes as she looked over the edge down at the dangerous outcropping. The team pawed at the ground, fighting the anchoring weight.

"Serena, don't look down. Step across me." But the instant he said it, there was a terrifying crunch as the wheel snapped off, sliding the rear-heavy carriage farther down the embankment.

The horses neighed in panic as they were dragged down with the carriage. Serena lost her foothold and screamed as she dangled precariously over the edge of the dashboard. Malcolm held on to the seat rail above him, holding Serena against his chest.

"Climb over me!" he shouted as he lifted his knee to support her. Every muscle in his body ached with the strain of holding on while hauling Serena up over the side of the overturning vehicle. With all the strength she could muster, Serena lifted herself up along his body, and scrambled onto the edge of the disappearing ground.

He felt an immense relief at seeing her to safety. But now he had to rescue himself. If he fell, he would become part of the Highland scenery forever. His arms and shoulders were drained from the effort of hanging on to the seat rail, and his sweaty palms were making the bar too slippery to hold on to much longer.

He brought both hands together and pulled. He lifted his body closer to the edge of the carriage. The horses' rear legs were tearing up the loose rocks, kicking stones and dirt into Malcolm's face as he tried to lift himself over the edge.

Suddenly, one after the other, the shafts snapped, jackknifing the carriage and jarring Malcolm's hold.

The team and crippled carriage slid farther down the gully. Vainly, the harnessed horses tried to claw their way out, but the immobilized carriage could not roll up the steep incline.

Malcolm braced for the shattering impact on the rocks below. Only one vision filled his thoughts—Serena.

And then he saw her. The carriage had slowed, caught on a fallen tree trunk. Serena was climbing down the brae, hanging on to bushes and tree branches.

"Serena, no!" he screamed. At worst, she'd fall into the ravine with him, and at best she'd watch him die. But she was driven by pure instinct. She gripped the horse's harness and unbuckled the trace that strapped its harness to the carriage.

"The reins, Malcolm!" she shouted. "Grab hold of the reins!"

He saw one dangling by his side, but if he let go of the rail to take it, he didn't think he could hold on.

"Hurry!" she shouted as she went to release the other trace.

Malcolm's life depended on whether he could reach the reins. His muscles screamed in pain as he used his leg to bring the leather strap closer. Finally, it was close enough for him to reach.

"Now, Malcolm!"

With supreme force of will, he let one hand go of the carriage and gripped the rein. Once the horses were freed from the weight, they were able to climb. The carriage skated out from beneath him down the rock face just as he was being dragged up the cliff.

Stones and loose debris raked his skin, but he would not let go. The horses continued to climb higher up the brae. A sickening crash on the riverbed below filled his ears. When they were finally on level ground, he let go the reins and let the pair run on.

He lay panting on the ground, grimacing at the sharp pain firing throughout his body. But Serena—he had to find out if she was all right.

He clambered to his feet and staggered toward the edge. Below, the carriage had splintered on the rocks. "Serena!"

There was no answer. A feeling of dread drained him. Not since he witnessed the lifeless bodies of his parents and brothers had he felt so much loss. If anything happened to Serena, he'd go mad. "Serena!" he shouted at the top of his lungs.

A voice came from far below. "I'm here!"

Then he saw her, a tiny form leaning on a sapling that angled upward from the slope. So far away. "Are ye hurt?"

"No. Are you?"

The relief of seeing her brought him to his knees. But as the tension and dread wore off, the pain escalated. He took stock of his injuries. He was bleeding from abrasions all along his left side, there was a nasty goose egg developing somewhere on his grit-dusted head, and his arms were killing him. "I'll live."

"I love you." The words floated up through the trees.

Malcolm never thought to hear that from the mouth of any woman, let alone Miss Serena Marsh. It filled his body with warmth, and made his heart lighter than the ether. She'd saved his life. And now she'd saved his soul.

"I love ye, too." He wished she were right there beside him, to be able to take her in his arms and show her what those words meant to him. To see her smile and read her eyes, and prove to her that her vulnerability was safe with him. Damned if the thought of it didn't take every last bit of pain away!

But now there was the problem of how to get Serena

out of the gully. He had no rope and no tools, only a battered body. There was no way of telling how far it was until the road connected with the river once more.

"Stay put," he called down to her. "I'll think of a way to get ye up."

"No, Malcolm," she responded, her voice nearly muffled over the rushing water. "I have to climb down."

"What?"

"My father's medicine is in the wreckage below. I have to retrieve it before the river washes it away."

"Ye'll do no such damn thing!" He wasn't about to let her risk her life . . . again. Beyond the small figure in the blue dress the terrain was rocky, gnarled, and difficult to negotiate. Any false step would result in a death slide.

"I must!"

He held up both hands. "All right. I'll get the medicine. Just stay where ye are."

There was no way Malcolm could get Serena out of the gully. He would have to find a way to go in.

TWENTY-SEVEN

Earlington had spent the better part of the day shivering with cold. The stone walls gave off a bitter chill, and though his nightdress had dried, it gave him no protection against the damp, fetid air. The cot smelled of sweat and fear multiplied over the course of decades. Never had he imagined an existence so tortured.

The injury to the back of his head had stopped bleeding, but it left a thick ache in its place. Added to that, worry about Serena plagued him. What if she had been captured? It made him miserable to think of her in a place such as this. But what if they had done unconscionable acts against her? What if they had raped her, or worse—what if they carried out their threat and mutilated her face? Pain pierced his chest and he clutched his heart. Both the pain, and the fear of the pain, locked upon his heart like a steel trap. Many anxious minutes passed while he held a hand to his heart. He grimaced, breathing through the constricting ache. Finally, the pain abated.

He tried to clear his head of the awful thoughts. But awful thoughts were like the foul smell that clung to these ancient stones . . . there was nothing to take their place.

Perhaps Malcolm had been able to protect her. Perhaps it was not Serena they were after. Maybe the

threatening letter had been only a ruse to distract him.
Perhaps he had been the real target after all.

But to what end? He could not envision His Royal
Highness bowing to the will of his captors just to get an
ambassador returned. Parliament would not negotiate
with revolutionaries, and the Crown would not be coerced by rebels. Otherwise, the government would be at
the mercy of every radical who abducted an official. If
he were in London and someone else was in this cell, he
would advise the Prime Minister to call the rebels'
bluff.

Of course, that did nothing to console him. But it did
clarify his thinking: It was completely up to him to get
himself out of this predicament.

Though faint, he heard a sound beyond the thick
stone wall. He wasn't tall enough to see out of the window, so he overturned the waste bucket and placed it
below the narrow opening to stand upon.

The window was still too high, but he managed to steal
a glance. In the courtyard above, hundreds of men,
maybe even a thousand, gathered. Someone, he couldn't
see who, was giving them instructions. He couldn't make
out any of the words, but the speech was punctuated
with cheers from the assemblage, which, he noted, was
armed with both swords and firearms.

Earlington sat back down. It was a soldiers' parade,
except that these weren't soldiers. They were militia
and mercenaries, just like the one who had abducted
him. This group was organizing for its defense.

The turning of the lock reverberated across his
chamber. The old man with the white beard appeared
in the doorway, flanked by two armed guards.

"Ye'll put this on," he said, handing Earlington a
shirt and a black woolen kilt. He was secretly grateful
for the warm garments. But he would not be manipu-

lated into thanking his captors for giving him the bar-
est of essentials.

"It is an outrage for you to keep me here. I demand
that you release me at once."

"Keep yer breath. Put on the clothes and then follow
me. The McCullough will see ye now."

The frightened horses had galloped over the broken
road and into a field. They would have easily run for
miles had not an ancient stone dyke cut short their
panicked dash.

They seemed miles away as Malcolm hobbled toward
them. The grays were still harnessed together, with
reins and straps dragging behind them. On one side,
they were still dragging a broken shaft that remained
wedged in the tug loop. He had to get to them, if for no
other reason than for the humane purpose of removing
their bindings.

When he finally reached them, the horses were still
wide-eyed and their ears were tipped back. He cooed
softly as he approached, inspecting them for injuries
from all angles. Miraculously, they didn't seem to be
hurt, with the exception of the horse whose rein had
pulled him out of the crevasse. The edge of her mouth
was torn and bleeding.

He made quick work of removing her bridle and
unbuckling the harness. But he kept a hold on both the
horses' halters, and he led them quietly but firmly back
to the road.

About a mile from where their carriage had dropped
upon the loose rocks, the road had begun to wend downward until it united with the river. Malcolm let the
horses drink before turning them back in the direction
they came from, this time walking along the riverbed.

Finally, Malcolm came upon the shattered carriage

at the foot of the rocky outcropping. He looked up: The crumbling slope was being held up by the remaining valiant trees, but it wouldn't hold out much longer.

"Serena!"

No answer.

He shielded his eyes from the late-afternoon sun as he scanned the slope. He'd give anything to be able to see a patch of blue fabric or a hint of blond hair.

"Serena!" he yelled louder. His voice reverberated across the canyon.

"Stop yelling," came a voice behind him. "I'm right here."

He turned, and there was Serena, smiling at him. He hugged her tightly, filling his arms with the feel of her, and spun her around.

"God be praised! Ye're all right! How did ye get down here?"

"I climbed down!" she said triumphantly. "Did you take me for a frail milkwater maid?"

His jaw tensed. "Ye've far too much confidence for yer own good. Didn't I tell ye to stay where ye were?"

"You said you were coming to get me."

"So I was!"

"You took your time about it."

"I had to fetch the horses."

"Where did they get to . . . Norway?"

He pinned his fists to his hips. "I've a good mind to kiss ye."

She smiled at him. "Well, what's keeping you now?"

He seized her by the arms and snapped her to a hairsbreadth away from his face. A fierce grin cut across his face. "Why do I get the feeling that any road I share with ye will be fraught with danger?"

"Don't worry," she said with a wry smile. "I'll protect you."

Her lips touched his, and he melted all around her. His arms wrapped around her back as he feasted on her lips. She snaked her arms around his neck, putting his body in full contact with hers. They fit together so perfectly, wholly and in every possible way. What foolishness was it that taught her men wanted only showpieces on their arm? Malcolm not only wanted to keep her all to himself—he wanted to erase every lowly, contemptible man from her memory.

She exhaled contentedly. "My goodness! You are . . . That was . . ."

He chuckled. Now he knew how to rob her of speech. "Next time, ye'll think twice about daring me to love ye."

TWENTY-EIGHT

Being able to live out in the open air was not a gift Serena could boast about.

Malcolm took her downstream to where the rushing water gentled to a brook alongside a forest. It was here that he announced they would set up camp for the night, and a peculiar sort of dread overtook her. For one thing, modesty protested. In London, relieving oneself out of doors was something that only dogs and drunkards did. For another, she was certain there were creeping things and crawling things that came out at night, and she did not want to meet any of them face-to-antennae.

There was very little that could be rescued from the wreckage of their town coach. What wasn't destroyed was washed away, including their provisions. However, Malcolm had found enough left with which to fashion rudimentary fishing equipment, including a net from one of her ruined chemises, which he used to pull a fat salmon from the brook.

"Right," he began, tossing down the fish onto the ground, "I got dinner. Now you, Miss Marsh, are going to cook it."

Her eyebrows flew into the air. "I?" She shook her head. "No."

"I know, too," he quipped. "Get to work."

"I'm not a domestic."

"If ye dinna cook, ye dinna eat."

The thought of going without food even one more minute was unbearable. "Malcolm, I don't know how."

"Start with a fire. And ye'll build it the Highland way. By yer wits, not yer assets."

Serena sighed in frustration. She looked around her at the forest, as if she might be able to spot a fireplace or stove nearby.

Malcolm handed her the knife from the sheath strapped to his leg. "Take this. See that dead birch tree over there? Shave off a wee bit of the bark. That'll be yer tinder."

Serena gave him a look that she hoped would convey her displeasure. But she went off and did as he said.

She returned a while later and showed him what she'd collected. "Here you go."

His eyes widened when he saw the pile of bark clutched in both her hands.

"Och, woman, ye only need a wee bit."

"Well, pardon me, but I have a difficult time quantifying the word *wee*. Next time, say when."

He laughed. "Looks like ye stripped the tree bare."

She held up the knife. "I'd like to strip you bare."

"Ye won't be needing that. Just ask me nicely."

She rolled her eyes heavenward, but the blush on her face confessed a different response.

"Come along." He grabbed her by the wrist. "Since ye're such an admirer of the blade, let me put it to another use."

He walked her deeper through the forest until they came to a vast open moor. His eyes continually scanned his surroundings until he found what he'd been looking for.

"Here we go. See this marshy area? This is peat. Get some of this, and it'll be fuel for yer fire." He pointed to a small overhang that faced the sun. "There. That part looks nice and dry. Slice off a portion from the outside. Not too deep, mind. The wet stuff won't do us any good."

"Won't that black muck get all over my shoes?"

He turned to her. "And yer point would be?"

Serena shrugged. "Just clarifying. How much would you like? A wee bit?"

"No. A fair bit."

She shook her head in exasperation.

"Keep away from that open bog to yer left. Get caught inside it and ye'll never come out."

Wonderful. She was in a wilderness, not another soul in sight, and even the terrain could kill her.

It was a woeful day for her boots. The muddy, black soil stuck to them, and she kept getting mired in the swampy marsh. It had a putrid, rotten odor to it, and she couldn't wait to leave this bog. She found the mound he'd indicated and carved off a dried portion. Once she had two brick-size pieces, she rejoined him. He had collected a couple of handfuls of thick green moss.

"Right. We're almost ready. Let's go find some kindling."

On the way back, he snapped off some dried twigs and collected them in his arms. When they reached the clearing, he assembled the fire, and they knelt at it.

"Here's what ye'll need to do, Serena. Rub this stick between yer hands like so. The faster ye rub it inside the notch on the wood below, the hotter it will become. When the wood below starts to smoke, place the birch bark on it. The bark will catch fire, and then ye can toss it onto the kindling. When that starts to go, put the peat on top of it. Understand?"

"I suppose," she said uncertainly, as she awkwardly rotated the stick between her palms. "And what, may I ask, will you be doing while I am rubbing calluses onto my hands?"

"I was planning to sit and relax with a cup of tea. But I thought it'd be better if I were to build us a shelter. All right?"

Serena grumbled, but resumed her rubbing.

At first, the only heat she felt was in her hands. But once she mastered the tricky skill of keeping the stick in place while it turned between her hands, smoke started to waft up from the notch. The more she rubbed, the thicker the plume became. Excitedly, she grabbed the birch shavings and put them into the notch. To her great surprise and joy, a flame licked up from the tinder.

"Look! Look!" she exclaimed, and excitedly threw the flaming bark onto the pile of dried twigs. In no time, the twigs caught fire. "Malcolm, I did it! I made fire!"

He came over and smiled down at her. "Ye've set me alight a time or two. Now I see ye can do it to wood as well."

She was elated at what she had accomplished. She looked down at the roaring fire and was immensely pleased with herself.

"Now," said Malcolm, "put the fish in between the sheaves of wet moss. This will keep it from charring when ye set it on the fire. And in about fifteen minutes, we'll set down to eat."

The salmon was exquisite.

Maybe it was Serena's hunger, or maybe it was the pride she had taken in building her own fire and cooking it herself. And the absence of mustard sauce or a glass of wine, or even one of her twenty-five dish sets, didn't matter in the slightest.

Malcolm had fashioned a shelter against a dried fallen tree by weaving together green branches and fir boughs, and he lined the inside with soft, dry moss.

"There ye are, milady. It's a wee bit rough, but it'll keep out the fierce wind and give ye a soft place to sleep."

Serena looked inside the crude shelter. "I can't sleep on grass, Malcolm," she protested apologetically. "If anything even vaguely resembling a spider shows itself . . ."

"Dinna fash yerself. If any of the little beasties should bite ye, I'm sure they'll expire from the venom in ye."

She waved away his friendly insult. "I'm sorry. I simply can't sleep out in nature."

He laughed roundly. "I don't know if ye've noticed, but at the moment, there's a lot of it about. 'Course, there is just one alternative."

"What is it?" she asked hopefully.

"Dinna sleep. I'm sure we can think of a way to while away the hours."

"Malcolm, I'm serious. If I even see a spider, I'll scream down these hills. Perhaps there's an inn not too far from here."

He sighed. "There are no inns for miles. But if ye like, I'll make ye a hammock with my fly plaid. Will that do?"

"My unending thanks." She watched him create a makeshift hammock with the black wool fabric, adjacent to the bed intended for her but about two feet off the ground. "In payment, how would you like a warm drink? I can boil some leaves of wild heather in the tin, and make us a nice cup of tea."

They sat around the fire, sipping the hot tea, which tasted quite delicious. As night fell, the winds blew back the blanket of clouds, revealing thousands of white stars. The only sounds were those of the leaves on the trees rattling in the wind and the crackle of the fire.

Silently, Serena watched him swallow the steaming liquid and lean his head back against a pine tree.

"They say you're a thief and a traitor. A man not to be trusted."

He opened his eyes and fixed them upon her. The flames reflected in what had become black eyes. "Who said that to ye?"

"Is it true?"

Malcolm shook his head and looked away. "Tell me something, Serena. Who do *ye* say I am?"

Serena leaned forward. "I say that you are someone much maligned, and unfairly so. I say that there is so much shame in you that you live in a suit of armor not to keep others out, but to keep yourself in. I say that you once had a compassionate heart, but it's been kicked about so much that it's callused over so it bleeds no longer. I think that that scar on your hand has compelled you to bury a lot of dreams. But equally I hope that whatever that scar may signify, it doesn't keep you from seeing the man you truly are."

A smile inched across his face. "My God. Now I understand the hold ye have over me." He reached out his scarred hand and placed it over hers.

She squeezed it and lifted it up, cradling it between her own. "Does it pain you?"

He shook his head. "I canna feel anything there. The scars have blotted out all feeling. I carry the pain . . . a little deeper."

"Who did this to you, Malcolm?"

He closed his eyes, and the furrow between his black eyebrows deepened. She sensed him going back in time to a place that he had visited many times by himself, but never with someone else.

"My own clansmen."

Serena's mouth fell open. "The Slayters?"

He exhaled. "Slayter isn't my real name. It's my label. My . . . title."

A cloud of confusion came over her. "Your title?"

"Aye." A note of sarcastic asperity pierced his voice. "I'm to be known forever as a *slaighteur*. It's Gaelic for 'knave.'"

"*Slaighteur*. So that's what the *S* stands for."

"Aye."

"What did you do to deserve that?"

Malcolm exhaled deeply. "I was born into a family of men that failed to present themselves in battle." He paused. "My father and my brothers didna stand with the clan, and the clan lost. For this, they should have been branded. But the clan was no' after justice. It was after revenge. They slaughtered my brothers, my father, and my mother, while the wee ones watched."

Serena had never heard anything so horrifying. "That's barbaric. Were the murderers caught?"

"Of course not. There is no justice in a place like this, Serena."

"We have British laws."

"But Highland ways. What law can exist here? The law of blood is all that is understood. Ye say it is barbaric, and so it is. At least I was thirteen. Almost a man. I could take it. But what sort of unrighteous justice would allow my young sisters and brother, three wee ones only this big, to be branded like so much cattle and taken as bondservants?"

Serena closed her eyes to the horror. "But why punish the little ones? Any of you? You were all innocent."

"To show the world that we came from a family of

cowards. Because children grow up, and they might take it into their heads to avenge themselves. So no self-respecting Scotsman would support a man with a brand like this one. Would ye help a criminal?"

Serena's voice dropped to a whisper. "And all this time I thought it was for something that you did."

He closed his eyes. "I don't deserve this for something I did. I deserve it for something I didn't do."

Her eyes snapped up to his face. He was staring at the *S* on the back of his hand. "They gave this to us for being cowards. Well, in my case, it's become well deserved, for so I am. I couldna prevent the wee ones from being hurt, but I'm the only one who escaped. I should have gone after them. I should have tried to find them. I should have scoured all of Scotland for a clue as to what became of them. But I didn't. I did nothing. I hid here, in the Highland wilderness. For almost a month, cowering in the fens and forests like a frightened rabbit. If it wasn't for that game hunter in the next village who found me, I'd probably be here still."

Serena raised herself to her knees. "Now you listen to me, Malcolm. You are not a coward. You were a little boy who *was* scared, and had every right to be. Even if you had been a man, armed with strength and wits, there was not much you could have done. Look at you now. Now you have the privilege of choice. You could have chosen not to protect me. You could have chosen not to go after my father. But instead you faced the danger. At great cost to yourself and with no promise of reward. I don't know what other people see when they see that brand. But to me, you are a hero."

He threaded his fingers in her hair. "Aye. And that's enough for me."

He leaned over and kissed her mouth. It was not just a kiss of affection; it was a profession of appreciation.

She returned it with equal fervor, pledging her indebtedness to him for showing her what a man's love ought to be, and then being that man for her. Until she'd loved him, she'd never loved enough.

Malcolm . . . a look from his emerald eyes could stop her heart, and his kiss could make it start again. She had been seasoning in her longing for him for weeks, and now the opportunity had arisen to indulge her desire. Here, with not another human soul for miles, was the chance to forget that she was Serena Marsh, the proper daughter of an English ambassador, and just let herself be a woman who desperately wanted to pleasure—and be pleasured by—the man she had come to love.

Her hand trailed down his chest. His body felt like a marble statue enrobed in warm velvet. The legs beneath the kilt were long and sculpted, and she yearned to see what was covered by the black wool garment. Her prior experience with a man had resolved the mystery of what such an organ looked like. But she couldn't help wondering what Malcolm looked like. He was such a large man otherwise. Was a man's manhood proportionate to his height?

Slowly, she let her hand descend to his thigh. What a muscle that was. His lap went on forever, firm and inviting. But it was inward her hand wanted to go. Suddenly she felt as men must, driven mad by desire to reach what was underneath a skirt. So easy to get to, and yet . . .

And then she felt it. His penis had raised the front of his kilt. Though she touched it only briefly, her question as to length was finally answered.

She tried not to, but she couldn't help smiling through their kiss. It gave away her bashful naughtiness.

Malcolm seized her by the waist and hauled her onto

his lap. "Come here, ya wee besom, if ye be wanting it so much. It wants to meet ye, too."

Serena shrieked. Now that she was in full contact with the object of her curiosity, she burst into giggles.

Malcolm laughed, too, a deep-throated rumble that thrummed against her body. "I love how yer big blue eyes disappear when ye smile," he said.

She placed a hand on his cheek, delighting in the emerging roughness. The firelight danced upon his masculine features, making him even more handsome. The crease in his cheeks deepened when he smiled thus, and his eyes acquired a warmth she had never seen before.

"I'm no' a man of tender words, Serena. I dinna know how to express m'self too well. But I want ye to know how much I love ye. And I'll always look after ye."

His breath was warm on her face, but it was the light behind his eyes that made her warm all over. If only time could stand still in this one moment . . .

But well she knew that life was made up of many moments, some just as memorable but wholly unpleasant. The last time a man told her he loved her, it was also a good moment. But the ones that followed were anything but. And though she knew that Malcolm truly loved her, lurking somewhere in her mind was a niggling doubt about his intentions. What if she gave herself to Malcolm, and then lost him because of it? What if all men were just like Ben, her Mistake, charming until they get a woman to give her most precious, intimate gifts, only to then walk away—in search, no less, of a woman who wouldn't be as promiscuous?

She couldn't bear it if Malcolm turned away from her for that. She would be angry with him for a short while, but she would hate herself for years to come. She couldn't go through that again. And though out here in the wilderness, no one would ever find out if they had made love, she would know it. And her mirror would give her no solace.

And God forbid she should emerge from their tryst with a belly. She was lucky enough to have escaped that humiliating fate with Ben. But that particular sort of luck runs out every month. And if there was one thing that Malcolm had taught her, it was that danger always struck when everything appeared safe.

His hand caressed that particular spot at the bend of her elbow, the spot that always disintegrated her resolve.

"Malcolm," she breathed before her strength gave out. "I love you, too. And I know you love me not just in words, but in actions. Tonight, I need you to show me how much you love me. By waiting."

He closed his eyes and let his forehead touch hers. She watched him as he talked his body down. Regret twisted her features for putting him through that again.

"Do you ken how difficult it is for me to keep m'hands off ye? It's getting harder and harder. No pun intended."

She chuckled nervously. "I'm sorry. I wish I could make love to you as well."

His hand tightened on her waist. "Tell me one thing. Are ye still comparing me to him?"

Her chest caved. She'd had no idea he could read her so. Her chin tucked into her chest. "In some ways, yes. We . . . made love . . . only the one time. Afterward, it was disastrous. But you should know, Malcolm, that there is no more 'him.' There is only you."

He nodded. He lifted her off his lap, stood up, and then lifted her onto the hammock made from his plaid. Once she was comfortably ensconced in the floating bed, he placed a kiss upon her lips.

"I wish to God I had been yer first. Because then ye

would have bonded with me, and not with some arse
who broke yer heart."

Her heart twisted inside her. As Malcolm lay down
on the moss-covered floor, she realized he was right.
She *had* bonded with Ben first. In her hurry to know
the pleasure that other women knew, she gave away the
beautiful opportunity to bond forever with Malcolm.
The regret returned, as strong and insistent as the day
Ben told her it was over.

As she curled up in the black woolen hammock, enveloping herself in Malcolm's woodsy smell, she valiantly kept from crying herself to sleep.

*The chirring of the nightjars roused Serena from sleep.
She opened her eyes to the diminishing fire, a weak
flame beneath a prison of charred twigs. Beside her,
Malcolm slept peacefully on the moss-covered ground.*

*She'd been to balls that boasted dancing, drinking,
and parlor games. She'd been to operas, galleries, and
the exalted houses of England. She'd had conversations with the most informed and erudite people in the
world. But none of those experiences even compared
to just watching Malcolm sleep.*

*She rolled herself off the hammock, falling sound-
lessly to the floor. Malcolm's deep slumber was undis-
turbed. His chest rose and fell evenly, his body
motionless.*

*She gazed into his face. Now that she had come
down off her high place and down to his level, she
could see him more clearly. Moonlight caressed one
side of his face and cast a blue glow on his raven's-wing
hair. His hooded brows cast his eyes into shadow, but
twin sets of eyelashes feathered down from the recess.*

The fire sparked and crackled to life. Serena sat

upon her haunches as she eyed Malcolm's body. His white shirt draped over his massive chest, outlining the divide down the middle and each of the hard lines that furrowed across his muscled abdomen. The shirt fell open at his throat, exposing a V of skin. His wide shoulders hung from a cobra hood of muscle at his neck.

Serena backed away on all fours, her loose mane spilling down the sides of her face, until she was kneeling at his feet. His long legs were relaxed, falling open slightly. Serena's gaze wended up the sturdy calves, the powerful thighs, and came to rest on the mound in between his slender hips.

Flames licked up from the gathering fire in response to the mounting hunger between Serena's legs. She let out a tense breath, reveling in the rising heat. She wedged herself between his legs and placed a hand on each of his knees.

Malcolm's eyes fluttered open, and he looked down at her. "Serena? What are ye—"

"Shh," she whispered, one finger at her lips. Slowly, she pushed back the fabric of his kilt, higher and higher up his tensing thighs, until she exposed the object of her desire.

In the intensifying orange light, Serena could see his sleeping cock lying over one thigh amid a black nest of hair. It was long and dark, sheathed in plaited skin all the way to the tip. Malcolm rose to his elbows, regarding her in curious excitement. She reached out a hand and covered it with her palm.

Malcolm's chest expanded with the unexpected touch, and so did his cock. Instantaneously, it shifted under her touch. She closed her eyes to the sensation, marveling at how the lifeless organ slowly thickened and hardened. She wrapped her inquisitive fingers around his rising manhood, defying gravity with each passing second. Beneath her hand, his furred sac, the softest skin she'd ever touched, tightened under his shaft.

Malcolm's breath came in rough gasps as her hand climbed higher on the veined pole. Between her legs, she could feel her own organ tightening, demanding connection with his rigid cock. Her chin jutted with the infusion of her sexual power over him. Behind her, the fire blazed, enveloping them both in consuming heat.

Malcolm was panting, begging for release from the gathering pressure in his loins. She would give him what he asked for.

She walked on all fours up his body until she was face-to-face with his passionate scowl. Her knees imprisoned his narrow waist, her breasts hanging decadently over his broad chest. He tried to kiss her but she pulled away. Serena was not now a creature to be coddled.

She pulled up her blue-printed muslin dress, a thing that now seemed completely foreign to her. Her sheath constricted within her, squeezing the slippery moistness from her folds. She lowered her hips, her opening seeking out the erect phallus beneath her. Just then, she found it, his tip kissing her nether mouth. Something feral awakened in her and she sank down upon him. But his girth was far too great for her slender channel, and she grimaced in pain. Involuntarily, she let out a cry as her body adapted itself to his size. The pain was fierce, tearing almost, but she endured it.

She opened up her eyes to find Malcolm gazing at her with passion and devotion. Then something happened inside her heart. Her desire and her care was for him. Her respect and her love was for him. She became for him alone.

In that moment, Serena bonded with Malcolm.

She let out a satisfied sigh. But her unmet need spurred her to action. She raised and thrust her hips, sliding his stiff cock in and out of her slick passage. The pain had diminished to a dull ache, but pleasure at her fullness quickly overcame any discomfort. Up and down, in and out, their bodies coupled in mutual pleasure. Malcolm writhed on the ground, his hands on her hips holding her to him. Her hands helped themselves to the feel of his chest and abdomen, her long hair caressing his neck. Serena rocked back and forth upon him, savoring the sensation that altering speeds and positions afforded her own gratification. The tiny bud between her folds was heated with the stimulation of their joining, and his enormous cock stretched her beyond herself.

Her moans began to signal her upcoming release. Serena bounced on top of him, hastening her nearing ecstasy. The wanton position, the heat from the fire, the wilderness around her, the animal lust, the bruising coupling—in a delirious, memorable moment, Serena exploded in a blaze of passion and contentment.

Serena gasped, opening her eyes. Her womanhood was still pulsating as she looked around in the pink-tinged dawn. Perspiration sheened on her face as she looked over her shoulder from the cocoon of Malcolm's fly plaid. There, on the ground, Malcolm lay sleeping.

She sighed in satisfaction as she relived the glorious dream, detail by delicious detail, still enveloped in the heady scent of his plaid. A wicked smile cut across her face as one day she vowed to make this particular dream come true.

TWENTY-NINE

In the morning, memories of Serena's wanton dream filled her every thought. Every word that Malcolm uttered seemed to have a double meaning. When he asked her to please put out the fire, she chuckled. When he asked her to give him a hand with something, she giggled. And when he complained how hard he slept, she laughed outright.

But her merriment was short-lived, coming to a halt the moment he offered to help her onto one of the horses.

"Bareback?" she exclaimed, aghast.

He steadied the horse against a fallen tree. "Certainly bareback. Can't ye ride?"

"Of course I can ride. But I use a sidesaddle, as propriety dictates."

"Well, *necessity* now dictates that ye not only ride without a sidesaddle, but also without a saddle. I'll use my fly plaid to put between ye and the beast."

"That is not the only consideration. My skirt will simply not allow me to spread my legs over the animal."

"I can fix that," he said, lifting her onto the fallen tree trunk. He pulled out his *sgian achlais* from the sheath strapped under his arm and began to cut a slit up the side of her skirt.

"What are you doing?" she exclaimed, but it was

already too late. He had sliced open the narrow skirt from ankle to hip.

Malcolm stood back and eyed his handiwork, resheathing his knife. "Hmm," he began with a wicked grin. "I like the look of it even more."

She pinned her fists to her hips. "I wouldn't hang up your couturier's shingle yet if I were you. Just look at me!" It was surely a grievous sin to mutilate such a beautiful garment. But her modesty objected to the exposed stockinged leg that protruded from the slit. "I can't go riding into Cannich like this, like some version of Lady Godiva."

Malcolm chuckled. "I doubt that the men in Cannich will have the decency to avert their eyes when they see ye coming. Come on, then. Up ye get."

He helped her seat the horse, which was no easy feat without stirrups or pommel. The horse blustered and tossed back its head. She felt completely insecure, as if she was about to slide off at any moment.

"Now, just relax. Don't squeeze the horse with yer legs, or he'll think ye want him to go faster. Just move with the horse. We'll go at a slow pace. If ye feel like ye're slipping, grab the horse's mane to steady yerself, not the reins. And dinna fret. I'll be right next to ye the whole time."

It was just about midday when they arrived at their destination. Cannich was a small village nestled in the valley at the foot of the Cairngorms. It was green but largely deserted, except for a pub, a church, a smattering of cottages—and Ronan McLeish.

McLeish was a great bear of a man, with an explosion of curly brown hair and a beard as thick as a fox's tail. His house was as far removed from the village center as it could be, shouldered by thick forests and scattered with chickens, goats, and a passel of children.

He greeted Malcolm with a large, booming voice and a noisy embrace.

"Jesus, Mary, and Joseph! Look at what the road vomited on my doorstep!"

Malcolm's feet left the ground as McLeish lifted him in the air. "And ye're a sight from best-forgotten days. I can't think of yer face without seeing prison bars in front of it."

His large belly jiggled up and down with his guttural laugh. "And who's this sweet ye brought for my dessert?"

Malcolm put his hand on her shoulder. "Serena Marsh, this is Ronan McLeish, the most slippery fugitive I've ever had the displeasure of pursuing."

"What a comely lass. Come in, come in. Meet my wife. Una!" His voice trumpeted across the rustic house.

A full-bosomed woman came down the stairs with a rosy-headed child on her hip. She was thick-necked and tough looking, but the dusting of freckles on the apples of her cheeks and her smooth ginger hair gave her a youthful, friendly quality.

"I want ye to meet Malcolm Slayter, the man I told ye aboot."

She smiled at him, crescents of cheek forming under her blue eyes. "Welcome to oor home, Mr. Slayter."

"And he's brought this beautiful young thing that he intends to share with his host."

"Wheesht now, ye peppery auld sod." She clouted him on the arm. "Where are yer manners? He isna always a boorish lout, my dear. Only on days that end in *day*."

Serena smiled. "You'll have to forgive the state I'm in," she said, clutching the panels of her skirt together. "I'm afraid Malcolm has taken up elementary dressmaking."

Una blinked. "Ye're English?"

Serena glanced uncertainly at Malcolm before returning her attention to Una. "I hope that's all right."

"O' course, o' course. It's just that we don't see many English up oor way unless—" Now it was Una's turn to look uncomfortably at her husband. "It's a verra pretty frock."

Serena shrugged nervously. "Just something I threw on."

McLeish stroked his beard. "I should throw it off again."

"McLeish!" cried his wife in mock despair. "Ye'll get yer head in yer hands to play with!"

"I only meant that ye should offer her somethin' to change into, ma dear heart." As soon as Una looked away, he turned to Malcolm and shook his head. He meant what he had said.

Una nodded suspiciously. "Ye'll have to overlook ma husband's randy mooth, Miss Marsh. He's as harmless as a dead bee. Come along. I'll show ye where ye kin freshen up from yer journey."

"Noo then. Ye come wi' me, Malcolm Slayter," said McLeish. "I'm sure I kin find a dram of whiskey for us to share."

"So long as ye don't tell me where ye got it from." Malcolm pulled up a chair at the long kitchen table. Una seemed to have been plucking a chicken for white feathers billowed across the wooden tabletop.

"So," he began, pouring the amber liquid into two small glasses. "Where did ye find that English filly?"

Malcolm gave a sidewise smile. "She's my current job. I'm her *seastnán*."

McLeish's bushy eyebrows knit together. "Why would

she need one? Who would want to hurt a pretty thing like her?"

"There are wicked people about. As well ye know."

"Aye, I do. So . . ." A naughty gleam illuminated McLeish's eyes. "Have ye plowed that field yet? Eh? Shaped the passage to yer measure?" McLeish jabbed an elbow into Malcolm's side.

For the first time in all the years since he'd been a boy, Malcolm blushed. "Not yet."

"Come on, man! Dinna spare the details. I saw how ye ripped open her dress. Give me a little image to rest ma head on. Una's fair boilin' at me for no' fixing the roof, and she won't let me in oor bed. D'ye knoo how desperate I am? Ye know me—I live for only two things. A pail full of ale—"

"—and lasses with fine asses. I remember." Malcolm laughed, and then his face sobered. "McLeish, I'm after ye on another matter. A matter I hope ye can aim some light on. There's been angry words against the English. I hear tell about war for independence. And to draw first blood, someone's taken the English ambassador hostage."

"Aye. I heard the whisperings."

"Do ye also know who took him?"

McLeish nodded. "Some Sassenach expatriate named Neville. Bad seed, even among us colorful folk. A real brutal sort. No honor in him."

"Who hired him?"

"I hear tell it's the McCullough. The son of Duncan McCullough."

"The one they call Brandubh?"

"That's the one."

"Where have they taken him?"

McLeish leaned back in his chair. "What is this

aboot? Why all the interest in the McCullough? And what's the connection with the Sassenach lass?"

Malcolm leaned his elbows on the table. "I know ye're not in the game anymore. And I don't want to put ye in harm's way. Let's just say ye don't need to know what ye don't need to know."

"Dammit, Malcolm. If ye're asking me to put ma family's life in danger, then give me the truth of the matter."

Malcolm thought quickly. A partial truth was better than none. "I'm no' after the McCullough. I just want to get the ambassador back."

"Why?"

"I don't care about the politics. War, no war . . . it matters not to me. I want to rescue the man . . . for the sake of his daughter." Malcolm's head jerked in the direction Serena was taken.

Illumination dawned on McLeish's florid face. "I see. So ye're willing to go and take back the McCullough's own hostage because of this girl."

Malcolm nodded.

"Ye're more than just her *seastnán* then."

Malcolm nodded.

McLeish shook his head. "I feel sorry for ye, Malcolm. Women make us do strange things. Raise chickens, fix roofs. Risk our lives by challenging the most powerful chief in the whole of the Highlands."

"Will ye help me?" Malcolm asked.

McLeish shook his head. "No. Ye were a pain in my arse for years. But I don't want to see ye killed, either."

Malcolm's eyes took on a fierceness. "Leave that to me. Just tell me where they've hidden him."

"Sorry, my auld friend. I've done a lot of my work in the dark, and I've been called a good many things. But I'm no *slaighteur*. This here is McCullough land now.

And though I don't belong to the McCullough, I've a family to look after. I want to help ye, if for nothing other than good times' sake. But not at the expense of my family." McLeish stood up, placed a conciliatory hand on Malcolm's shoulder, and walked out of the kitchen.

Malcolm's heart sank. Without McLeish's direction, they would be going into this blind. It would take weeks—months even—to track down where McCullough could have taken the ambassador. And given the current political climate, there was very little chance that the ambassador would be found alive.

"I simply can't take this," said Serena, smoothing out the dress Una had given her to wear. "It's yours."

"Och. The last time I wore it, I had nineteen summers. Before the children came. Ma waist will ne'er be this tiny again. Nor ma teats."

Serena blushed. "But surely you'd like to leave it for your daughters."

"The only daughter bairn to me died at two, may she rest in peace. And the seven boys willna be wantin' it. Besides, I was wearing it when Ronan and I were handfasted. 'Twould be a shame to cut it up and use it for somethin' else."

Serena smoothed out the striped skirt in white and green. Though the waist was lower than the fashion currently dictated, she had to admit that it was much more comfortable having a belt cinch at her natural waist than at her rib cage. And the full skirt allowed for ease of movement. The white camisole had yellowed somewhat, but it was still beautiful. And though the brown jacket was less ornate than any of her spencers, it fit her perfectly.

She gazed at her reflection in the windowpanes. She

hardly recognized herself. Who would think that the woman in the glass was London's celebrated sophisticate, the chronicler of balls and parties, the paradigm of fashion and Society? She smiled at the image she now presented.

But it suddenly occurred to her that her opinion alone was not enough. "Do you mind if I show Malcolm?"

"'Course not. And if he doesna like it, I've a cast-iron skillet ye can use to convince him that he does."

She went downstairs with Una close behind. She found Malcolm sitting at the kitchen table.

"How do I look?"

Malcolm turned around and got up out of his chair. He looked her up and down. And smiled such a great big smile that it took her breath away.

"That's my girl," he said, his chest swelling with pride.

Una came up behind her. "Doesn't she look a picture?"

"Aye. That she does."

Serena bit her smile. His approval made her feel giddy. She had always dressed up to impress, but now it seemed it was her state of *undress* that impressed him the most.

Una stuck her head out the window and yelled something at the children playing in the forest behind the house. She then turned to Serena. "Do me a blissin', Serena. Can ye bring the little ones in to dinner? I'm just about to bring the pot to the table."

"Certainly." Serena walked out the front door.

Malcolm leaned his hands onto the windowsill, watching her walk between the trees.

Una put the plates on the dinner table. "She's an amiable one, that one. Pretty, too."

"Aye," he said, his gaze riveted to Serena. His lips began to move, silently, mouthing inaudible words.

Una watched him for a few moments. "What are ye doing?"

He gave her a sidewise glance before looking out of the window again. "Praying."

"Aye. These be troubled times. Are ye praying that nothing happens to ye?"

Malcolm straightened. "No. I'm praying that if something should happen to me, He'll take care of Serena."

Laughter cracked across the kitchen table again. Serena had never seen so much cheerfulness before. Though eleven people crowded around the wooden table, and a pot of chicken soup was all that was to be served, not a bite was taken without a joke or a humorous gibe to gladden their hearts.

Whereas the English spoke in quiet whispers, the Scots had bold voices. No Scottish mother ever shushed an ebullient child, it seemed, and certainly not Una. The parents and their boys, who ranged in age from two to eighteen, spoke in brash, loud voices among themselves. Their accent and dialogue were hard for Serena to comprehend, and she desperately wanted to. She half wished there was a libretto, like at the opera, to follow their conversation along.

Malcolm lifted the pitcher. "Will ye have another drop o' ale, Una?"

McLeish positioned his glass under it. "Don't mind if I do."

"I was talking to yer wife," he responded.

"She doesn't mind if I do, either."

The boys laughed.

Una shook her head. "Och, Ronan! Ye must have been bairn on Wednesday 'cause ye're always in the middle! Haven't ye had enough?"

"I dunno. What time is it? I've only been drinking since . . . 1798." His openmouthed guffaws infected everyone at the table.

Malcolm filled Una's glass.

"Thank ye, Malcolm. This sets me to rememberin'. When I was a wee lass—"

McLeish whispered behind his hand to Serena. "That was a while ago."

"—my father told me—"

"Not to marry me, probably," he whispered.

"—that a man without a woman is no man."

"In that case," responded McLeish, "I must be a real hell of a man, because I've landed myself a hellion of a woman."

Malcolm tossed McLeish a piece of bread. "A real man doesn't go around calling himself a real man."

"He does if he has the ballocks to prove it! What do ye say, lass?"

A wicked smile cut across Serena's face. "Oh, I never judge a man by the size of his . . . caber."

"That's right," said Malcolm. "Size doesn't matter."

"Spoken like a true deficient," quipped McLeish, sparking an outburst of laughter. "Ha! Hang on, lasses. It's about to get wild now."

Malcolm smiled at Serena. "That's what he said to his wife twenty years ago, and she's still waiting." Amid the laughs, Malcolm downed his ale and stood up.

"Well, I'm afraid Serena and I must be on our way."

Serena took her cue and stood, too. "Thank you all for an enjoyable meal. And for the beautiful dress, Una. I shall treasure it always." She gave Una a firm hug.

McLeish tapped his eldest boy on the shoulder and told him to fetch the horses Malcolm and Serena rode in on. "Come, Malcolm. I'll see ye oot."

McLeish took Malcolm aside. "Look, I've never

been one for doing the right thing, as ye well knoo. But I didn't want my sons to follow the life I led. One McLeish on the game was enough."

Malcolm grinned and nodded.

"But," McLeish continued, "I don't want English troops quartered in my home or burning me off my property. I don't trust them Sassenach soldiers, and God help them if any one of those devils lays a hand on my Una. What I mean to say is that if that ambassador fella that McCullough's got is able to stop a war, then I'll tell ye what I knoo."

Malcolm's eyes widened, his jaw jutting firmly. "Go on."

McLeish gave a quick glance over his shoulder. "Mc-Cullough is organizing his troops at Ramh Droighionn Castle. He's got himself at least a thousand men there, Scots and Irish, plus several more divisions stationed throughout the Highlands. They're armed to the teeth—muskets, pistols, broadswords. I dinna knoo where Mc-Cullough got the weapons, but I heard tell that he vowed that his soldiers would not be outgunned like the Jacobites were at Culloden Moor. But Ramh Droighionn is where the McCullough is headquartered. If yer lass's da is imprisoned anywhere, it'll surely be there."

Malcolm's chest fanned. "How far is Ramh Droighionn?"

"Aboot fifteen mile north of here. In Ross-shire."

"Thank you, McLeish. Ye're a decent sort."

"Sort of what?" McLeish guffawed. "Och. I may be a stupid man, as my parents often told me, but even I knoo there's no such thing as a good war. Or a bad peace."

THIRTY

Swathed in an ill-fitting black kilt, Earlington was escorted from the dungeon by the bearded man and two burly guards.

The McCullough. He wondered who it was he was about to be presented to. Was it Duncan McCullough, the man who at last report was on his deathbed? Was it another named successor? Or was it, he shuddered to contemplate it, Brandubh McCullough?

Brandubh. His name in Gaelic meant "black raven." And how apt it was. He now realized, after so many broken dialogues between them, that Brandubh was a scavenger by nature. He'd been known to pick over the carcasses of weaker politicians, putting on their mantle of power. An exceedingly intelligent man, he had the mental acuity of any great leader or hero—except that he used his faculties for personal gain rather than for collective prosperity. And if he assumed power, there was no telling how much damage he could do to his country.

Earlington was taken to the castle's long dining hall. Hanging from the ceiling were a dozen colorful but dusty banners bearing coats of arms, presumably of the families who had fought for the McCulloughs. There was a relief plaster frieze running across one wall depicting a continuous line of Roman soldiers on horseback. Along the opposite wall, weapons of antiquity were hung on display.

He was escorted down the length of the hall, which was filled with kilted men, most of them armed. The majority were men his age, a sea of white hair and gray resembling dirty snow. But he also saw boys no older than twenty, their youthful heads topped by the earthy shades of red, orange, brown and all the mixtures therein. The men's enmity toward Earlington was palpable. There had been so much fighting between their respective countries in the last few decades that they didn't want him to be in the same country as them, let alone the same room.

At the far end of the hall, there was a man seated atop a dais, surrounded by a retinue of Scotsmen who were speaking to him. Earlington felt as if he was back at Carlton House, being granted an audience by the Prince Regent. As he approached, the features on the face of the seated man became clear. There was Brandubh, looking for all the world like a king on a throne.

"Commissioner!" Brandubh's face lit up like a tiger that had spotted a wounded fawn. "Welcome to Ramh Droighionn Castle. I hope ye're being treated well."

Earlington had only been given one meal each day he was here—a slice of hard bread and a thin brown soup made from beef drippings. "As well as can be hoped for in a house of mourning. Your father must have passed away, for in his place you sit."

"Aye. He was frail and sickly. Men of a certain age should never be allowed to remain in positions of command, for their leadership will reflect their own weakness. Isn't that right, Commissioner?"

A ripple of laughter went out from the men surrounding the throne.

The barb grazed him, but Earlington ignored it. "My condolences on your loss."

"Thank you. 'Tis considerate of ye to wear black."

The advisers around him laughed again.

"I brought ye here so that ye may hear what yer regent has to say to his Scottish subjects." A man next to him handed him a parchment scroll, which he unfurled and read aloud. "From His Royal Highness the Prince of Wales, Regent of the United Kingdom of Great Britain and Ireland, in the name and on behalf of His Majesty, a proclamation. Whereas His Royal Highness has been made aware of and seeks to suppress unlawful insurrections fomenting in the counties of Caithness, Sutherland, Ross-shire, Cromartyshire, and Invernessshire, to the utter destruction of the public peace, be it enacted that henceforth, all persons who are found in these areas must surrender their arms and weapons, and any persons unwilling to do so are to be arrested and transported to England for trial. Be it enacted that persons who assemble for the purposes of planning or implementing a rebellion will be charged with treason against His Royal Highness's grace, and if convicted, will suffer execution. Be it enacted also that for better regulating the governance of Scotland, the present council is to be immediately disbanded. All members of the governing body in Scotland must prove themselves to be true and faithful subjects to the kingdom by swearing allegiance to His Highness's grace, and paying a fealty of one-quarter of their holdings to the Royal Treasury, the sum of which will be used for the betterment of his loyal subjects in Scotland. Royal Army regiments will be dispatched to enforce compliance with these measures."

Brandubh rolled up the parchment. "Tell me, Commissioner, what say ye to this?"

Earlington was nonplussed. "His Majesty wishes an end to the strife that has been caused here. How do you see it?"

"I see it as a tactic to humiliate, impoverish, and weaken the Scottish people. The troops quartered in Perthshire have confronted ordinary citizens and ordered them to surrender not pistols or swords, but pitchforks, scythes, and hammers. I have learned reports of old men asked to surrender their walking sticks. According to this edict, Commissioner, anything can be used as a weapon. I shouldn't wonder if it next be asked of a Scotsman to surrender his cock."

The comment drew chortles from the assembly.

"I know mine will be," chimed in one man. "Long as a broadsword, and just as hard."

"That's not what his wife says," said another, and the room erupted with laughter.

Earlington interrupted their raucousness. "May I remind you, McCullough, that it was your hue and cry that rallied the rebels in the first place."

"Rebels?" Brandubh shook his head. "We're not rebels, Commissioner. We're patriots."

"Not in the eyes of the law."

"And who wrote that law? A king . . . or a tyrant? History will tell whether he be noble or abusive. And so will it me."

"Men of violence can never be called noble. You oppose the king to the detriment of all your people. Think before you set these people alight."

"Not I, Commissioner. Their own unhappiness spurs them to their flammable tempers. Ask them yerself. Go on. See if ye can sway them from the cause."

It was a taunt, but Earlington was willing to take up the challenge. He turned to face the crowd. "Men of Scotland, listen to me. These speeches—this assembly—is treasonous. The king will not abide the insult to his majesty. England will oppose you in force, and you—shall—be—put—down."

The crowd jeered at him, shouting epithets and insults.

He continued. "I know that we are in the midst of a situation that is boiling with political hatreds. But defiance will not bring about the resolution you seek. Let me negotiate a peace between us. Even now, there are regiments at Fort William ready to march on Inverness. Some of you have no experience of soldiering. Tell me then . . . will you have another Culloden? Or another Glenshiel? Will you not prefer peace?"

Several men answered him at once.

"To stand against tyranny is to face death!"

"We would rather fall dead one across another than surrender!"

"We are Highlanders after all. If we die, we die as heroes!"

Earlington turned to the man who answered him last. "No. You will die as traitors. And history will remember you as such—if it remembers you at all. A dead man cannot testify to his motives. And if you are killed, who will care for your wives, your children? Here, now, the lines are being drawn. Question your own loyalties. Will you be on the side of the law? Or will you betray the trust our king reposes in you?"

A young man interrupted him. "Ha! Ye would have Scotland be called North England! We will not have it! Look at the French and the Americans. They fought for greater participation in their ruling class . . . and won. We will do the same!"

Earlington turned to the man who spoke, a mere boy in comparison with the rest of the assemblage. "But at what cost? The Americans lost twenty-five thousand lives, and the French lost a hundred and seventy thousand. There aren't that many people in the whole of the Highlands. Gentlemen, no one questions the courage of your convictions. But there is a right way to move the hand of government, and a wrong way. Use your power not to fight with your adversary, but to reason with him.

"I have great power. A word from me will bring all the military might of the Crown of England, or a different word can allay the anger of the monarch. You, too, have great power. You have the power of choice, and it is a great and awesome thing. Submit, and you will receive the gracious pardon of His Royal Highness for this insurrection. Rebel, and there will be loss of life and deprivations such as you cannot imagine. Think carefully what you will do, for your decisions will be lived by you, your families, and your countrymen for generations to come. Now is the time, gentlemen. Will you lay down your arms?"

There was silence throughout the room. Earlington looked from face to face in that hall. A spirit of patriotism was battling with one of peace, of loyalty warring with fear of reprisal. One of them had to emerge the winner.

A shout came from a man in the center of the assemblage, like the first arrow released in a battle. "A free Scotland!"

A roar of assent exploded from the others.

"We will not submit!"

"War, not words!"

"Let's rid ourselves of the English contagion."

Earlington's shoulders drooped, and his head sank. He had never felt a defeat so keenly.

Brandubh McCullough leaned back in his chair, a smug look on his face as he tried to speak above the hurrahs. "Ye see, Commissioner, we speak with a single voice. Scotland *will* be an independent nation."

Earlington looked at him through slitted eyes. "You make a very costly mistake, McCullough. You will never be king."

Surprise passed over his face, but his arrogance overtook it. "Why not? These same people will carry me to the throne."

"No, Brandubh. After this conflict is over, there will be no one left for you to govern."

Brandubh's nostrils flared. "My father had the audacity to speak those same words to me. He expelled his last breath shortly after." His words were pregnant with meaning, and Earlington suspected there was more to Duncan McCullough's death than most people knew.

Brandubh stood. "Friends. Our hands are at our swords. The English think themselves gods, but they are not. In our presence, with our swords at their necks, they will realize they are naught but men."

A man called out from the rabble. "The Commissioner's a *slaighteur*! Brand him!"

Brandubh held his hands out. "No. He is not for branding. The Commissioner will serve another function. We will send his head to the Prince Regent. Let him see the strength of our resolve." He turned to Earlington. "Let them both see."

Malcolm and Serena reached Ramh Droighionn by nightfall. The town at the foot of the hill was bubbling with activity as women tugged small children on their way home from the baker or the butcher.

Malcolm alighted from his horse at a corner pub. The wooden sign swinging in the wind above the door read KING'S ARMS, but someone had scrawled the word SCOTTISH above the emblem. Its wooden door was propped open to let in a breeze.

He helped Serena slide from the horse, but held her fast. He whispered in her ear. "Ye're dressed like a Highland woman, but don't open yer mouth. Do ye understand? No one must know ye're English."

Serena nodded fearfully. Una had also given her an arisaid, and Serena now draped the length of wool fabric over her head to help obscure her features.

Together they walked into the pub, a cramped establishment with three odd tables and a scattering of mismatched chairs. The wood paneling looked as if it had been replaced in sections throughout the years without any regard to matching it to the original woodwork. The smell of stale liquor wet the air.

Malcolm stepped up to the man behind the bar and spoke to him in Gaelic. "Evening."

The pub keeper was a slender man crowned with white hair and weathered skin that sagged around his face. "It be a mighty warm one. What can I get for ye?"

"The missus and I would like a room. Have ye got one?"

"Aye. There be one behind the bar. It isn't much, just a place we put the ones too drunk to negotiate their carriage home. One shilling."

"We'll take it. Is anyone around to stable our horses?"

"Sorry, got no stable hands. Can't offer you warm food, either. All we have is bread and cheese."

"Why so bare?"

The man shrugged. "All the food we be making in the kitchen is for them up at the castle."

"Why?"

"Don't ye know? From where do ye hail?"

"Up Cromarty way. We're traveling down to Dumfries. The wife wants to be with her family when she gives birth."

The old man looked Serena up and down. "Hmm. Congratulations to ye." Without a shred of emotion, he turned back to Malcolm, and leaned an elbow onto the bar. "Listen, friend. If I were ye, I'd ride straight down to Dumfries. It's a troubled climate here. There's bound to be a war soon, and our chief is organizing for when the English attack. All able-bodied men have been taken to the castle and given a weapon. They've taken my stable lad, my cook—even my son, who's nearly forty but whose mind is like a child's. And if ye're not careful, they might even call *ye* up to fight alongside them. I'll give ye a room, but a word to the wise—set out as soon as ye can."

As soon as the pub keeper spoke, Malcolm heard a commotion outside. He darted out onto the cobbled street, and saw a lone horse and rider galloping up the high street.

"Make way! Make way!" the rider shouted as his horse's hooves clattered on the ancient stones. He was headed straight for the path that led up to Ramh Droighionn Castle.

Malcolm's instincts leapt into heightened awareness. A messenger on horseback at full gallop bound for the clan chief . . . this did not bode well.

They hid their horses in a thicket at the foot of the hill far removed from the road up to Ramh Droighionn Castle.

"We go on foot from here," said Malcolm. "From now on, we must rely on stealth."

Serena adjusted the dark arisaid around her to cover as much of her light-colored dress as she could.

"Well done," Malcolm said. He pulled out a pistol from the waistband of his kilt and handed it to her. "Ye may have need of this. Have ye ever used one before?"

She shook her head as she turned the weapon over in her hand.

"Do ye know how to shoot?"

"No, but many is the time I've wished I had one of these to shoot you with."

A grin appeared on his face. "Funny enough, the same thought had occurred to me." He took the gun from her and modeled a stance for her. "Ye shoot like this. The trigger is very stiff, and it requires a lot of strength to squeeze. Ye may have to use both hands to pull back on it. Like this." He showed her how to do it. "Ye only have one pistol ball, so shoot only if ye have to, and only if ye have a reasonable expectation of putting yer man down."

Putting her man down. It was a sobering thought. All of a sudden she realized what the implement of wood and metal in her hand was capable of. Malcolm must have sensed her apprehension, for he put his hands on her shoulders.

"If it comes down to yer life or another's, shoot to kill. Do ye understand?"

Numbly, she nodded. That made it worse. It wasn't the weapon that would *put her man down*. It was she herself who would be doing it.

"Stay low and out of sight," he added. "Remember, nothing can happen to ye if ye're invisible. Use the bushes to hide behind. And if anything should happen to me, don't stay here. Make yer way back to Lord Askey's home in Fort Augustus. All right?"

"Yes," she lied. She was not about to leave Malcolm behind, even at his own insistence.

They crept up toward the castle on the forest side,

hidden from sight by the undergrowth. It slowed their steps, but they were able to approach undetected. Malcolm's footsteps made no noise, even to Serena, who was only a few feet behind. He was clever enough to step only on earth or moss, avoiding the fallen leaves that crunched under Serena's feet. Despite her pervasive fear of spiders, Serena gave them only a cursory thought. She was consumed with the hope that her father was just beyond the thick gray stone walls, and with the fear of anything happening to either of the two men dearest to her in the whole world.

Malcolm halted in mid-stride, tensing. Some sound pricked his ears, and he stilled to hear it. Serena's heart raced in her chest. Suddenly she heard it, too. It sounded like distant thunder, low in the sky, but it grew louder and stronger, until she felt it vibrate the ground underneath her feet.

"The soldiers are on the move," he said. "They're marching out."

Serena gripped his arm. "What if they take Father with them?"

His jaw tensed. "Come on. We've got to get a look."

They left the safety of the woods and ran to the stone dyke that ran along the far end of the adjacent sheep pasture. Crawling along behind the low wall, they reached a good vantage point. From here, they could get a better look at what was happening at the door of the castle.

Ramh Droighionn Castle was a fortress built about five hundred years earlier. It comprised a high square keep surrounded by thick walls, which encased a courtyard in the center.

From the portcullis emerged a line of armed soldiers four men thick, who followed in formation behind a cavalry of regimental leaders. On and on the line continued, hundreds and hundreds of men marching off to war. The infantry held lit torches in the air, making it appear as if the castle was spewing fire from its fanged mouth. It was a terrifying sight.

"It's hard to tell if the ambassador is with them. I have to find out for certain if he is still inside." She made a move to follow him, but he halted her. "No. Ye stay here. No one will see ye behind this dyke."

"I want to—"

"If I'm no' back in fifteen minutes, find yer way back to the horses and return to Fort Augustus. Is that clear?"

She was a jangle of emotions. She wanted her father back, but she didn't want Malcolm to go. Her entire relationship with Malcolm flashed through her mind in an instant. At what point had she stopped being afraid *of* him and started being afraid *for* him?

Her eyebrows tented in worry. "Be careful."

He placed a reassuring kiss on her mouth. "Tell that to whoever stands against me."

She watched him run silently across the meadow. He jumped over the stone dyke on the far end, and then he disappeared.

The seconds slowed to a crawl, and the minutes dragged by. Serena's eyes watered as she scanned the sight of the forbidding castle for a sign of her beloved. Her anxiety made her lose all sense of time. Malcolm could have been gone only a moment, or the unending moments could have swallowed him up entirely.

A shadow shifted in the distance, and she saw a man's body being dumped over the stone dyke into the sheep pasture. It landed with a thud on the ground and lay lifeless. Malcolm! Her heart was ready to beat its last. And then she saw a man jump over the dyke and run straight toward her.

The moon was nowhere to be found, but she would recognize him even in utter darkness. "Malcolm!" She threw her arms around him and squeezed. "Thank God you're all right."

"Yer father's inside," he panted. "He's alive. They're keeping him in one of the dungeon cells."

"Oh!" she breathed, joy fanning into her chest.

"I also found out that the British have marched on Inverness. McCullough's gone to engage them in battle."

"Can we go get my father now? Is it safe?"

Malcolm shook his head. "The castle has reinforcements. McCullough has kept reserves."

"How many?"

"About a hundred."

"A hundred men? How are we going to get my father out?"

"I'll figure out a way. Ye stay here."

"The hell I will!" Serena's curse word surprised even herself. "I'm not going to be left behind again. *We* will get my father out."

"I can't allow it. If anything should happen to ye—"

"Malcolm," she said forcefully. "You are here because I need you. But I can't let you go in there alone. Now you need me."

She watched his face transform as he carefully weighed her proposal. "All right. But do only as I say."

She raised her pistol and cocked it. "As long as you say it nicely."

They ran across the meadow. Serena saw a lad lying unconscious on the ground with his hands bound behind him and a cloth in his mouth. A few sheets of paper danced in the wind beside him. "Who on earth is that?"

He waved away her question. "Just the obliging page who told me what I needed to know. Don't worry about him. When he wakes up, he'll have a hell of a headache, but he'll be fine."

They stole through the raised portcullis and darted behind an unhitched wagon situated just inside the courtyard. A wheel, broken in half, leaned against the crippled carriage. The oil lamps hanging from the walls around the keep cast a yellow glow on the enclosure. A couple of lads—pages, she assumed—were glumly walking around picking up rubbish and other debris after the regiments marched off.

"Dougal," one of them called out, but got no answer. "Dougal!"

Serena's heart started pounding. He was no doubt calling the unconscious boy from whom Malcolm had extracted information.

The ginger-haired lad came right toward them. "Dougal, if ye're hiding behind the carriage so ye can draw yer dirty pictures again, I'll tell the captain in the dining hall. He'll give ye what for."

Malcolm picked up a bone from the ground and tossed it through the portcullis. The thud distracted the boy, who walked outside calling his friend.

Soundlessly, Malcolm grabbed Serena by the wrist and pulled her out from behind the wagon. They ran to the shadowed crevice behind one of the smaller baileys.

Just then, an armed soldier walked past them. Malcolm darted his head out to follow the man's movements. He went through the courtyard and stood his post, guarding the entryway. Malcolm ground his teeth.

"The boy told me that the dungeon lies through that arched door in the keep," he whispered. "We're going to run for it." Malcolm waited for the sentry to turn his head. "Now!"

Malcolm held Serena by the hand as they ran headlong toward the opening in the keep. They were confronted by stairs going up, and another set going down. Malcolm took the downward stairs, hugging the cold stone wall as he tread silently. Serena could feel a dark sense of foreboding as she descended to what she knew was a dungeon. If they were caught down here, they'd be surely trapped with no other way out.

The stairs yawned onto a room, a shaft of light glowing on the ancient stone walls. Malcolm stole a quick look within and saw two men sitting upon stools in the vestibule to the dungeon. Behind them was a thick metal gate. The opening to the prison cells.

He turned to her and made a gesture to stay still. He pulled his *sgian dubh* from his sporran and ran to the bigger of the two guards. He plunged the six-inch blade into the man's thigh, and the man screamed. Malcolm pulled the *sgian achlais* from under his arm and brandished it at the other man, but the guard was ready for him. He swung his sword at Malcolm's dagger, knocking the weapon from his hand. Malcolm swung a fist at the guard's face and jumped on him to wrestle the sword from his grasp. With his free hand, the guard punched Malcolm in the ribs, making him curl sideways. Still, Malcolm refused to let go of the guard's sword fist. A taller man than the guard, Malcolm pushed him backward and wedged him against the stone wall. Malcolm succeeded in wresting the sword from his hand, but he left himself vulnerable to the meaty fist that came swinging at him. Disoriented, Malcolm stumbled backward and the man got in another blow to his face. He swung again, getting Malcolm in the abdomen. Malcolm collapsed to the floor. The man came at him, and when he bent to lay hands on Malcolm's back, Malcolm grabbed hold of the man's ankle and yanked on it, sending him sprawling to the floor. Malcolm fell upon him and began to rain blows on the man's head.

The other guard finally succeeded in extracting the dagger from his bleeding thigh. Just as Malcolm's opponent finally lost consciousness, the stabbed guard lifted the bloody knife high and staggered toward Malcolm's unprotected back.

Serena stepped in the path of the armed man and pointed the muzzle straight at his face. "Touch him and you die."

The man's already pained features contorted into one of shock at seeing not only a second assailant, but a woman, no less, with a gun. Slowly, he lowered the bloody knife.

"Drop it," she said.

The man hesitated.

Serena took a step toward him, her determined scowl blackening. "You've already got one hole too many in your body. How would you like another?"

The man opened his fingers, and the dagger clanged on the stone floor.

Malcolm stood behind her and took the gun from her steady hand. He aimed the pistol at the guard. "Open the gate."

The guard raised his bloodied hands. "I can't."

"Now!" Malcolm yelled, his scream echoing through the chamber.

The man quaked. "I haven't got the key."

"Where is it?"

A voice came from beyond the barred gate. "I have it."

Malcolm and Serena turned to look. It was an old man with a white beard that reached halfway down his bony chest. Several large iron keys dangled from a ring in his hand.

The guard chuckled. "What are ye going to do, now, eh? Key's inside. Ye'll never get it out."

Their failure flashed red in Serena's mind. So close, only to fall short now. With the key to opening the gate on the other side of it, they could not get her father out. And the pistol had only one shot. Even if they did succeed in shooting the old man, the key would still be out of their grasp.

Malcolm stepped behind the guard and put the pistol to the man's head. "Open the gate, old man, or we'll shoot yer friend."

The old man's voice rasped. "He ain't m'friend. How do I know ye won't kill me next?"

"We're here for Commissioner Marsh. Let him out, and we'll trouble ye no more."

The guard continued to chuckle. "Ye're wasting yer time. Guthrie's not aboot to let a prisoner escape."

Malcolm met the old man's gaze. Malcolm was at a disadvantage. He knew it. The guard knew it. Guthrie knew it. Malcolm had gone as far as he could. His success or failure was in the hands of the old man Guthrie.

Serena walked up to the iron gate. She reached into the pouch that dangled from her belt and pulled out the bottle of digitalis.

"Sir," she whispered, her eyes beginning to water, "all I ask is that you give him this. It's medicine . . . for his weak heart. Please."

The guard chuckled some more until Malcolm thumped him in the temple with the barrel.

Guthrie's mouth turned down at the edges. He eyed the brown bottle in Serena's hand. His gaze lifted to Serena's face.

"Give it to him yerself." He put the iron key into the lock and turned it, its mechanism grinding and clanking within. The door opened on its hinge. Serena gasped, glancing at him with something between suspicion and gratitude, then flew inside.

The dungeon was a warren of small cells, each enclosed by stone walls and an oaken door with iron bars. The air was polluted with the smell of unwashed bodies and human excrement. She ran down the narrow passageway, looking into every cell. Each one was occupied, but not by her father.

"Father!" she cried, despair darkening her voice.

"Serena?" came her father's voice.

She flew to the cell the sound came from. "Father!" Inside was Earlington Marsh, looking drawn and pale, but miraculously alive. The sight of him tore sobs from her.

"Poppet! I thought I would never lay eyes on you again." Tears streamed down his face as he put his hands through the bars to stroke her hair. "What on earth are you doing here? How did you find me?"

Guthrie walked up behind Serena. He put the key into the lock and opened the door. Earlington emerged and pulled Serena into his arms. Serena hugged her father so tightly that the bottle nearly slipped from her trembling fingers.

Malcolm came up behind them, urging the guard ahead of him. He shoved the wounded man into Earlington's cell, and the man stumbled to the floor with a grimace. Malcolm took the key from Guthrie and locked the guard inside.

Earlington put a hand out to Guthrie. "Thank you. I'm more grateful than you can ever know."

Guthrie shook it. "Remember what I told ye. And if ye get to talk to the Prince, tell him that we wish to end the feud. The soil of our country should never be watered by the blood of its own children."

Earlington nodded, squeezing the old man's hand.

"Ambassador," said Malcolm. "We must away. Now."

The three of them ran out of the dungeon and up the stairs to the courtyard. Malcolm led the way, stopping at the arched door. He glanced outside. The pages were gone, but the sentry was in the center of the courtyard. There was no way they would be able to run across undetected. They had to sneak back the way they came, creeping behind the small bailey.

They waited until the sentry's back was turned, and then darted across to the shadows behind the bailey. Just as they were about to sneak out past the broken wagon, the dungeon guard emerged from the arched doorway, his face bloodied from Malcolm's beating.

"A prisoner's escaped. Lower the portcullis! Lower it now!"

From a tiny window above the archway, a man rattled to life and began to lower the heavy wood-and-metal grille.

Malcolm shouted. "Run!"

Serena and her father took off hand in hand. They got halfway to the portcullis when Earlington's hand slipped from Serena's. She turned to look. He was doubled over, clutching his chest.

"Father! Malcolm, help!"

Metal screeched against stone as the portcullis continued to descend. Malcolm lifted Earlington into his arms. Thinking quickly, Serena grabbed the broken wagon wheel and wedged the arc of metal and wood underneath the opening.

Serena was already outside, but Malcolm was running as fast as he could carrying the full-grown man in his arms. The heavy door lowered to the level of the wagon wheel and slowed as it made contact.

"Hurry!" she shouted. The wheel would hold the portcullis, but only for a few seconds.

Malcolm reached the gate and threw Earlington under the opening. But the sentry laid his hands on Malcolm and tossed him to the ground.

"Malcolm!" A sense of alarm froze her blood. She realized with dismay that she no longer had possession of the pistol. Malcolm had taken it from her in the dungeon.

The sentry, a large man, had Malcolm pinned to the ground facedown, unable to reach for the gun wedged in the waistband of his kilt.

The spokes of the wagon wheel splintered as the weight of the portcullis bore down. The wheel would snap at any minute.

"Malcolm, hurry!"

Malcolm's hand connected with the small dirk wedged in his hose. He unsheathed the knife and rammed it into the man's calf. Screaming, the man jumped off him. Malcolm crawled out from under him and through the opening under the teeth of the portcullis, a single moment before the wagon wheel shattered.

A cluster of soldiers reached the arched entry. "Raise the portcullis!" they shouted to the man in the room above the archway.

Serena ignored the impotent shouts. She knelt beside her father, swiftly pulled out the bottle from her pouch, and poured a swallow of it in her father's mouth.

"Take this, Father. The pain will pass," she said, the confidence in her voice hollow but the hope strong.

Through his twisted expression, Earlington swallowed the bitter draft. He gasped for breath, and within seconds his heartbeat returned to an even rhythm.

Slowly, the portcullis lifted from its groove.

"Time to go," shouted Malcolm. "I'll carry yer father. Just move!"

Serena led them back across the sheep pasture. By the time they reached the forest, the soldiers were on their trail. Their escape was downhill, which gave them extra speed. Soon they found the horses they had hidden in the clearing. Malcolm helped Serena and Earlington onto one horse, and then he jumped on the other.

They left the soldiers behind as their horses leapt into flight.

THIRTY-ONE

Earlington Marsh gazed out of the window onto English soil. *British* soil.

The morning sun peeked through the clouds, warming the gentlefolk below as they went to church. Newcastle ladies underneath ornate parasols strolled through the park, accompanied by well-dressed gentlemen clicking their walking sticks on the pavement. And though he was far from the nightmarish experience of being confined to a Scottish dungeon, the scene of bustling tranquility on the streets below did nothing to gladden his heart.

Earlington was staying as a guest of Lord Torrence Patterson, a Member of Parliament and friend, who insisted that Earlington recuperate from his ordeal under Lord Patterson's personal care. Earlington was only too happy to accept, especially since he did not feel well enough to journey all the way to London just yet.

He heard a knock on the door. A footman entered.

"A General Frobisher here to see you, sir."

"Thank you. Please send him in."

Moments later a uniformed army officer was escorted into the study.

General Frobisher was a man of singularly hard looks, with a slather of brown hair and determined brown eyes.

A man of imposing breadth, even without the epaulets
and gold braiding, he had a soldier's bearing. He carried
his plumed bicorn in the crook of his arm, and he moved
with great purpose, as if he were always walking against
the wind.

"Ambassador Marsh," he said in a thick voice as he
shook Earlington's hand. "I came at your summons.
What may I do for you?"

"Please sit down, General. I would hear your report
on the Highland insurrection."

The general shifted his sword and folded himself
into the proffered chair after Earlington took a seat.
"Forgive my familiarity, Ambassador, but ought you to
be so concerned with the battle at this point in time? It
has been less than a week since your rescue. And even
though your escape to England aboard ship was swift, I
am given to understand that the journey was especially
arduous. Perhaps you should be resting."

"I find it difficult to sleep of late, General. I'm sure
you can understand."

"Sir, I have my best men—experienced soldiers—
posted both inside and outside this residence around the
clock. Please take your ease. There will *not* be a recur-
rence of the abduction you suffered."

"I thank you for your concern, General, but I assure
you that I am well on the way toward making a full
recovery. However, I cannot in good conscience rest
while our Scottish brethren are under attack. Please tell
me all you know, and withhold nothing."

General Frobisher cocked his head. "Very well. Our
troops engaged the insurrectionists on three fronts—
two in Ross-shire, and one at Inverness, the last being
the decisive victory. To their credit, the insurrectionists
were well armed and well trained; however, they were
greatly outnumbered. It helped also that the infantry's

resolution weakened with each passing hour of the battle. Desertion was rife among them. By the time the battle was over, more than half their troops had fled into the hills."

Earlington nodded. "How many dead?"

"Our army lost nine hundred fifty-three enlisted men, twenty-three officers, fourteen—"

Earlington stopped him. "Not us. Them. How many Scottish souls were lost?"

"Oh." The general's eyebrows came together in puzzlement. "Scottish losses numbered in the thousands, sir. At last count, approximately thirty-two hundred dead or wounded."

Earlington's expression collapsed in a beleaguered frown. *In the thousands.* He stood back up and went to gaze out the window at nothing. His mind skipped back to the day at Ramh Droighionn Castle, when he pleaded with the assembled soldiers to lay down their arms. His memory could still recall the faces belonging to those too old and too young to fight. They were the expressions of men opposed to war, but even more afraid of reprisals for speaking out against it.

The general shifted in his chair. "Ambassador, I must admit to a little surprise at your reaction. I would have thought you would exhibit much more satisfaction at hearing about the loss of your enemies."

Earlington shook his head, his eyes closed to the prejudice. "The men who fought at Inverness are not my enemies, General. Nor are they yours. Had this escalated, it would have been nothing less than civil war. A war between brothers. Don't ever forget who it was you really fought."

The general was quiet for a few moments. "Nevertheless, I hope you at least applaud the suppression of the rebellion against the king's majesty."

Earlington sighed, and changed the subject. "What of the instigators? Skene, Kinross . . . McCullough?"

The general's voice acquired a more triumphant note. "Skene and Kinross were killed on the battlefield. McCullough is not yet accounted for. If he is found alive, he will be arrested and sent to London to answer for his treason. Surely you are contented to be bringing your abductor to justice?"

"Yes. But not because he attacked me. It is because he and the others attacked the peace-loving Scottish people, using acts of violence and cruelty as political weapons."

The general sucked in his cheeks. "If I may be so bold, Ambassador, each man on that battlefield had a choice. If he picked up a sword in defiance against the king, then he deserved to be put down as a subverter of the king's peace."

Earlington resumed his seat, and folded his hands upon his lap. "Peace exists where there is also justice. Something that the Scots do not enjoy in abundance." Earlington inhaled sharply. "Which is why I intend to seek an audience with the Prince Regent and beg him to ask Parliament to repeal his tax on grain, and levy it instead on a different commodity. Perhaps this will alleviate the poverty of the Scottish people. And reconcile His Highness to his northern subjects." Earlington nodded at his own course of action. "Yes, it will mean a lot coming from me."

"As you wish. Will that be all, sir?" The general came to his feet.

"Thank you, General Frobisher," he said, gripping the man's hand. "I'm sure the Prince will reward you graciously for your victory in the Highlands."

Earlington leaned back in the chair, lost in thought. Time slipped away as he contemplated the future.

"Father?"

He turned to look. In the doorway was his precious daughter. She was a reminder that his age and infirmity had rendered him incapable of protecting her; in fact, it was she who protected him.

"Serena!" he said, a smile spreading across his face. "Come in, come in."

She went around the desk and behind his chair, and threw her arms over his neck. "I didn't see you at breakfast this morning. How are you feeling?"

"Better each day. I woke early, and decided to write some letters."

Serena clasped her hands in front of his chest. "You know that the doctor told you to rest," she admonished.

"He's just being overly cautious. I refuse to lay about like an old cat. I feel fine."

"Why are you so headstrong?"

"You had to get it from someone."

She planted a kiss on his cheek and sat down opposite him. "Are you feeling up to traveling back to London?"

"Soon. But I don't see why you shouldn't journey ahead."

"Actually, Father," she began hesitantly. "I find that I really have no wish to return there."

Earlington exhibited only a slight curiosity. "Oh?"

Serena's eyebrows drew together. "You don't seem very surprised to hear me say that."

His face softened to bemusement. "Actually, Malcolm came to see me yesterday. It seems that he has a question he'd like to put to you."

A blush colored Serena's cheeks. "Ah."

"Do you love him?"

The blush darkened. "Unfortunately, Father, I do."

"I always suspected you'd be a begrudging bride,"

Earlington teased. "He's a good man, poppet. And he loves you. Quite desperately."

"He must. Since he's met me, he's been pummeled black and blue twice. I shudder to think what a lifetime with me will do to him. I don't seem to be very good for his health."

He laughed, and then his expression sobered. "You do know that tongues will wag. News of your marriage to a man with a profession will no doubt make the rounds in the parlor rooms of London."

"I don't plan to be around to listen to them."

Earlington looked quizzically at her.

"I intend to be in London for the proclamation of the banns—and for the wedding, of course—but I wouldn't want Malcolm to live there too long. Aside from the fact that he'd be a fish out of water there, I couldn't stand it if he were somehow tarnished by any of Society's foppery or foolishness."

"You mean the way you were?"

She arched her eyebrows. "I won't dignify that with an answer, Father."

Earlington chuckled. "Where do you intend to live?"

"Er—"

He looked incredulously at her. "You're not serious."

Serena shrugged and bit her upper lip. "It does have its charms."

His shoulders drooped. "After all this, you're telling me you now want to *live* in Scotland?" He shook his head. "We'll have to see about that, Serena. I'm not certain I like the idea of my only daughter moving to a distant and remote locale."

"You mean the way you did?" she replied archly.

"I won't dignify that with an answer, Serena." He reached his arm across the desk and took her hand in his. "What am I going to do without you? Home will seem so empty once you're gone."

A gleam flashed in her eyes. "That is precisely the point on which I came to consult you. I've been thinking very hard about the staffing in our household back in London, and I realized that we really do need another member to help run it."

"What are you talking ab—"

"So I've taken the liberty of looking for an administrator to help keep our affairs in order. And I thought that you would like to interview the most promising candidate this morning." She jumped up and went to the door.

Earlington sighed. "Serena, this really is too presumptuous of you. We really don't need—"

His protests died on his tongue when he saw the figure in the doorway. Even though she almost disappeared under the tartan shawl and the plain gray bonnet, he recognized the lady immediately.

"Gabby."

Her piercing blue eyes lit up like a fine Scottish sky. The corners of her mouth lifted, and her expression fairly illuminated when she laid eyes upon him. "Good morning, Commissioner Marsh."

He could hardly speak. To him, she belonged to another time, a whole world away.

She gave a brief sidewise glance at Serena, and then returned her gaze to him. "'Tis good to see ye again, sir. And so fit. I trust ye're well."

That lovely lilt was like music to his ears. "Yes, quite well, thank you. Please come in." He wanted to take her into his arms, but he didn't dare. "How came you to . . . that is, how did you know I was here?"

"Miss Serena sent word to us. We were all worried

sick aboot what had happened to ye. I'm glad to see ye're safe noo."

Earlington looked Gabby Walker up and down, thinking her the rarest and most beguiling creature put on this earth.

Serena exhaled. "As you can appreciate, Father, knowing our desperate need for someone to take over the affairs that I once oversaw and of Mrs. Walker's willingness to apply for the position, I simply had to fetch her straightaway. I understand that she is willing to relocate to London, and is amenable to the conditions of a long-term relationship in our household. I'll withdraw now, and leave you two to discuss the terms in greater detail."

Serena took hold of the doorknob and stepped outside the room. Slowly, she brought the door closer and closer to the jamb, until only a sliver remained through which to see.

Serena watched her father and Lord Askey's former housekeeper. Without taking his eyes off Gabby, her father took her in his arms and held her firmly against his chest. His look of happiness was so great that it almost brought tears to Serena's eyes. Gabby's arms locked around him, too, and silently they held each other for a long time. She raised her head toward his, and their mouths connected in a loving, sensual kiss.

Serena shrugged mischievously at the joy she'd brought to her father's life. She could almost sense his heart beating stronger already. He might not have many years left, but at least he had someone to live them for.

"What are ye doing?" The loud voice spoke over her shoulder, and she nearly cried out in surprise.

"Malcolm!" She spun around and clutched her chest in shock. "Don't sneak up on people like that. You just about stopped my heart!"

He wrapped his hands around her hips and drew her body into his. "Well, we can't have that. We shall just have to think of a way to start it back up again." His head disappeared into her neck, and his hot breath warmed the shell of her ear.

"Malcolm, someone will see."

"Ye little hypocrite. Weren't ye just spying on yer father?"

"I was not spying. I was making sure they were all right."

"Yer father does not need a chaperone." A wicked smile razored across his face. "But with all the things I have in mind, *ye* might."

She smiled back at him. "You're going to be a handful, I can tell."

"Aye, ye can fill both hands with what I have for ye."

She giggled at his ribaldry. "I've heard it said that those who brag the most have the least to show for it."

His lips thinned with determination as he lifted her in his arms. "Care to put me to the test?"

She wrapped her arms around his neck and gazed down into his face. "Aye. Every single day."

Since she was twelve years old, Serena had been fantasizing about her wedding day. But never, in all those years, did she expect it to turn out as it did.

It all started when they finally arrived in London. Serena was proud of her betrothal to Malcolm, but she was concerned that the same Society bluebloods in her set would look down upon him and make him feel inferior or excluded. She needn't have worried. The Prince Regent himself had requested to meet Malcolm, and when news of his part in the rescue of Ambassador Marsh was circulated, Malcolm became quite a celebrity in social circles.

To be sure, Prince George had a particular interest in their marriage. There were political fences to mend following the Crown's victory in the Scottish uprising. He made a gracious, albeit very public, tribute to Serena and Malcolm's nuptials. The wedding of a daughter of England and a son of Scotland would go far in healing the rift in the kingdom and would celebrate the unity of the British people once again.

To Serena's great surprise, everything Scottish became all the rage. Tartans were splashed upon window coverings and tablecloths, and whiskey became more prevalent at parties than champagne. And when Serena and Malcolm were called to Carlton House to sup with the Prince, evidence of his support of Scotland could be seen in everything from the food that he served to the entertainment he commissioned.

More than a hundred people were at this dinner when Prince George announced that he had a wedding gift for the couple. He waved his arm, and a page brought forth a plush purple cushion on which rested a leather portfolio. The page lowered the cushion before Malcolm with a sober bow.

Quizzically, Malcolm took the leather folder. "Yer Highness is too kind," he said, and loosened the ties that kept the folds together.

Serena, who was sitting opposite Malcolm at the table, watched his expression dissolve from pleased curiosity to utter disbelief. "Malcolm? What do you see?"

Serena had never thought to see this particular emotion on the face of her betrothed. Her eyes jumped from the Regent back to Malcolm. "What is it?"

He held it up. "It's the deed to Ravens Craig. My ancestral home."

An appreciative applause rippled down the table. Malcolm faced Prince George.

"Yer Highness, I have no words adequate enough to thank ye," he said haltingly. "This gift is beyond anything of value to me, save my bride. How can I ever repay ye?"

The Prince shifted his considerable frame in his chair. "By living in it. It was forfeited by one of the leaders of the insurrection, whose goods and property were seized by bill of attainder. It is especially fitting that a Scotsman and *loyal* subject should own it instead."

"Ye overwhelm me, sir."

Serena hadn't seen Malcolm so moved since she first told him she loved him. "And I wish to thank you as well, Your Highness. Malcolm and I hope you will honor us by considering it your home when in Scotland and that you favor us with your presence very soon."

The Prince nodded in appreciation. "There is one more gift. Ambassador Marsh has told me that Slayter is not your true last name, as this last was stricken from you for some offense. Is this so?"

A troubled look cast a shadow over his face. "It is, sir."

"Well, then, by royal proclamation, in gratitude for your acts of bravery and loyalty to the government of our people, we hereby end the proscription of your name, restoring it to its former honor without blemish or prejudice, and decree that you will never again be forced to bear the designation of *slaighteur* again."

The guests at the table applauded, but no one could have been happier than Serena herself. It meant everything to her that the world would recognize Malcolm for who he was, and honor him with the simplest of gifts—his own name back.

"A toast." The Prince rose to his feet, and everyone

at the table rose in deference. He lifted his glass, and everyone followed suit. "To the rechristening of our honored guest, henceforth to be known as—"

Malcolm closed his eyes and smiled, forming the unspoken words on his lips. "Malcolm David MacAslan."

The din of the thunderous applause dimmed as she basked in the contentment of seeing his expression. Serena beamed for Malcolm—and because of him. She'd become a new creature once Malcolm edged his way into her life. Now she, too, would carry a new name . . . Serena MacAslan. And she loved it.

Malcolm nodded at the people who applauded him, and slowly, his smiling green eyes landed on Serena. He raised his glass to her, and without words, the curve of the smile on his face told her how much he loved her.

Their wedding day was glorious. The weather had cooled, bringing a crisp chill to the London air. Serena's dress was made of white silk taffeta with gold ribbon at the sleeves, bodice, and hem, with gold threading up the front of the skirt. Her modest tiara dripped with teardrop pearls, and a string of them hung around her neck. The bodice was tight enough to delicately lift her breasts over the hem, but ruched so as to give the appearance of looseness. Long white gloves snaked up her arms, leaving just a narrow band of pale skin showing on her arms. It was a costume of her own design, and she hoped Malcolm would like it. She thought of him when she ordered her bouquet, a singular piece with white roses interspersed with purple thistles and sprayed with heather, a subtle nod to the union of their two cultures.

And when Serena walked down the aisle on her

father's arm, her apprehension evaporated when she saw Malcolm's face. He smiled broadly as she approached him, his eyes shining into hers. She *pleased* him.

And he pleased her as well. His masculine beauty had been the object of more than a few whispered comments behind open fans, and now it was resplendent for all to see. His thick black hair waved over his head, echoed in the eyebrows that hovered above his luminous green eyes. His alabaster smile shone brilliantly against his healthy complexion, shaved smooth to see the dent in the middle of his prominent chin. Dense eyelashes lined the mischievous eyes that now dared her to desire him.

Malcolm was wearing a garment she had become quite used to seeing him in—a kilt. But its hue was not black, devoid of any identity, but the vivid blue, red, and green of the MacAslan tartan. *Her* clan now.

His cutaway double-breasted jacket in the same tartan formed a triangle of his torso, and was made even more elegant by a fly plaid tied around his torso and over one shoulder like a sash. His sporran had a silver cantle, and was made of black fur with six small tassels in white fur dangling from the front. He looked like a prince of Scotland.

Her father dropped a kiss on her cheek, and placed her hand upon the back of Malcolm's outstretched hand. It was a moment full of poignant symbolism, and the tears began to well up as she left her father's side and joined Malcolm.

Breaking tradition, Malcolm turned his hand upward, and their palms touched. His warmth and strength spread to her, even through her gloves. The meaning of the gesture was not lost on her. They would face the future not merely as gentleman and lady, but hand in hand, joined together, as one.

"My hero," she whispered as they approached the clergyman.

"My hero," he answered right back.

THIRTY-TWO

The wedding festivities were held at Ambassador Marsh's home, Greywood House, located in Highgate. Although the current fashion was to have an intimate gathering for the wedding breakfast, Serena had determined to buck every fashion to which she had ever confined herself. Besides, she reasoned, the circumference of her circle of friends was so large that it was difficult to leave anyone out.

Malcolm unwittingly provided the greatest revelry when he began to tell the guests how easy it was to marry in England. Bridegrooms in Scotland, he said, would be forced to endure any of several customs, which included blackening—when townspeople would pour treacle, soot, and boot polish over a couple about to be married—or creeling the bridegroom, in which a man about to be married would have a basket strapped to his back, and his friends would fill it with stones. He'd then be forced to carry the basket up and down the street until his betrothed willingly deigned to kiss him.

Three young gentlemen at the party looked at one another impishly and insisted that Malcolm demonstrate this custom on the spot.

Twin French doors connected the ballroom to the garden court. The three young men seized Malcolm and playfully rushed him outside. Some of the guests went outside into the garden, and others, like Serena, watched from the open doors and windows. They didn't find a basket, but they grabbed an empty wooden box, and with some rope secured it onto Malcolm's back. One by one, they grabbed stones and empty bottles and threw them into the box. The guests laughed as Malcolm began to buckle under the heavy weight strapped to his back. Up and down the garden paths Malcolm ran, to the jeers and taunts of the wedding guests. He gritted his teeth as some of them continued to throw in a stone or two as he ran past them.

"Will you not put your husband out of his misery?" laughed one of the ladies.

"Yes," shouted the man next to her. "Give him a kiss. He's been subjected to enough torment."

Serena grinned wickedly. "This is a good lesson for him. Let him prepare himself for the burdens of marriage."

Malcolm stopped dead in his tracks. "Will you no' give me my ease, woman?"

"No. I'm having too much fun watching you from here."

His jaw jutted forward. "That's it. I'm through indulging you."

He stomped over to her. She shrieked and tried to back away, but the crowd behind her prevented a retreat. He bent over and swept her into his arms. Mortification and excitement shook her to her core. He paraded up and down the garden path, carrying the weight both behind and in front of him. Serena clung to his neck, her feet hanging in the air. Unsettled at being the object of this spectacle, Serena finally turned his head and planted a lingering kiss on his lips.

Malcolm stopped, relishing their first passionate kiss

since being proclaimed man and wife. "Aye. That's my girl," he said lovingly.

A short while later, Malcolm and Serena were seen off. In another Scottish tradition, Gabby had baked a special bannock, which was broken over Serena's head to ensure happiness and wealth.

But the journey to their wedding night was only a short one. As part of Serena's dowry, her father had given them a small cottage in Stratford, where she and Malcolm had planned to spend their honeymoon. The cottage had been in her mother's dowry, but because Earlington's career in foreign service required his presence in London or abroad, he and June had rarely used it. Serena herself had only vague recollections of it as a child. But Stratford was a day's ride from London, and they would have to set out in the morning. Tonight, they'd stay in her bedroom at Greywood House.

Serena walked up the stairs slowly, nerves weakening her knees. Malcolm was just behind her, his heavy footfalls pounding upon the steps.

She'd never had a man in her bedroom before. Had her Mistake occurred in her rooms, she would have moved to a different part of the house. But even though Ben had never been here, she carried the memory of him—and the scars—inside. Now she was about to let a man into her room who would reside there forever. What happened next in her room would shape the entire course of her sexual relationship with Malcolm.

Her hand shook as it reached for the doorknob.

Malcolm stopped her before she walked through. "Another Scottish custom." He scooped her into his arms and carried her over the threshold. With a kiss, he set her back onto her feet.

Malcolm walked around her suite of rooms. Serena's living space comprised a sizable part of the second floor of Greywood House. In addition to her bedchamber, there was also a private morning room, dressing room, and privy. The walls were cornflower blue and dripping with relief plaster. Her windows nearly reached the floor, and looked out onto the back garden.

"Ye grew up here?" he asked incredulously.

"Yes. Terribly cramped, I know, but I made do." Remembering how the child Malcolm had been adopted by a village game hunter, she felt a stab of shame at the opulence of her surroundings. "I don't suppose you had as much when you grew up."

He shook his head, chuckling. "But I've learned a few things in my time. 'Twasn't how much I had that made me rich. It was how little I required."

Serena reflected on his words. She glanced around at her room's fancy appointments, each one picked personally by her. She had *required* all these things because it was what had given her life meaning. Now she didn't care for a single one of the brocade pillows or silver hairbrushes or gilt-framed paintings. She had found what made her life meaningful. It was the man who stood in the center of her room—the center of her existence.

He walked up to her and took her hands in his. "I never felt myself poor. Until that moment when our carriage fell down the brae. When I called out to ye and ye didn't answer, for a single, terrifying moment, I thought ye'd died. That's when I felt it. Because losing ye would have impoverished me beyond redemption. I knew then that I loved ye. I can't think of my life without ye, Serena. I don't need anything else but ye."

She wrapped her arms around his torso, her cheek pressed against his chest. "And the difference is that I don't *want* anything else but you. If you swept me away to live in the middle of the Highlands, in that forest with nothing but a fire and a salmon, I'd be contented. As long as you were there, I'd be happy."

His arms tightened around her. "Then it looks as if we're the two richest people in all the earth."

She tilted her head up to him. "What can I give you that would make you happy?"

"Ye've already given me yer heart. That's made me the happiest of men."

Serena cast her face away. "I wish I had remained a maid until this night. You deserve to have been my first. But I wasn't virtuous enough for you, Malcolm. I didn't think any man would ever love me the way you do. I didn't know that one day I'd be in love with a man to whom I wanted to give something of mine very special, something that only he could ever claim. I was so very foolish. I sold myself for nothing more than romantic words, words that gave me a sweet illusion of love. But it wasn't real. And after I gave myself away, both the words and the love evaporated into nothingness. You taught me what real love was. It's not in words, it's not in romantic flutterings. It's in actions. Your actions, Malcolm. It was what you did for me. How you put me above yourself, your own life. I'll never be able to repay you. Not ever. And not tonight."

He put a warm hand on either side of her face. "I don't want repayment, Serena. I can't help loving ye. It's as natural to me as breathing. But there is something very special of yers that ye can give me. And as valuable as yer maidenhead was, it's so much more special than that."

"What?"

His thumbs caressed her cheek softly. "Yer lifetime. Give me forever with ye. By my side, hand in hand. In my bed."

She smiled at him wistfully. There was so much to

say, so many things she would promise. But she knew it would never be enough. Actions, not words—that's what mattered.

"Will my bed do for now?"

A wicked grin cut across his handsome face. "Oh, aye."

His lips touched hers. Warm, moist, delicious. She could still taste the sugar and brandy from the wedding cake upon his lips.

Her arms snaked up his chest and around his neck. Such a tall, strong man. She had always felt safe with him at her back, and now she felt safe in his arms. His hands rested on her waist. He walked backward until his thighs touched the edge of her four-poster bed, and sitting upon it, he wedged her between his knees.

Her fingers disappeared in the black currents of his hair that looked like a storm-tossed sea at midnight. She feasted her eyes upon each of his beautiful features, from the sensual mouth to the sensual glare from his eyes. Her fingers danced upon the silvering sideburns, which ended just above his square jaw.

"Do you know how much I love your beauty?" she asked.

He smiled. "No. Show me."

She sucked in her lips as she contemplated it. "I love this part." She leaned over and kissed his eyes, which fluttered closed as she did so. "I love this part." She kissed the dimple on his chin. "And this." She placed her hands on his face and pressed a kiss on his full lips.

"Are there no more features that please ye?"

She blushed. "There may be one or two. But these clothes are in my way."

He revealed a row of white teeth. "Let's have them off, then." He unfastened the tartan fly plaid and threw it over his head, letting it slide down the opposite side of her bed. He reached for the buttons on his jacket, and she stopped him.

"Allow me," she said. Men's clothes were always objects of fascination for her. And Malcolm was like a giant present that she wanted to unwrap.

Slowly, she unbuttoned the six silver buttons of the double-breasted jacket. She slipped her hands inside, wedging the MacAslan jacket off his shoulders. She let her fingers slide over his massive shoulders, then down his arms, relishing the undulations of the muscles under his black linen shirt.

His hands began a slow exploration of her thighs. She halted him. "Not yet. I want to see you first." Visions of her dream that night in the forest danced through her head.

The voluminous sleeves of the black shirt gave him the appearance of having larger arms, but Malcolm did not need the same affectation as other men did. Serena well knew how heavy with muscle his arms already were. His waistcoat, an especially sensual garment as it hugged the V of his torso so tightly, was warm beneath her fingers as she undid the buttons at his chest.

A black silk cravat gave him a dangerous, roguish look. She undid the artfully arranged knot, letting the smooth fabric slide through her fingers.

His impatient hands began to play with the hemline at her bodice. She slapped the back of his hands.

"I said, *wait!*"

He retracted his stung hand. His jaw jutted forward as he playfully smacked her on the behind. "Cat! Keep yer claws sheathed, or I'll give ye what for!"

Her eyes narrowed upon him in mock anger. She tightened the cravat around his neck until he coughed. "Those that board with cats may count on scratches."

He fell backward on the bed, bringing her upon him.

"Are ye after making yerself a widow so soon?" He unknotted the cravat and slid the fabric from his neck. "Keep that up and I'll tie ye down to the bed."

She smoothed her lips over his. "As if that could keep my hands off you."

A sultry determination surged in his eyes. He seemed to be the type of man who appreciated brazenness in a woman. Effortlessly, he rolled her over onto the bed and got on top of her.

"Ow. Malcolm. Ow." The silver-framed sporran was digging into her thigh.

He raised himself to one knee. "Sorry," he chuckled. He unhitched the offending article and let it fall to the rug.

"I want my go." His head descended upon her chest, kissing the round flesh that mounded up from her bodice. She shivered as his warm lips sizzled on her cool skin.

His palm flattened on her breast, and cupped her bosom in his hand. The pressure upon her nipple made her arch into him. The sensation added a physical arousal to her heightened mental one. She wanted to see his chest, not through the shirt, but naked before her. She grasped at the fabric tucked into the waistband of his kilt, and yanked it free of its confines. Taking her lead, he sat up on one knee and threw it off his back.

Despite the scars that speckled his torso, Malcolm was glorious in semi-nudity. His skin was taut over his heavily muscled frame. A smattering of hair curled in the valley between his small brown nipples. His abdomen was bricked by muscles down the center—but her view was halted by a black leather belt.

Shrouded in a mist of arousal, Serena grabbed the belt and unfastened it for him. His breathing accelerated and his back curled toward her like a cobra about to strike.

She gave her hands free rein to stroke the soft skin on his hard abdomen. "I once had a dream that I was making love to you," she confessed. "How I longed to make that dream come true."

"By God, woman, ye've a fire in you. Come here." He slid his hands beneath her arms and lifted her toward the middle of the mattress. The bed creaked as he threw himself next to her, his mouth devouring her pearled neck. The warm sucking felt heavenly, and she shuddered in anticipation of what that would feel like on her breast. He threw one long thigh between hers, and its sinews caressed the ache between her legs. Her fingers splayed across his back, feeling the hard muscles beneath the warm skin. As he shifted downward, her fingertips learned the movements of his strong back.

Somewhere in a nearly forgotten part of her mind was the memory of her bridal trousseau, and of the new lace sleeping gown she was supposed to wear to bed for him. A voice growing ever fainter admonished her to have her bed turned down, comb out her hair, or at the very least have the common decency to remove her shoes.

But as he pulled down on the hem of her bodice, tearing at the delicate fabric with his mighty strength and laving at her exposed nipple, none of that mattered. Their hunger for each other drove them forward inexorably, their bodies demanding to be united as mates. It was animal. It was feral. It was heaven.

He reached under her dress and stroked her stockinged leg from ankle to pink garter. She felt a rush of honeyed lust course between her thighs. Sensing her readiness, he slipped a finger inside her and was met with a slippery passage.

He sat upon his haunches. Her eyes became slits as she gazed upon him. He looked like a conquering warrior,

a man about to ravage a captured female. Underneath
the fabric of his cobalt kilt, his full erection threatened
both pain and pleasure. His mouth hanging open, he
gripped one slippered foot and threw it to the other side
of his thigh. Now she was defenseless before him, her
legs scissored open like a wanton on the dark streets of
London. His eyes boring into hers, he lifted the skirts of
her wedding dress all the way up to her waist.

She was exposed to his eyes—and to his cock. The
memory of her dream came flooding back, except that
their roles had been reversed. *Her* body was now at *his*
mercy.

Her rapid breathing caused her breasts to rise and
fall over her bodice. Anticipation thrilled her senses as
she tried to read his next move. There was so much of
him she wanted to see, to touch. But she was already
wet for him, and she wanted him *now*.

"Do ye know how long I've wanted to do this, to see
that look upon yer face? Now there's another look I want
to see, and I'm no' going to stop until I get it."

He gripped her by the ankles and yanked her toward
him. She gasped as her body slid onto his thighs. One
deft move later, she found her calves upon the curve of
his elbows. Never in her whole life had she felt so vulnerable. Blood rushed through her body, hips to head,
as she contemplated the impending penetration.

She felt the woolen kilt rasp her backside as he
yanked it upward. And then she felt his member, tall
and rock-hard, at the mouth of her splayed opening.
Fearfully, she gripped the bed coverings, twisting the
fabric in her nervous fingers.

He leaned forward, simultaneously entering her with
his cock. She gasped sharply, his thick cock stretching
her to the limit. Her unyielding tightness pained her, her

vagina unused to the assault of so large a member. She winced, wishing for the hurting to recede. Had she been a maid, she would never have been able to accommodate him.

His face was mere inches from hers, and he watched her intently as she took him in. Her hands clutched the muscles behind his arms, her nails biting into the flesh, returning pain for pain. His jaw clenched and his nostrils flared, but he absorbed her stabs just as she took the piercing he gave her. Yet he waited, patiently, as she adjusted to his girth.

When her nails released him, he moved. Slow, steady thrusts at first, stoking the fire that had sputtered when the pain of penetration left her winded. But when that fire blazed to life again, it began to burn her up, and only Malcolm could extinguish it for her.

He kissed her mouth, his tongue dancing upon her own, and she moaned at the double penetration. His thrusts became shorter, faster, and she gasped for air. She was one long sleeve for his penis. Her body rocked upon the bed, the headboard banging against the wall. She thrashed upon the bed, crying his name and gasping for release. The invisible thread that held her control in check stretched tauter and tauter, until finally it snapped and pleasure exploded through her body.

Involuntarily, her body squeezed upon his still-erect member, organically pumping upon his penis to draw in his seed. When the fog cleared, she found him staring at her in seductive amusement.

"That's the look I wanted to see."

"Oh, Malcolm," she cried, wrapping her arms around his neck. "I love you so much."

He smiled. "Come. I'll give ye a chance to love me again."

Her legs slid down his sides, and he sat upon his haunches, taking her with him. Now she was seated upon his member, supported by his hands clasped under her bottom. Her hips were unaccustomed to the rocking motion, so Malcolm helped her move upon him. Her breasts bounced over the shredded bodice, giving him something to kiss while she thrust herself upon his shaft. Though her need had been sated, she found the movement upon him to be very stimulating. But she wanted to watch his expression as her body accelerated his pleasure. He closed his eyes, a deep moan rumbling in his massive chest. Her arms upon his wide shoulders steadied her as she sped up her movements, creasing his brow. As he begged for his release, Serena exulted in the feeling of power over his unresisting body. She stroked the hair at the back of his neck, something she knew brought him pleasure, and watched as his orgasm hastened. Suddenly every muscle in his body tightened, bringing them more snugly together, and his body shuddered in a lightning flash of passion.

She accepted inside her all he had to give. As his last shiver died away, she stroked his face. And when he opened his eyes, she grinned at him.

"You're a passionate animal, Malcolm MacAslan."

"So we're fairly matched, then."

"It would appear so."

"But now, this animal needs a wee rest." He threw himself on the bed, basking in the glow of the moment. "Come lay beside me."

She rested her head on the pillow of his bicep, watching his handsome face. He was a great lion of a man, able to scatter lesser men from his path with just a low growl. But Serena Marsh could bring him low with just an expression of love.

They lay together for some time, his mighty arm

wrapped around her head and her foot stroking the inside of his leg.

He turned to her, the sheen on his pink lips returning as he smiled at her. "Let's do this properly."

"Properly?" she asked, bewildered. "I'm no expert, but I thought we did this fairly well."

He smiled broadly. "Wait here."

He sat on the side of her bed and began to remove his shoes and stockings. From her vantage point, Serena watched his back in motion. Light and shadow danced upon the muscled V, outlining every unexplored crevice and ridge. He stood up and unbuckled the small leather strap that held his kilt to his narrow waist. The garment slipped to the floor, revealing a pelt of hair above his penis. Its skin was darker than the rest of him, but smooth all the way to the rounded knob. It rested upon his sac, which to Serena's amusement resembled two eggs in a dark nest. It was naughty and unladylike to regard him so brazenly, but she wouldn't have missed it for the world.

The servants had left a decanter of wine and some fruit on her tea table. She watched his backside as he padded to her morning room to pour out two glasses. What a beautiful bottom it was, to be sure. Twin squares of muscle perched atop two long thighs, each dented at the hip. Damn that kilt for hiding such a gorgeous feature.

Taking her cue from him, she got off the bed, holding the ends of her wedding dress together at her bosom.

"Where are ye going?" he asked.

"To change into my nightgown."

Gripping her wrist, he spun her in the opposite direction. "Ye won't be needing that. Come with me."

He handed her a glass and took a swallow from his

before setting it on her night table. He spun her around and began to undo the hooks at the back of the dress.

"I certainly made a mess of that," he said, tossing the tattered garment onto her chair. He looked at the remains of her torn muslin shift. "And that."

He raised the shift over her head. She met him with a kiss. Their naked bodies touched, lips on lips, skin against skin.

His callused hand rubbed her back. It was scratchy but manly, as was the hair that touched her tummy. He was so delightfully masculine, so ruggedly male, that it called to something naturally female within her.

His hand went to the side of her breast and cupped its heaviness, making her nipples bloom at his touch. The hand then traveled up the side of her face and pulled at the pins holding her chignon in place. One by one, tendrils of blond hair cascaded down her shoulders. He lifted a handful of it onto the back of his hand, and kissed it tenderly.

He threw off the twisted bedcovering, revealing the soft sheets. He bent over, scooped her up, and laid her gently on the bed. He feasted his eyes upon her naked body, and she could almost feel his dark gaze upon her breasts, tummy, and muff. He pulled off her heeled slippers, and one after the other gave the soles of her feet and toes a gentle rub. A grin spread across her face at the relaxing ministration.

The white silk stockings were the last remaining garment. He sat next to her on the bed and tried to unfasten her garters. But they proved tricky to remove, thwarting his best efforts. She struggled to keep from giggling as he pulled on the pink strands. Finally, he got one off and in a fit of pique, threw it across the room.

She chuckled behind her clenched fist. Slowly, he unrolled her stocking, exposing the sensitive skin to the air. With the tips of his splayed fingers, he contoured a path down her leg from upper thigh to ankle. By the time he got to the other leg, the heat had already begun to pool inside her.

With the backs of his fingers, he trailed a path down the very center of her body. The tiny blond hairs all along her core quivered at the tender touch. Her skin demurred from the passing fingers, unaccustomed to their intimacy. Wordlessly, he bent over upon her chest and placed a hot kiss upon her right aureole.

She inhaled sharply at the sensation. It felt as if he was breathing fire upon her already tight nipple. Even so, she lifted the soft breast higher into his sensuous mouth.

When he moved to the left one, a moan escaped her lax mouth. His palm smoothed a trail down her waist and covered the soft fur between her legs. The sensation stimulated her desire to be entered, and she relaxed her legs.

But he ignored the invitation. Instead, he traced each rib and slope of her hips, studying her, learning her shape and contours. His fingers passed through the sensitive valley between her chest and arm, and the skin alongside her bent elbow, taking careful note of her shudders. Her breathing started to come shallower and more uneven, at once enjoying his touch and wanting the sweet torture to end.

"Turn over," he said, his voice a low whisper.

She did as he said. His hands lifted the blond tresses over her head, exposing her nape. His head descended and she felt his torturous mouth on the back of her neck. She moaned pitiably, delighting in the ravishing

sensation. Something impeded his sumptuous mouth . . .
it was the strand of pearls that still clung to her neck.
How she wished they would disappear!

Malcolm climbed over her on all fours. The heat
from his body wrapped her in a cocoon of warmth. His
mouth kissed her shoulder, feasting upon her back. His
tongue flicked a trail down the middle of her back,
which undulated with the surprising sensation.

Farther down his tongue went, eliciting a moan with
every inch. But when his tongue passed her waist and
climbed up the ridge of her lower back, she stiffened. He
was leaving no spot on her body unexplored. His hand
rubbed the slopes of her bottom, cupping the flesh in his
giant hand. She was still wet between her legs from their
earlier lovemaking, but a new, hotter flow warmed her
passage.

Instinctively, her back arched, jutting her bottom upward. She was ready for him again. Kneeling on the bed,
Malcolm lifted her hips up to meet his own. She, too,
was on all fours, her legs open for him. Malcolm brought
his penis to her caramel-colored curls, and plunged
deep inside her.

She moaned loudly, the length of him reaching all
the way inside her. She wasn't sure if it was the prime-
val position or the erotic caresses beforehand, but his
thrusts stoked a ruthless lust within her that she found
impossible to contain. His driving hips bounced against
her bottom cheeks, making her dangling breasts sway
beneath her. She used the headboard to curl upward,
closer to Malcolm. He stroked her neck and hair, bringing
as much of her body into contact with his as he could.

The closer his body came to orgasm, the louder his
grunting became. Her breaths came in short rasps, and
before long they had turned into moans that echoed his
sounds. The fire grew inside her until she could no lon-

ger withstand the heat. Together they reached their release, exploding with heated pleasure. Together they
stayed mated until their breathing evened. Together,
they lay entwined until the morning came.

And somehow, Serena's pearls fell away altogether.

THIRTY-THREE

Serena had learned by experience that the weather in Scotland could be fickle. But as their brand-new town coach rumbled up the lesser-trodden roads in the Highlands, she gloried in the cool air and the bright sunshine.

Ravens Craig House was all Malcolm could talk about since they left Edinburgh. He talked of his earliest memories of the house—fond memories that Serena doubted he had ever unearthed until now—and what the place would be like once they moved in.

But as they neared his lands, he grew quiet. There were memories hidden in the forests and hills that sent him to another place. It was here that Malcolm lost his innocence, learning of evil firsthand and all alone. How she pitied that child. The twenty years since that boy had been here had been bleak, but she silently promised herself to make the next twenty his happiest.

At first, the furrowed road to Ravens Craig seemed to be nothing more than a path overgrown by rhododendron shrubs and beech trees. Then it began to peek out at her. A window pane flashing between laurel branches, a hint of a turret peeking through the lofty oak trees. And then it appeared, springing from the top of the hill.

The house was wreathed in centuries. It slept atop a

green field, surrounded by acres of forests and meadows. The walls were bricked with gray and brown stones that seemed hewn from the very mountain behind it. A crenellated tower overlooked the view of the neighboring rises, dotted with sheep and lambs. A massive door, reinforced with black iron strap hinges, remembered the house to a bygone age.

The carriage turned onto an ancient stone bridge painted by a thick coat of moss. They traversed a stream that wept around the hill.

Serena turned to Malcolm in disbelief. "You lived here?"

"Aye."

The house was not at all what she expected. She wasn't sure why, but she had assumed Malcolm had lived in a tiny cottage. Though Ravens Craig was no manor or palace, it was far from being a one-room croft.

Malcolm stepped out of the carriage and took a lingering look around before helping Serena alight.

"Welcome home, wife," he said, grinning into her face.

Serena glanced at the impressive structure. "Welcome home, husband."

As they approached, an elderly couple came to the door.

"I'm so glad ye've arrived safely," said the woman from the door. "Mr. Brooker here can see to the horses. I've a warm stew and some fresh-baked bread waiting for ye. Come in, come in!"

The lady had on a simple apron, and she wiped her hands on them. "My name's Mrs. Brooker, sir. I used to be the cook here. When the sheriff came here aboot a month ago with orders to the previous owner to vacate the premises, he let Mr. Brooker and myself stay behind to look after the house until ye arrived."

Serena looked around the house. It looked as if it had been cleaned out of all its belongings. Hardly a stick of furniture was left behind. "And who was the previous owner, Mrs. Brooker?"

"It belonged to the McCullough."

Serena's eyes flew open. "Brandubh McCullough?"

"Aye. 'Twas him who lived here since the time he came of age. His father be the man who took hold of it, aboot eight year ago."

Malcolm looked at the yawning emptiness. "And took all its antiquities with him."

Serena was in shock that Brandubh McCullough was still alive. "McCullough is a wanted man. Didn't the sheriff take him into custody?"

"He wouldna do that. The sheriff is the McCullough's kinsman."

Malcolm walked away into another room. Serena was about to follow him, but Mrs. Brooker stopped her.

"Pardon me, missus, but would it be asking too much if me and the husband could stay on awhile longer? Just until we find another situation for the both of us, mind. Only it'll take a bit of looking, and we're not as young and strong as we used to be."

Serena nodded. "I'll consult the matter with Mr. Slay—that is, Mr. MacAslan. But I don't think he would be opposed to letting you stay on for as long as you wish. We don't have anyone else to assist us at the moment, and we'd be grateful for the help."

"Oh, thank ye, missus! Thank ye! We'll do our best to please ye."

Serena followed the path Malcolm had taken. She found him standing in the kitchen.

She looked around the room. There was a fireplace big enough for her to stand in, where Mrs. Brooker had a pot hanging from a spit. There was a long wooden table at the other end. And there was Malcolm, lost in a world of memories.

Mrs. Brooker came in behind them. "The table's all set for ye in the dining room. I'll bring the pot out straightaway." She seemed somehow embarrassed, as if they were inspecting her cooking area.

But Malcolm didn't hear her. There was a door that led out into the rear of the house, and Malcolm walked through it.

Serena followed Malcolm through the rear garden, down the hill, and to a patch of gravestones under a shady oak. Her eyes darted around at the ones still standing. Most of them were smashed, the names of the honored dead unrecognizable.

A surge of anger welled up inside her. Whoever had desecrated the gravestones had tried to obliterate the MacAslan name.

"Don't worry, Malcolm," she said, putting a hand around his elbow. "We can rebuild them. We'll put up whole new ones even more beautiful than these. Marble ones, if you like."

He shook his head. "No need. My ancestors . . . they're no longer here. Beneath this ground are only bones. There's no need to venerate the dead." He picked up the corner of a stone slab that had fallen facedown, pushing away the grass that had grown high around it. "I only care to know where my brother and my sisters are. If they're alive, or . . . if they also need gravestones." The slab fell from his hand. "I feel ashamed somehow . . . being the only one to return to the house."

She turned him around to face her. "You must never say that. You belong here. And so do they. If they're alive, then we will find them . . . together."

She hoped that some of her optimism would splash

upon him. His countenance shifted, and a look of hope twitched the corners of his eyes.

"Do ye think then that I am no' the last of the Mac-Aslans?"

She smiled. "No. You're looking at one now."

He chuckled, and engulfed her in his mighty arms. "No wonder I delight myself in ye."

EPILOGUE

Tossing his blue-patterned fly plaid casually over one shoulder, Malcolm sauntered into Serena's morning room while she was scratching furiously at a lettersheet with her quill.

"I'm going down to the village."

She dipped her quill in the inkpot. "Mm-hmm."

"I'm after buying some seed to have the crofters plant the north field."

"Mm-hmm."

Malcolm sighed at her obliviousness to him. "And then I'll play the lute while the pixies braid yer hair."

"Mm-hmm."

He placed a hot kiss on her neck. "Why do I get the feeling ye're no' listening to me? Must I resort to doing what I did to ye last night?"

Serena feigned a cross expression. "It took me half an hour to pull all the hay from my hair."

He peeked over her shoulder at her lettersheet. "Is that a new article for the *Edinburgh Gazette*? What is it this week? A scathing indictment of the conditions of the working class in industrial living quarters? A plea for the plight of children in workhouses?"

She set down her quill. "No. This is not an article for the new 'Rage Page.' This," she said, folding the lettersheet, "is an invitation for my father to come visit at Easter. I'm planning a very special event, and I don't want him to miss it."

"Another party?"

She nodded. "Of sorts. It's a birthday party."

Malcolm frowned. "Yer birthday isn't until January."

"It isn't for me. I wasn't planning to tell you until dinner, but . . . it's a birthday party for the next Mac-Aslan."

Malcolm's eyes flew open. "You mean—"

Her eyes lit up. "Oh, aye."

He lifted her out of the seat high over his head. "Our very first babe!"

She tightened her arms around his neck as he lowered her to the floor, and placed a slow kiss on his mouth. "And I can hardly wait to start on the next one."

AUTHOR'S NOTE

Social studies. The two most dreaded words of my adolescent school life.

I can still remember how my teeth used to grind whenever it was time to pull out our social studies books to learn about some dead people who did some boring stuff a long time ago. Like everyone else, I had to memorize the preamble to the Constitution (easier if done to the tune of the *Schoolhouse Rock* song) and be able to identify the funny-looking men whose pictures were on our coins. I skated by with Cs, grateful just to have passed, and contented myself with more interesting classes like English and science—subjects that felt more relevant to me.

But something changed when, decades later, I began to write *Secrets to Seducing a Scot.* In creating a fictional revolution in Scotland in 1819, my research took me to an event very recent to my story, the American Revolution. Both of these events had, at their roots, similar discontentment with the British government of its day. Suddenly, by putting the characters whom I loved in those unsettling times, the topic began to become very relevant indeed.

I began to look at the American Revolution in a more profound way. I became fascinated by the forces that would lead a largely pacific people to revolt against one of the greatest and most powerful empires the world had ever seen. I went to Washington, D.C., and toured the Smithsonian. I bought a life-size copy of the Declaration of Independence and read it in its original script form. I studied the writings of our founding fathers, and learned the extent of their passion for freedom. I even developed a crush on the humorous and colorful Benjamin Franklin, whose quotes, some may notice, have leaked into this story.

In short, I discovered *who* those men on our coins were, and understood that to call them "heroes" devalued their humanity. In trying to do what they believed to be right, they faced opposition from their families, their friends, and their king. They didn't set out to be heroes; in fact, standing up to the established order probably made them wonder if they had a screw loose. They suffered fear, experienced heartache, and endured deprivation. They did so not to be on coins, but because they felt that the goal—freedom from injustice—was more important.

Some lessons are not learned in the classroom. Some lessons take a lifetime to learn. The important thing is that they are learned.

Is it too late to get an A?

Read on for a sneak peek at the next book in
Michelle Marcos's Highland Knaves series

Lessons
in Loving a Laird

Coming in 2012 from St. Martin's Paperbacks

Ravens Craig House
Ross-shire, Scotland
Twelve years before

"Mumma?" asked Shona, her pink lips pouting.

Fiona straightened, her unlaced ghillie still clutched in her hand. "Aye?"

"If God made spiders, why did ye try to squoosh that one just now?"

Fiona shook her head as she searched for the beastie beneath the table. It took her a moment to compose an answer for her eight-year-old daughter. "Well, he doesna belong in my kitchen. If the Good Lord made a creature with so many legs, He must've meant for it to be ootside where there's plenty of room to run around."

Shona's mouth formed an O as the sense of it dawned on her. Excitedly, she jumped down from the chair. "I'll take him ootside for ye, Mumma." Her black hair splayed around her shoulders as she crouched on the wooden floor.

The black spider was no bigger than the tip of her finger, and she watched it slowly climb the leg of the kitchen table. Mumma was cutting tatties and neeps for supper, and it was dangerous for the wee spider to be here. Her younger brother, Camran, was playing on the floor, surrounded by toy king's men their father had carved. Shona took the empty wooden box and placed it on the floor underneath the spider.

She leaned closer, her large green eyes rounding over the tiny creature. He seemed so alone, so far from home. Everyone should be home with his family. *I'll take ye home,* she thought at it, feeling sure he understood her. She puckered her lips and blew.

The startled spider let go of the wooden surface, and, supported by a single thread, landed squarely in the wooden box.

"I got him, Mumma!" she shouted excitedly. She lifted the box so her mother could see.

"Well done, Shona," Fiona cheered flatly, barely able to suppress a shudder. "Mind ye put him ootside where he belongs."

Her older brother, Malcolm, always kept the woodpile outside well stocked. Shona had seen spiders among the chopped wood, especially around the base of the pile where the logs were oldest. This must be where Wee Spider's family lived.

Shona upended the box onto the pile, and Wee Spider scampered out and disappeared between the dried logs.

"Ye've got too many legs to be in the house," she said, bouncing an admonishing finger in the air. "Mind ye don't stray inside again."

In the distance, beyond the footbridge, she saw three figures approaching. Her father and older brothers were returning from the hunt. From a pole shouldered by Thomas and Hamish swung a large dead boar.

"Mumma!" cried Shona. "Da's come back!" As she ran through the house shouting the news, she passed her thirteen-year-old brother, Malcolm, who'd been sullenly dragging about the house, moping because he wasn't allowed to go hunting with them. Her twin sister, Willow, squealed in delight. She dropped the bannock she was shaping and ran out of the house.

Shona wanted to be the first to greet her father, but Willow raced ahead of her down the footpath into John's arms. John lifted Willow in his meaty arms, swinging her 'round and 'round until she laughed convulsively. Even in the waning light of the setting sun, Shona could see the radiant smile upon her father's face as he embraced her pretty blond sister.

He carried Willow in the crook of his elbow, her corkscrew tendrils dripping around his cheeks. "Have ye been a good lass, then, Willow?"

"Aye, Da. I made the bannocks for tonight."

"Happy I am to hear it," he said as he strode toward their front door. "I'm as hungry as a bear in the springtime. I want them all for m'own!" Willow giggled as he tickled her.

Shona hugged her father around his waist.

"And ye, Shona? Did ye mind yer mother while we were away?"

"I saved a spider."

"Is that for my dessert?"

Shona laughed gleefully. "He's not for ye to eat, Da!"

"Oh!" He tousled the black fringe of hair over her forehead.

As they walked across the threshold, Fiona came to greet them, wiping her hands upon her pinafore.

"Happy I am ye're home," her mother said as she kissed her father on the mouth, something that always struck Shona as repulsive, even though they always smiled when they did it. "I'm over the moon for ye, John MacAslan."

"I'll meet ye there, Fiona MacAslan."

Her older brothers flopped the boar upon the butchering table, and pulled the pole out from between his tied legs. Malcolm trudged over to see the kill he hadn't been permitted to make. John promised to take him hunting next year, when Malcolm would be strong enough to hunt boar. Thomas and Hamish pounded Malcolm on the back reassuringly.

Blam! A forceful pounding on the front door startled a scream from her mother. A group of men battered through the door, and began to stream into the house. Their clothes were soaked red and blood caked around their wounds.

Fiona grabbed Shona's arm, and shoved her behind her along with Willow and Camran. John pulled out his hunting knife and shielded them all from the intruders.

"Who the devil are ye?" demanded his father.

An angry bearded man spoke. "Aye, the de'il indeed. Did you no' expect a visit from yer own clan? Or did ye think yer cowardice would go unnoticed?"

"Get out!" her father ordered.

The bearded man laughed hollowly. "Ye see that, lads? Now he's found his balls! Where were they when the clan was musterin' for battle yesterday, eh? Where were *ye*?" The bearded man held his sword to her father's chest.

Fiona turned around and knelt in front of Shona, Willow, and Camran. Her hand was trembling upon Shona's arm. Shona had never seen her mother so frightened. "Hide yerselves. Go!"

Breathlessly, Shona nodded. She took hold of Camran and shoved him inside the larder cupboard. Willow refused to let go of her mother, her tiny fists balling Fiona's skirts. Shona yanked at Willow's hands, and folded her into the cupboard next to their brother. But now there was no more room, so Shona crouched beneath the scullery table.

"I made my case before the chief personally," John explained. "I have no quarrel with the McBrays—my son Hamish is to be married to a McBray lass. I could not fight them."

"Ye mean ye *would* not fight them. Ye and yer tenants would have increased our showing on the battlefield. It may not have come to a head if they had seen us strong in number. But without ye we were outnumbered, and the McBrays saw it. They tore us to strips. The battle was lost in only two hours."

From beneath the scullery table, Shona could only see the dirty, muddy legs of all the men. *Too many legs to be in the house.*

"I'm sorry," she heard her father say.

"Sorry?" A man advanced upon him. "I saw both my sons slain on that battlefield. I found my William with a claymore in his chest. My boy Robert had his neck broken. It took an hour for him to die." His voice warbled with anguish. "Ye don't know the depths of sorry yet!"

"I know ye're grieving," said her father, "but the blame for yer boys does not rest on me."

"Aye, it does," said the bearded man. "His sons' deaths, as well as every man oot there who lost life or limb, is on *yer* head. Ye and every man jack of yers who hid with yer womenfolk inside the safety of yer homes. Lads, let it not be said that there is no justice among our clan. An eye for an eye. If Angus here lost two sons, then John must not be allowed to keep his!"

"No!" her mother screamed as she dove in front of her older sons.

Shona heard a crack, and her mother crashed to the floor, clutching her cheek. Then she saw her brother Thomas take a run at the man, just as two more men joined the fray. With his dagger high in the air, her father swung into the mob.

And then everyone was fighting. Her heart pounding in her chest, Shona began to cry.

Fists and daggers flew inside the kitchen for what seemed like forever. She could no longer see her father among all the angry men. Her mother grabbed her kitchen knife and dove on top of a man who was beating Hamish. But one of the angry men grabbed her from behind and called her a bad name. Then he raked his knife across her throat.

Her mother fell to her knees, blood oozing from between the fingers clasped at her throat. Her face was twisted in horror, and she made an odd, gulping sound. Mumma's pretty yellow frock ran red with blood. Shona watched in terror as her mother's eyes flew around the room like those of a frightened horse. Finally, Fiona's gaze landed upon the tear-streaked face of Shona, huddled under the scullery table, and a strange serenity came over her face.

"Mumma," Shona whispered, the saliva in her mouth stringing between her lips.

But her mother didn't answer as she fell forward into a pool of her own blood.

Horrified, Shona watched as the lifeblood poured from her mother in an ever-widening pool. The image of her mother's face blurred as tears crested over Shona's green eyes. She cringed against the wall as the awful red syrup inched closer and closer.

The yelling and the noises suddenly stopped. The angry men were no longer fighting, only breathlessly talking with each other. Shona's gaze lifted from her mother to a spot beyond the kitchen table. Her father lay upon the floor, a *sgian achlais* sticking out from his chest.

Get up, Da, she thought to him, but knew he would not understand. His body only convulsed slower and slower as blood poured from the wound.

Suddenly, a shod foot stepped right in the puddle of her mother's blood, and a hand gripped her wrist. She screamed.

A man lifted her into his arms. "Is this the wee mouse ye're after then? Ye're a pretty thing, aren't ye?" he said.

Her despair turned to rage as she beat her fists against the man's hairy face. The vinegary smell of sweat and hate assaulted her nose. Though Shona was only eight, she was strong, and his head jerked backward with each of her punches. Aggravated, the man dropped her, and she fell hard on the floor. He seized her by the hair, and dragged her over to the fireplace where another man held an iron in the fire.

"Here's yer first *slaighteur*, Seldomridge. Burn her."

Shona tried to pull away, but her hair was wound tightly in the bearded man's fist, and he wouldn't let go. The shorter man grabbed her wrist and held it aloft while he aimed the glowing iron at the back of her hand.

Shona struggled against them, but their strength was too mighty. She watched as the iron drew closer to her hand, her fingers splayed impotently. Then she heard a sizzling sound, and pain exploded inside her. She screamed shrilly as the darkening iron seared her skin. She had never known such pain. Or such malice to inflict it.

They let her go, and she ran into the corner. All her insides ached, and no amount of crying was enough to quench the pain. She looked at the back of her hand. Blistering on her skin was a squiggly figure. They had burned a snake onto her hand.

But she soon realized that she wasn't the only one blubbering, and she could easily hear her twin sister from within the cupboard, her sobs disclosing her hiding place. Instinctively, Shona ran in front of the cupboard, shielding it. But they had already heard—already expected—the presence of her siblings. The bearded man grabbed her by the shoulder of her frock and threw her forward. She landed upon her dead mother.

He threw open the doors of the cupboard and pulled Camran out. He, too, fought, but his child's body was no match for the man's strength.

Just then, Malcolm's eyes fluttered open and he groaned.

"Malcolm!" Shona cried, grateful he was alive. If he helped, they might be able to escape. But he never moved. Blood seeped from his ears.

She heard Camran screaming, his small boy's voice filling the air as they branded him, too. Shona had to do something. She reached into the cupboard and yanked on Willow, whose eyes were clenched tight. Pain flooded her as she curled her fingers around Willow's arm. But Willow wouldn't budge.

"Come with me!" Shona cried, and Willow's eyes fluttered open. Fixing her gaze upon her twin sister, Willow climbed out of the cupboard. Hand in hand, they ran over the bodies of her family on the kitchen floor.

But a mob of kilted men were looting in the hall, blocking their escape.

"Where do ye think ye're going?" said a voice that Shona would never forget. The bearded man seized both their arms in his meaty fists, and yanked them backward toward the kitchen fireplace.

"Leave my sister be!" Shona cried as the bearded man hauled Willow into his arms. Shona's other half, the one that her father delighted in, was about to be painfully disfigured.

And as the iron drew closer to Willow's little hand, her legs scissoring helplessly in the air, Shona cried over that vision of suffering and thought just one thing.

Why?

ONE

Miles' End Farm
Dumfriesshire, Scotland
1811

"I'll kill her!"

The front door slammed, thrusting an exclamation point on the threat.

Iona rolled her eyes as she wiped her sticky hands on her apron. "What did Shona do this time?"

Her husband lumbered into the kitchen and wedged his hatchet into the wooden table.

"It's no' what she did. It's what she has no' done. I ordered her to bring in the flock from the field before midday. Farragut will be here any minute to take the lambs to be butchered. She's disappeared and taken the damned sheep with her!"

Iona's loose bun wobbled as she turned back to the task of stuffing the chicken with the oniony skirlie. "Well, what did ye expect? Ye know how she gets. As soon as ye mentioned the word 'slaughter,' she was bound to rescue the lambs. I told ye to send her off to market today. Getting those lambs away from Shona will be like tryin' to pry the cubs from a she-bear."

Hume jerked the worn tam off his head, revealing a shiny white scalp. Though his face was bristling with thick ginger hair, there was not a single strand above his bushy eyebrows. "Every blessed spring we go through this."

Iona hoisted the pan heavy with two stuffed chickens and hung it from the hook inside the fireplace. Her back screamed as she righted her rounded frame. "After near ten years workin' for ye, ye should know the lass well enough by now."

"If I had only put my foot down in the first place. I knew she'd be trouble from the moment I laid eyes on her. I told ye so, didn't I? I told ye we should ha' only taken in the fair one. Every time I listen to ye, I end up having to eat ma own liver." He stuffed a hunk of bread into his mouth.

"Och, Hume. Ye know perfectly well we couldna take one sister and no' take the other."

"Aye, we could ha'!" Crumbs of bread flew out of his mouth. "'Twas required we take only one parish apprentice, no' two. And *slaighteurs,* no less! Two mouths to feed, two backs to clothe—"

"And two pairs of hands to do all the work that ye're too old to do, so shut yer pie-hole."

Hume grumbled. "Why can't Shona be more like her sister? I don't understand it. They eat the same food, sleep in the same bed, wear the same clothes. We grew them alike. Why is the one so obedient and docile, and the other so full of her own mind?"

Iona's thoughts turned to the gentle Willow. The twin sisters could not be more dissimilar. Not just in looks, but in disposition. The murder of their parents must have affected them in entirely different ways. The fair-haired Willow was a beauty, but terrified of her own shadow. She was not docile; she was dominated.

Shona, on the other hand, had grown fangs and claws. Since the night she had witnessed the brutal slaying of her parents and older brothers, Shona had grown into an untamable wildcat, and it was not to Hume's liking. Oh, they got along well enough, whenever they shared funny stories in the evening or when they were of one mind on an issue. But if Shona Slayter had to stand up to him, stand up she did, and woe betide him if he tried to put her in her place. Yet there was a chink in her armor, and Hume knew what it was. She had a weakness for all things defenseless, especially her twin sister. And, of course, lambs destined for slaughter.

"If she doesna bring back those sheep before Farragut arrives, I'll . . . I'll—"

Iona ignored him, and began to slice the carrots. Hume never could finish that sentence.

The sound of carriage wheels crushing the gravel outside made Hume groan. "Och! Farragut has arrived! Damn that lass! So help me, Iona, I'll make that girl obey me if it's the last thing I do!" He wedged the cap back on his head and stormed off as fast as his bowed legs would carry him.

There would be the devil to pay for this. And Shona Slayter was about to become the chosen currency.